Sons of the Tropics

Wayne Parrish

Morro Press

Sons of the Tropics

Cover Design by
Rocki deLlamas

ISBN: 0-972-5000-3-0

Printed in the United States of America

We shall not cease from exploration
And the end of all our exploring
Will be to arrive where we started
And know the place for the first time
When the last of earth left to discover
Is that which was the beginning
At the source of the longest river
The voice of the hidden waterfall.

-- T.S. ELIOT,
Four Quartets

This novel is dedicated to my gypsy children – Kip, Trisha, and David who have taught me so much about living, loving, and exploring; to David Lasisi, New Guinea poet and artist; to the Australian Patrol Officers who served in Papua New Guinea and to the Native Constabulary.

PROLOGUE

The morning was warm and muggy as the sun climbed over Port Moresby. The stench emanating from the mangrove swamp and tidal muck mingled with the odor of decaying and rotting mangoes and papayas that the prisoners habitually tossed over the stockade walls attracting rooting half-wild pigs from the village as well as a host of insects, rodents, and vermin from the surrounding rain forest. The billowing clouds held no promise of rain as they drifted unhurriedly through the azure sky and faded ignominiously into the cobalt sea.

Giant chartreuse bird-wing butterflies fluttered through the clusters of magenta-colored bougainvillea. On the edge of the rain forest, flame trees in full bloom competed with violet flowering jacarandas. Orchids, nature's floral aristocrats, grew like weeds and contrasted vividly with the deep green of the forest. Rainbow-hued bromichulae trellised their way up the lanai vines providing havens for a multitude of tree frogs that chorused even in the daylight. The scent of the fragrant frangipani mixed with the other smells bringing total confusion to one's nostrils.

Behind the harbor, the canopied rain forest stretched across the surrounding hills, untouched by any sign of human habitation. In the branches of the smaller trees, soft furry black-and-tan couscous, the favorite diet of the Papuan people, scurried through the branches, seeking yellow paw-paw and breadfruit to feed their youngsters. Tree Kangaroos contently munched flower buds and peered down from their perches eyeing the deadly venomous tai-pais and the equally fearsome carpet pythons on the forest floor below.

Red-and-blue parrots joined their green-and-blue brethren and flitted under the forest canopies squawking raucously. Birds of Paradise, the emperors of the air, flitted across an open meadow and disappeared into the trees on the other side of the hilltop. Fruit bats, looking like overdressed Bela Lugosi's, hung upside down from the tallest trees. The odor from their droppings was so strong that Jack could taste it and, checking an urge to vomit, he swallowed forcefully.

Patrol Officer Jack Reed was wearing his best tropical white dress uniform, replete with dress-white pith helmet, dress-white chalked putties and white calfskin shoes. Jack adjusted the back of his collar with his finger allowing the accumulated perspiration on the nape of his neck to further soak his already deeply stained jacket.

Turning to the large black companion on his left, who was dressed more casually in a native lap-lap which almost disguised a girth of magnificent proportions, Jack remarked, “Damnably hot. Wouldn't you say?” The Prime Minister unclasped his hands from his enormous belly, nodded and adjusted the navy blue cap with a wide red band, his “official” cap, which was perched precariously on a huge foot-high mound of kinky white hair.

“You should have learned by now to dress like me! You wouldn't sweat so damn much... Shall we get on with it?” Without waiting for a reply, Somatu waved his cap signaling the Sgt. Major who came to attention, turned, and faced the Police Drum and Bugle Corps standing at Parade Rest.

On his command, they quickly snapped to attention and straightened their ranks. He turned and faced forward, placing his baton smartly across a chest bedecked with ribbons that adorned his black-and-blue parade uniform. Pointing the baton skyward, he bellowed, “Forward march!” and forged ahead, swinging his baton stridently from side to side as the Corps Band quick-marched behind him. The Police Cadets, smartly dressed in their dress blue uniforms and white gloves with swagger sticks tucked neatly under their arms, trailed a few paces behind.

The entire corps of Native Constabulary, or at least those who could be spared from duty, had been assembled on the Parade Field. Each policeman carried a .303 rifle, a bayonet in the scabbard on a leather belt, and bandoliers of ammunition crisscrossed against the red-piped navy blouse-shirts they wore with a short navy wraparound. Barefooted, with weapons clasped in front of them, the Native Constabulary moved forward with precision and élan, and cued by a shouted cadence from the Sgt. Major, broke into a stiff-legged march.

Caught by surprise, the mixed bag of ruffians, refugees, and former prisoners known as the Loyal Native Trackers sprung off their haunches and swaggered along behind the other formations. Last in line, witch doctors, "Big Men", magistrates, and sing-sing groups wearing their finest decorations did their best to imitate the martial manner of the professionals in front. They waved to the assembled crowd as they moved forward. Cymbals crashed and drums thundered as the Royal Constabulary Marching Band burst into "Hail Britannia".

The sudden din sent flocks of blue-green and yellow-red lollikeets racing into the sky. The lollies circled the parade ground and then swept down the dark brown turbid river passing swiftly over mounds of lazy crocodiles dozing in the sun. A few alarmed reptiles slithered back into the primordial ooze that pretended to be a river. Unmoved by the uproar, the rest wriggled deeper into the mud and returned to their slumber.

A few frightened cassowaries crashed through the brush and onto the parade ground and seeing the crowds of women and children edging the meadow, fled back into the bush. A signal cannon boomed from a ship anchored far below in the harbor sending a faint plume of smoke skyward to join the motionless clouds above. Bells from the abandoned Catholic Church lent their voices to the cacophony of sound.

Jack forced his slightly stooped shoulders erect. The Military Cross suspended by a blue garter from his neck flopped and settled on his chest as he returned the Sgt. Major's salute. Behind him, the Prime Minister, who was born with the taste of long pig in his mouth, shifted his huge bulk, leaned forward and spoke softly, "Did you think back then it would all come to this?"

The slowly dissolving morning mists on the hills beyond the promontory created a glare that caused Jack's blue eyes to water, forcing tears down his face that merged with tears of joy, sorrow, and remembrance that he could not suppress. So many years and so many memories ago ... Kandi, Isi, Dekadua, Tenoso, Coffee, Manu... They were all gone. Lost in the mists and clouds of the unexplored territory. Jack remembered them all. How could he ever forget? "No, Prime Minister. I never imagined we would live to see a time like today."

PART ONE

PORT MORESBY TO DARU

The settlement of tin-roofed houses lay between two rock-clad hills. Rain came only in three or four months of the year, and in the dry season, the rocks were bare and the landscape was parched and trying to the eyes. Port Moresby faced a beautiful harbor. Since Jack's last visit, colonial buildings had spread up the hillsides. Workmen had been kept busy laying concrete sidewalks and planting thousands of flowering trees and bushes. Brown-skinned natives were walking or riding bicycles down tree-lined boulevards. Occasionally, Jack spotted colonials driving the streets in old worn out Ford Sedans and pick-up trucks, honking their horns madly and waving their arms in vain attempts to coerce the slow moving Joes and Meris off the roadway. Some people who had come to town to sell pineapples and fish were startled and jumped aside, but most were only mildly amused by the antics of the white mastas and waved at them good naturedly, steadfastly refusing to be hurried aside.

A rotund Meri with large bare breasts flopping and a small child suspended on her back in a large net supported by a headband, struggled up the gangway that led from the mud flats onto the pier. In each arm, she clutched a clay pot and supported them on her large hips. She paused in front of the Oroko bearers who were busy stacking a mound of supplies on the planking.

"You boys wantun kai kai belongum me?" she asked as she laughed and deposited her pots on the planks. Ceremoniously she undid her headband and lifted the girl child gently to the deck, cautioning her to stay put. She rolled out the net and spilled a generous amount of cut yams in front of them. "Three shilling," she said simply to the men, holding up the stubs of three fingers, the tips of which had been sacrificed in mourning for a departed husband or close relative.

"We have no money, woman," Somatu, Jack's orderly, shouted. "You must ask the Kiap," he said as he pointed down to the end of the pier where Jack stood with Patrol Officer O'Rourke, who was the expeditions second in command. Big, broad-shouldered, and generous-minded, O'Rourke signaled an OK to her by circling the air with a large clubby hand and smacking it into his fist.

“Woman, you are a thief,” Somatu shouted in the fish-monger's face. “One shilling only,” he bargained and then ran to where the officers were supervising the loading of supplies onto the cutter. “One shilling only Kiap. The woman is a no-good robber.”

The Meri waved her tattooed arms in the air saying, “Kai Kai belongum me. No sellum to no-good Orokos.” But it was too late. The men had already snatched up the yams and were busy plundering the dried fish from her pots.

“It's alright, Somatu. I know her. That old bloody Meri always brings me good luck,” O'Rourke drawled. “Tell the men the treat's on me.”

Somatu left muttering to himself sourly about no good robbers, but in a moment, he was laughing with the Meri and her child as he bit off the head of a fish and swallowed it... eyeballs and all. Finished with their meal and with jaws packed with betel nut and lime powder, the Oroko men were squatting on their haunches and spitting the red juice into the murky tide pools below.

Sergeant Manu appeared on the edge of the shore, followed closely by ten armed native policemen. He had them stack their arms and stand at ease under the shade of a poinciana tree. Then he stepped smartly over the mud flat and up the gangway. He stopped short in front of the lounging Orokos, storming angrily at them.

“What's the matter with you lazy men? Do you think you are white men and that you can sit down all day and do nothing? You lazy men, move kai kai into the lakatoi! Now!” He began rapping the startled men on their heads and shoulders with his swagger stick. He aimed a few curses and kicks in their direction as the men quickly scrambled to their feet. The Orokos were no match for Sgt. Manu, and they knew it. Sgt. Manu's patrol work was legendary. He had once tracked eight escaped convicts into the bush and had single-handedly captured and brought them back to the Port Moresby stockade. He was a veteran of a hundred patrols and at least two expeditions into unexplored territory.

Sgt. Manu came quickly to the edge of the pier where O'Rourke and Jack were standing and saluted smartly. They stood at attention and respectfully returned his salute. “Sorry, Kiap,” Sgt. Manu said. “It's no good to spoil Oroko men. They must be made to obey.”

“Thank you, Sgt.” Jack replied courteously. “Please instruct your men to assist the porters. We want to embark early in the morning. I want two constables to escort the Oroko men to the bivouac in Hanga town and return with them to the pier by five a.m. I don't want to spend the morning searching the streets and the gaols for strays. The rest of the constables will sleep in the police barracks. Is that clear?”

“Yes, Kiap. No worries. I will keep the Oroko boys in line. They no run away with bisong ladies.” Sgt. Manu lined up the porters and constables and herded then toward Hanga town. Patrol Officer O'Rourke followed them ashore and set off to secure additional mosquito netting and flannel shirts for the carriers.

The crushed-coral streets bustled with porters, errand boys and miners who scurried back and forth like aimless ants, pausing only to exchange greetings with one another before resuming their vague tasks. A haze of dust stirred up by bustling builders and countless drag carts hovered over the town. White-shirted merchants sat on shaded verandas vainly waving flywhisks, puffing their cigars, and shouting orders at indolent haus-boys. It was a familiar sight to Jack, who waited for the first whiff of the late afternoon trade winds in the cockpit of the Valhalla. I grew up here, he thought, in this backwater of the world that clings to the edge of this island continent like the mythical Mu. It exists only due to its sheer persistence. But was Canberra, where I attended school, any more real?

Now he was headed for the unknown territory, a place of dreams and legends, a place covered with clouds and mists of unknowing. The roof of the world was up there somewhere, according to Nandi. No white man, not even the great D'Albertis had been there.

Why am I going? Jack asked himself for the hundredth time since Judge Murray, the chief administrative officer had inveigled him to lead the expedition into the highlands. "It's an opportunity of a lifetime," Murray had cajoled. "You'll be Stanley and Livingston, Perry and Admunsen, Lewis and Clark, all rolled into one. It's the last unexplored territory left on this planet. God knows what you'll find up there!"

"But why me? You've got Ryan, McCarthy, a dozen seasoned officers who are senior to me."

"You are my choice. You are a natural born explorer, Jack. You are healthy and strong and curious. You have imagination. You relate well to the natives. You understand them better than any officer I know. Most of all, you have perseverance ... that most of all. If you go in, I know you'll see your men through even if it gets to be a sticky wicket. McCarthy is too old. So is Jamison," Murray paused and stared at his fingers clasped in front of him.

"The others are too quick to shoot and ask questions later. I need a man who knows when to use restraint. Roberts shot up the Kukukukus, and ten years later we're still fighting them. You proved your merit in Daiwo. You brought in that old cannibal, Sigiwa, for trial, and established a first-rate station. We've had no trouble up there for the past two years." Murray's eyes met Jack's.

"Judge Murray, my trackers found Sigiwa and brought us both down to the peninsula. My restraint earned me an arrow, remember?"

"Yes and no fault of your own. But you didn't shoot down some innocent tribesman. That's what counts."

"Constable Agoti and Corporal Dekadua led me in and out of Daiwo. That's their territory. Without them I wouldn't have made it back to the mission station."

"Agoti and Dekadua are Bushmen, and they are also Constabulary. Jack, you trained them and all the rest of that lot you salvaged out of the stockade, and you turned them into police trackers. Which brings me to another point. You and your men have done a tremendous job, but you're not popular here anymore. The miners and some of the plantation owners think you were too soft on the Daiwos. The miners want the bush babies to clear out of the territory, and the plantation men complain they can't work the land when its chock full of untamed heathen cannibals. It's the Daiwos who are a thorn in their side. They want to get rid of them, and they can't while you are up there. On the other hand, the missionaries have convinced the do-gooders and the world-betterers down in Canberra that you are the ticket, so I am caught between the two mobs."

"If that's the case, then I'm for sticking it out in Daiwo."

"Jack, like it or not, our work is pacification. Every moneyman and misfit in Australia who can book passage is coming up here. They see Papua as their last chance to make a fortune. No one, nothing can prevent it. I'm sending Jamison and McCarthy up there. They'll look after your people. They won't let the miners or the planters pull any shenanigans. They are truly first rate 'Outside Men'."

Jack briefly relived the relief he felt when Murray had told him he was posting McCarthy and Jamison to Daiwo. Tonight he would be joining the two veteran officers at the hotel bar to pass on his notes and briefs on the territory. Better men than me, Jack thought.

He trusted Murray's judgment, which was based on thirty years experience as a judge and administrative officer in Moresby and in the field. Murray had picked up and held MacGregor's torch high, dealing justly and righteously with the native inhabitants. In his time, Murray had traversed more of the bush districts than most of his DO's. Even today, in his early 70s, Murray would don a backpack and shorts and do a walkabout through the hill country, visiting the more remote villages, settling disputes and conferring with the elders, who had a high regard for his courage and wisdom. "Coconut counting" he called it. The native constabulary was devoted to him, and took pride in calling themselves "Judge Murray's men".

Murray had struck while the iron was hot. "You're my man," he shouted, and slammed his fist on the table. "There's nothing more to do but to do it!" he exclaimed. He clinched the deal by telling Jack he was bringing O'Rourke down from Rabaul to give an assist. "If you should get whacked on the skull up there, I've told O'Rourke to carry you home on his back, if need be, and he's strong enough to do it."

Tim O'Rourke, the amiable red-haired giant, four years his junior, but more than a match in strength, had grown up in the Queensland outback, and had a good sense of the bush. He had a steady way of working with the native police. A good man. A good choice.

Relaxing in the chair, Jack gradually felt his body and then his mind, acquiesce to the judge's persuasive powers. Secretly he felt pleased. The unknown territory? What was its promise? To explore a pristine country, unseen and untouched by civilized men? Possible encounters with some primitive culture? No, it was more than that. It was a chance for freedom. A chance to be locked into nature and all its power, to be free from the boredom and monotony of civilization.

"I'm your man, Judge," Jack heard himself say. "I'll want Corporal Isi and Corporal Dekadua, and I'd like Sergeant Manu if you can spare him."

"Done. Here's my hand on it. You're a good man to volunteer. See to it that you don't set your tent on fire like that fool Roberts did and you'll be back home by Anzac Day. Pull that off and I'll give you the pick of the districts. Rabaul, Madang, or back to Daiwan. Just give me the word."

The wind stirred the tarpaulin, and Jack felt the freshness of the sea breeze on his cheek. He shifted his gaze toward the small foothills that ringed the harbor. He rested his eyes on the blue and white shuttered cupolas of the Homestead House. The largest turret had served as his aerie when he was a boy. The window was unusually large, and Jack would spread out his arms on the sill and stare with his binoculars at ships anchored in the pallid blue waters of the bay. The tossing palm trees combined with surging waves, and at that height created a dizzying sensation as well as giving him a feeling of power. Jack smiled when he remembered as a boy wanting to be King Arthur and pretending that the turreted Homestead House was his castle.

He loved spying on the inhabitants of Hanga Town. From his turret he would survey every pigsty, every stick house, and every hovel roof. He would watch the men squatting on their haunches, smoking and talking quietly as they mended their nets, and the tattooed bare-breasted fisherwomen, with naked babies straddling their hips. Their raucous laughter and shrill scolding would drift faintly across the bay and waft up to his tower. When the men began pulling the huge butterfly nets off the rusty red tin roofs, Jack would let out a yelp of glee as he sprinted across the gabled roof and scrambled down the arms and branches of the huge Jacaranda tree. He would make a wild, bare-footed rush, fists flying, down the lane that led to the fishermen's shanties, perched like eccentric stork nests, along the bay.

"Big fish today," Nandi would call. "Hurry. We must not be last."

Together they would push Nandi's canoe into the water and would paddle out to join a circle of outriggers far out in the bay. On Nandi's signal, the men would paddle toward the shoreline while the younger boys splashed the water and each other, making blood-thirsty cries as the line of canoes worked itself slowly shoreward, driving the startled fish toward the waiting women waving and dipping their butterfly nets.

In less than an hour, the men and boys would return and beach their outriggers high above the tide line. Their work over, they would light up their pipes and watch the women divide the catch. The fish-wives would quarrel noisily among themselves for a prize fish, but in the end, each woman headed home with a basket of fish balanced on her head, leaving the men and boys to follow with the nets. Jack would join them on the high porches where the women had fired up their tin stoves with coconut hulls, and the copra-scented stench drifted inland toward the hills behind the village.

Jack would devour the fish raw as the native children did. He often stayed in Hanga Town into the early evening, sharing fish, rice and spinach cooked in coconut oil with the men and boys.

He would sit with his back resting against a shanty wall as far from the cooking fires as possible, and yet be close enough to hear the man-talk when it began. While he waited, he would let his eyes wander slowly from the mossy sea wall to the kelp-covered kitchen middens, across the turbid bay and on to the great red setting sun, until it sank like a fiery mushroom into the translucent sea.

The gurgling tide as it sucked the accumulated shanty offal out to sea and mingled with the babbling voices of women and children often induced a euphoric state and a subtle peacefulness would gently cloud Jack's mind. He would be only vaguely aware of the contented mutterings of the old men as they filled and fired their pipes.

The scent of acrid smoke from their green tobacco soothed rather than disturbed his reverie. He would remain in this trance-like state until Nandi initiated the man-talk with his stock invocation: “May the mother of us all bring food, live children and tea. Most of all bring us tea!” The men always grunted their approval.

Afterward they would dip their Burns-Philips store tin cups into a great iron pot, fill them with steaming black tea, and return to their perches, squatting contentedly on their heels. When the women departed with the noisy young children, the story telling would begin. Tales of the days before the white men came to Moresby, told over and over by Nandi and the old men.

“Those were good times,” Nandi would say. “We used to fight the men in the hills, and people came from everywhere to trade for our Kona shells. We were rich then.” His pointed teeth would gleam. “But today it is better,” he would finish. “We love tea and we have beer and rice. There are no more battles,” but the light would dim in his eyes. The older men would shuffle their feet and stare into their cups. “Judge Murray's men have made us safe, and our children now go to school.” And the older men would grumble and mutter to themselves, forgetting that young Jack, a white child, sat at their feet.

Jack knew that he had lived a blessed youth, that his mother trusted him to be with Nandi. The other town boys were raised behind stockaded walls, protected by haus-bois on their way to and from school. Jack, on the other hand, had been free to roam the snake-ridden hills behind Moresby and the viscera-ridden alleys of Hanga Town under Nandi's watchful eye. He would return home later in the evening, calling all the village curs by name as he wended his way up the hill to the stockade under the star-studded tropic sky. He hadn't yet realized that he was a somewhat lonely, only child who flitted between the two cultures, belonging to neither, and he wouldn't have cared. He truly felt he was a child of the universe.

When Jack's mother died, he sold the Homestead, on Judge Murray's advice, to an English couple newly arrived from Sydney, and moved his belongings into a bungalow next to the hotel.

"No time to grieve, Jack," Judge Murray had advised. "Nothing for it but to move forward. You can't go back and you can't stand still. I've found you a posting with the constabulary if you complete the course of study at the cadet academy. You'll make a fine patrol officer, Jack. You have all the makings for it. You were born here and lived here all your life. You understand the Papuan. You won't be like those second-rate, second-hand, pampered misfits coming here to get a service record. Papua needs men like you.

So Jack had left Papua, and two years later he returned from Canberra as a cadet intern. True to his word, Judge Murray posted him for six months to the stockade, and then sent him north to learn the ropes under McCarthy and later under Jamison. Two years later he was directed to establish a post in the Daiwan country.

Among the Daiwos Jack first realized he was somewhat of a loner; he felt comfortable being the only white man in a region of semi-barbarous savages. His mission was to prepare the people for the eventual invasion of their territory by first the missionaries and traders, and if all proceeded well, by the planters and cultivators.

He truly liked and enjoyed the Daiwo people. He established a tribal council to help him govern the district. Together they set up a village school and a rudimentary sanitation program. Overall, he managed the district well. Surveying and mapping the district, building his headquarters, and providing basic health care took up much of his time.

The two years had passed quickly, when his temporary replacement arrived following an inspection tour by Judge Murray. "First rate job you've done here." Murray had told him. "No more than I'd expected. Something's up. I'll tell you more when you are back in Moresby," he added cryptically.

A month later, Jack packed out to the coast and took a cutter to Moresby. Although at times he yearned to be among his own kind in Moresby, he didn't belong there. I don't like civilized society with all its limitations and restrictions, he thought. I don't like bureaucratic intrigue. I don't like the way most colonials treat the Papuans. The rub is that I know what I'm against, but I don't know what I'm for.

Judge Murray had put it to Jack: "You'll find social injustice everywhere, Jack. Our first task is always to raise the level of our existence. But the trick is to remember the real prize to be won is our freedom." Murray was right of course, but there are many kinds of freedom. What kind of freedom am I searching for? He wondered.

It was nearly sunset when Jack looked out over the town again. Shades of inexpressible yellow and green blended with the purple grasses on the hills. The moringas, the bougainvilleas, and the acacias were all in bloom casting a blanket of color over the nearby slopes. The main boulevard was lined with poincianas spaced about forty feet apart, adding a soft pink glow. On the steep embankment facing the waterfront, stood a wide ribbon of blooming oleanders. Ferns draped over crannies in the rock sea wall and a hundred yards further on, a small creek crossed a thin strip of glittering yellow sand, emptying into the bay, which in turn fed out into the dazzling ocean.

The wild landscape of a millennium ago had taken on a lovely sophistication and charm. Jack lingered until the sun suddenly vanished over the horizon with a final green spark calling up the night. When the electric lights of the town burst into brilliance, Jack left the Valhalla enjoying the sweet perfume of frangipani and moringa blossoms as he walked down the tree-lined boulevard.

A horse-drawn cart was stationed in front of the hotel; both the horse and driver were asleep. The hotel and its grounds included a rambling series of structures that sprawled over several blocks and overlooked the bay. The largest building contained a barroom and an enormous dining room. Encircling the entire building was a wide veranda that served as sleeping porch at night and sitting porch during the day when the plantation owners and Moresby businessmen and their ladies met to gossip about the latest scandals, social affairs, and mediocrity of the government planners and officials. Any serious deal cutting was accomplished by men standing at the bar. The dining tables were set around a wide polished floor which was also used for dancing. The building was open on all four sides for added coolness. Punkahs were hung from the ceiling. These were operated by small boys with cords tied to their toes. The boys stood silently in the small corners of the room where they pulled the punkah fans back and forth. The buildings were decorated with an astonishing variety of fancy woodwork and railings; minarets protruded here and there adding to the bizarre effect.

The hotel and the adjoining plantation had been acquired by two brothers who were ex-troopers of the “Light Horse”. Both were splendid horsemen, one of whom on occasion would ride his horse into the bar and shout, “Drinks for the house,” including his horse who was a well-known beer drinker. When he was officially reprimanded for this, he retorted, “It's my horse and my hotel!”

Jack met O'Rourke as he came out of the dining room. “Are you ready for this?” he asked as he eyed Keith McCarthy and Bill Jamison, grizzled veterans of numerous patrols.

“Right as I'll ever be,” O'Rourke smiled. Together they strode across the large room and joined the “Old Men” at the bar.

“Oh, here are the young lambs about to be led to the slaughter,” McCarthy teased.

“Here it comes. Be ready for the worst,” Jack said to O'Rourke with a grin.

“Not yet dry behind the ears,” McCarthy added taking a swipe with a beery wet finger behind Jack's ear. “Not too wet,” he said examining his finger approvingly. “At least it's beer wet,” and he winked at Jamison. “Can I shout you boys a beer? A last remembrance drink?”

“Now that you can do,” O'Rourke piped up.

“Four beers mate,” McCarthy bellowed at the barmen who were doing their best in the midst of the uproar to satisfy the clamor for beer and whiskey. Although one barman, Jack noticed, still managed to have time for a few moments of conversation with every man he served. Jack watched with fascination as the barman pulled four tall bottles of Resch's Pilsner out of a cooler, tossed them in the air, and juggled them professionally as he walked down to the men, where he sat them down with a flourish. He pried off the tops with a key and said, “How are you John Keith McCarthy?”

“Fit and ready,” said Keith. “Bill, I'd like you to meet some friends of mine. This would be Tim O'Rourke and this would be...”

“Jack Gregory Reed,” Bill said to Jack's surprise.

“How did you know my name?”

“Not hard,” Bill replied. “I study the *Government Gazette* and besides all Moresby knows you're going up the Fly River and then overland to the Purari... if you can find it.” He paused, “They all hope you boys will find a pinch of gold dust up there somewhere or land ripe for cultivation. Hell, even the missionaries are hoping you'll find more souls for them to save.” Bill let that sink in. “Have you met your new boss, George Wilford Townsend, yet?” he nodded towards the dance floor and went off grinning.

“Look at ‘em,” the brash, burly Jamison lifted his glass towards the veranda. “Here's to your new boss. May he rot in hell,” he belched. Jack and O'Rourke scanned the veranda and spotted G.W. Townsend, a short man about five-and-a-half-feet tall who was sitting with an attractive grey-haired lady who possessed the kind of charm that comes only with years of experience. The couple was drinking champagne and Townsend got up and limped over to the Victrola to put on a record, and they began to dance.

This happy scene enraged Jamison, who said, “Look at ‘em with his game leg, worrying poor Mrs. Stoddard and he never played cricket in his life.”

“What’s cricket's got to do with champagne and dancing?” O'Rourke blurted.

“You're ignorant,” exploded Jamison as he sputtered into his beer. “Plain ignorant. Don't you know Mrs. Stoddard's husband captained an English Eleven in Australia?”

“That was a long time ago,” O'Rourke responded.

“So it was, but for sure my memory for matches and players hasn't faded,” Jamison replied.

“It's not cricket that bothers him,” McCarthy said to appease the now red-faced patrol officer. “It's the man himself. He posted up to Moresby about six years ago. Just a second rate clerk and passed himself off as a former player who taught Ponceford to bat.”

“To hell he did!” challenged O'Rourke, no slouch at cricket himself.

“In Australia he'd have been lost among fools of his kind,” McCarthy mused, “but up here in charge of some pettifogging system, he's become somebody to reckon with. He's abused the plantation owners and natives alike. Jamie here caught him flogging a native lad and decked him on the spot. A 'King's Hit' it was.”

"And for that, I got busted and posted to New Ireland while that twit ends up second in command to Murray. He's in charge of all the land schemes; now everybody kow-tows to him. He is arrogant and insulting to anyone who questions his views on anything. He's a sorry replacement while Murray's on leave to get his gong. You blokes best hope that Murray's back before you are. That bastard will belittle your report and sell any inside information to the highest bidder. He's got the itch."

"He's also got the only refrigerator in Papua," said Bill as he sat four more beers down in front of them. "He invests in the ladies and keeps his fridge stocked with chicken, champagne, and ice cream."

"Let's move out to the veranda boys where the air is a bit fresher." McCarthy grabbed his beer.

"How does Jamison know so much?" asked Jack.

"They used to be roomies before he and Jamie had their spat. Then Jamie topped it off by having the kuk-boi pluck a rooster and stick it half-alive in the fridge. There was hell to pay when Townsend came home and found that featherless cold chook in the fridge," McCarthy said with a laugh. "Townsend tried to shiv him out of the service but Murray intervened."

Once again Jack was reminded that here on the edge of the frontier, you had to accept the banter, to take pride in all the cheeking. Even more, you had to prove yourself in the bush to be accepted by the brotherhood of Outside Men. They found a place at the table in a corner of the veranda where they could monitor the bar. Jack was thoughtful. Murray wasn't popular with the Europeans for he used his power and prestige to forestall the plundering miners and the greedy plantation owners.

"Coconut country," Murray called Papua, but he was the Papuans' staunchest advocate. "It's their country," he often reminded Jack and anyone else who would listen. "Not ours in spite of the fact that some people think New Guinea is part of Pax Australia."

Murray had been Jack's mentor, for other than a manual on handling natives there was little in the Patrol Officers training that prepared them to be an "Outside Man." "You learn from the experience in the field or you die out there somewhere. If it's not a disease, it's an arrow, or a snake, or a crocodile or you'll set fire to your hut and burn yourself alive like Roberts did. So keep your eyes and ears open, your mouth shut, your boots laced, and your fly zipped," was the advice Murray gave to all the young patrol officers.

Now the man was gone for at least six months or more and they would be under the direction of Townsend. Good thing we're leaving tomorrow. He turned his attention to the other men who were arguing about the merits of various cricket players, the rounds, the scores... the argument would be endless.

Jack took the opportunity to study his companion. O'Rourke was a good-looking, energetic, redhead. Diffident, keen and possessed with a good sense of humor. Jack considered him to be the best of the junior patrol officers. O'Rourke had learned his trade under D.O. Taylor, who seconded him to a lonely outpost in the Salonga country. Out of sheer boredom, O'Rourke wrote his reports in rhyming verse. Other than that oddity, he had a fine record. O'Rourke caught Murray's attention when he captured some Gori warriors who had ambushed and massacred a party of miners. O'Rourke dogged the men for weeks through trackless country and then brought them to Moresby for trial. He had acted as public defender and made a good case while they stood handcuffed to the dock.

"These men are stone age people," O'Rourke had told the court. "They are like children. Look how fascinated they are by the magic of the blades," he said dramatically pointing to the oscillating electric fan that sat on the bench. "In the eyes of their people, they are 'spearmen' because they were only righting the wrongs done to their villages. The fact that the murdered white men were not the guilt parties did not concern them. Look at them! You can see that they are prepared to meet their fate without whimper or complaint."

O'Rourke had done his best, but they were sentenced to be hung. Nevertheless, the young men were fortunate. O'Rourke appealed to Murray who rescinded the decision and ordered the men to Moresby prison for detention and retraining. Yes, Jack thought, Murray's choice for second-in-command was a good one.

A scuffle broke out between two miners at the other end of the bar; they went at each other for a few moments with flailing arms and fists but finding that no one was paying much attention, went back to the bar and resumed their drinking. Jack surveyed the barroom and verandas all now packed with administrators and their wives, contractors, packet boat skippers, policemen, planters, and miners mingling freely.

"Look at the swarm," McCarthy said. "What a lot. Before Murray those people ran roughshod over this town. The roads were a quagmire, a sea of bloody potholes a man could drown in. The Chinese wouldn't buy copra from the Papuans, and the owners would shoot down like dogs any 'Big Men' natives who tried to plant their own groves. The Papuans were all Joes and Meris with no rights at all and the Chinese 'cooties' were no better off." He tossed off the rest of his beer in a single swallow. "Oh, they all whinged at first, but now everybody's happy. The price of copra is up and there's no forced labor. All this in less than ten years. Now Murray wants the government to train the Papuans to look after their own country," he paused. "It won't work. I've done a few patrols in my time, plenty of them for Murray. Too many people ... too many languages... they'll never unite. The geography of this place is against it. They'll always be tribal in nature."

"Speaking of tribes. You boys are going into the Never-Never country. God knows what you'll find. The tribes on the Upper Fly are none too friendly, but after the Strickland, watch out," Jamison cautioned and signed his finger across his throat.

"You'll be running the risk of desertion but if you can get the porters across the mountains, they'll be afraid to leave you. Carry shot guns," McCarthy advised. "Food is going to be your biggest problem if you don't find people; and if you do find people, you both better take Winchesters."

"How many men are you taking?" asked Jamison.

“All together about 50. Sixteen Orokos from here and ten constables. We'll pick up 16 carriers and five more constables in Daru,” Jack said.

“Who's your head man?” McCarthy asked.

“Sergeant Manu.” Jack looked carefully at both men.

“The best there is!” they chimed.

“Three stripes and a hundred patrols. He took me and Jamison in many a time and he got us out. Trust him. Give him all the rope he needs,” Keith said.

“Barkeep,” bawled Jamison, “more beers.” A shriek and a cry of dismay came to them from the slightly darkened dance floor. Everyone glanced that way and saw Townsend struggling drunkenly up off the floor while his apparent adversary gamely adjusted her blouse. He stood glassy-eyed rocking back and forth, then he grabbed her by the arm, “Quiet!” he hissed at her. “I'm taking you home, now!”

“Let go of me,” and she slapped Townsend across the face, knocking him backwards.

Anticipating Townsend's reaction, Jack and O'Rourke raced to the rescue. One man grabbed each of Townsend's outstretched arms. They escorted him out of the hotel, both legs kicking in the air, trying desperately for a toe-hold, all the while cursing at the top of his lungs. Jamison and McCarthy followed close behind, as they carried him down the steps of the hotel and dropped him rather unceremoniously onto the ground.

“You bloody clods. I'll have you up on charges for this,” he cried as he struggled to his feet.

“Not tonight, you won't,” and Jamison knocked the man cold. “A King's Hit,” he laughed.

“We'll take care of this twit,” said McCarthy, “but you boys best be out of Moresby by daybreak. No telling what this piece of garbage will dream up.”

“Thanks, Keith,” Jack said and nodded at Jamison. “We'll get our tucker and camp on the Valhalla tonight.”

"Well, it's the knickers for us. Best be off," O'Rourke said and laughed as he and Jack headed back to the wharf.

The expedition embarked from Port Moresby early in the morning on the 20-ton Valhalla, a scow-like craft capable of navigating shallow streams and river bars. Their stepping-off place for the interior was the government station at Daru, situated 300 miles west of Port Moresby. A low island, with mud and mangrove-fringed shores, Daru lies near the estuary of the Fly River. The mouth of this mighty Papuan stream is thirty miles in width, and with its two great tributaries, the Upper Fly and the Strickland, it brings waters from the "Roof of New Guinea" down across hundreds of miles of grass and forested plains to meet the sea.

Prior to their departure for Daru, O'Rourke and Jack had been busy preparing requisitions for all the needs of the expedition. Food and medicines, ammunition, rifles and constabulary equipment, matches and kerosene, steel goods and other articles for purposes of trade; painted canvas bags to protect their precious rice from the torrential rains; tents and all the other necessities. Nothing could be forgotten; nothing could be overlooked. Once they had left the coast, they must depend on themselves alone, making their own world, and forgetting the one they had left behind, as if they were journeying to the moon.

The Valhalla was fully loaded with fuel, police, and the patrol's stores and equipment as it steamed out of Port Moresby harbor. Cobalt on cobalt, space on space, where the sky met the sea, a broken line of snow-white breakers thinly separating the spheres. Unwanted specters of unforeseen dangers cast shadows on Jack's thoughts. I hope I'll live to see those red-roofed bungalows and green hills once more.

Vaguely aware that he was more at ease in nature than most men he knew, Jack was willing to live by most of society's rules, but he had learned early to put an inner wall between himself and the material world. He did not aggressively reject society, but he put a distance between himself and most other men. At times he enjoyed Moresby for what it was, an island of order in the midst of a sea of chaos, but he preferred to live beyond civilization and its artificial reality, where he could at least reach for spiritual exile. The magic of the horizon lured him onward. He hoped that somewhere in the unexplored country he would discover a newer, more sublime world than the one he was leaving.

The cutter steamed down the west coast, past Kairuku and the Kekeo plain. It quickly swept by the mountains of the Loloupa and the ten-thousand-foot block of stone called Mt. Yule, and then slowed until it was northward of the even mightier Mt. Tofa.

The beaches disappeared and the coastline became fringed with mangrove swamp, shutting the passing vessel off from all view of the interior. Sea kestrels circled lazily overhead. The porters and constabulary were resting on the decks, somnambulated by the heat and the drone of the ship's engine. Jack also was being slowly hypnotized as he watched the sweeps and turns of a solitary sea eagle dwarfed by a giant cloud.

Out of the corner of his eye, Jack spotted a stowaway, a bright-colored goanna at least four feet long, glowing with iridescent colors, flicking its bright blue tongue was staring straight into the ship's cook's eyes. It never saw the steel machete coming that arched through the air and sliced off its head. Its world stopped. Yet it lurched forward, blood from its severed neck splattering the ship's cook as he leaped back as if he had been speared.

"Kai Kai," yelled Somatu as he grabbed the goanna by the tail and held it triumphantly over his head for all to see.

"Kai Kai!" shouted the porters suddenly aroused from their torpor. Jack was amused but didn't dare let a grin appear. "Bugger off!" the cook roared at the Orderly.

A crest-fallen Somatu went forward to join his mates who roared with laughter when he confessed, "Cookie no likum; Goanna belongum me. Somatu meke kai-kai, Cookie no eatum."

Troubles seem to follow Somatu like a plague, Jack thought. Somatu couldn't be more than sixteen, but he already showed signs that he was going to live up to his Iuma heritage.

His tribe had been massacred by a band of KuKuKuKus and the survivors had fled to the coast. Judge Murray had found the orphaned lad when the Moresby expedition had gone into the hills to restore order but the nomadic KuKuKuKus had already fled.

"I found a place for him at the mission," Murray told Jack, "but he didn't last two months. One of the sisters tried to discipline him with a steel ruler. It didn't come off well. He's already a man-child, the son of a brave warrior, not a child to be scolded in front of younger children. I brought him home with me, but in spite of Lady Murray's best efforts, Somatu's no hause-boi. He steals my cigars and my brandy. I'm sure even though I haven't taken to marking the bottle. He sneaks out of the compound at night when he gets a chance and hangs out with the local street Arabs. Shows up with a shiner more often than nought. Sets a bad example if I keep a wild one like him around. But in spite of it all, I like the boy. The last straw was when Lady Murray caught him trying to pull the knickers off the maid. He's got to go. I've told him I'd ask you to take him as you're orderly. He can cook passably and press a shirt and that's about all. I promised him if he did you right, that I'd give him a berth at the police academy. He could be a barracks boy the first year and after that we could talk things over again."

Not a chance, Jack had thought to himself, but when he saw the half-pleading look in Murray's eyes, his resolve slackened. "Let's meet the boy," Jack said and Murray called loudly from his chair for Somatu who appeared as if by magic onto the veranda. He grinned from ear to ear as he snapped a smart salute over a blackened eye. His kit and bedroll were already neatly packed, worthy of any police cadet, Jack noted.

Somatu's body was that of an athlete or even a middle-weight fighter. Somatu looked lean, lithe, and tough. Born and bred in the bush, Somatu was no town boy.

Jack liked the eager light in his eyes. Somatu's smile was infectious, no hint of sullenness showed in his expression. "Would you like to be my orderly, Somatu?"

"Yes, Kiap. Somatu would like that, Sir!"

"Do you know what your duties will be?"

"Yes, Sir, Kiap. Wash clothes and iron. Pack your kit. Do the cooking and dishes, and clean the weapons and carry your rifle," he said proudly.

"Do you know where the officers' quarters are?"

"Yes, Kiap," his eyes flashed.

"Then go to the quarter master and pick up my kit and carry it down to the Valhalla. Kiap O'Rourke will tell you where to stash it."

Somatu leaped over the railing, trampling one of Lady Murray's bushes, raced down the coral pathway where he slowed to a halt. He turned and saluted, "Thank you, Judge Murray."

"Off with you and see that you mind the Kiap. Good luck! You won't regret this Jack," Murray said. "He's a good lad at heart. If he doesn't work out by the time you reach Daru, leave him with Jackson and Buguru. They'll take care of him until I can think of something else."

Fat chance, Jack thought. The Judge knows me too well. He's counting on me to turn him into a police tracker before the boy ends up in gaol or something worse.

The evening meal was almost finished. A creamy yellow moon slithered its way over the horizon and beamed broadly across the water bleaching the tide pools white, luring the fresh frondescence from the delta shores. A fish slapped the water sending a phosphorescent wavelet towards the anchored boat. The porters were joking with Somatu, and on his urging they gleefully held up tender bits of charred goanna for the cook to see. The cook and his men ignored them, turned their heads away, and stared hard into the nightscape.

Cpt. "Sharkeye" Woodson was a brown leathery little man who couldn't have weighed more than nine stone. A salt-dried tarry toupee barely covered his scalp and when it shifted sideways the men could not help but notice a large indentation in his skull. Nothing could conceal the hideous scar that slashed downward over his left check. The Captain had to squint to hold a glass eye in place that otherwise would have revealed a gaping socket. The squint had earned him the sobriquet “Sharkeye” in the bars and saloons in Moresby, but no man called him “Sharkeye” to his face.

Jack and O'Rourke sat with the Captain in the cockpit of the cutter, sipping brandy and smoking cigars. “Order them by the cabinet from the Burns-Philips Company,” Woodson volunteered. Neither of the patrol officers had even heard of buying them that way, but they enjoyed the cigars nonetheless, as their faces lit cherry red with each puff.

“I came up from Sydney 34 years ago, and I've seen it all come and go. Nothing lasts up here. Not the missionaries or the miners, the government men, or the patrol officers,” Woodson said, glancing shrewdly at O'Rourke and Jack. “The plantation owners, their wives, and their children get sick and die. The miners get ambushed or split each other's skulls; all for a few flakes of gold. The missionaries get massacred by a bunch of howling Kukukukus who haul their possessions into the hills, so the sorcerers can piss on the crosses and relics. The patrol officers ruin their health trying to cram white man's law down the natives' throats or they take an arrow on some damn patrol hauling some murdering cannibal to justice. If they do manage to bring one of the heathens to Moresby, or Lae, or Madang, the cannibal sits in a gaol for a year or so, then some magistrate sends him back home fat and happy and twice as cunning.” Woodson drew on his cigar and continued. “You boys ain't got a chance to get from the Fly to the Purari, if you ask me. If you do get back, you'll be all skin and bones from malnutrition and your bodies ruined with fever.”

“Who asked us to help the Papuans? Look at them,” Woodson paused and nodded at the porters. “They don't want to be saved by you, the government, or the missionaries. If you try, first chance they get, they'll put a spear in your backside. You ain't baby-faced boys fronting life for the first time. Why would you want to bend over backwards to help them? Why don't you just get a nice post in Madang and send reports to Canberra and talk a lot about helping our brown brothers? No need to go on a walk-about in the Never-Never asking for trouble!" He paused and swallowed some more brandy and tossed his stogie into the delta waters where it dissolved with an explosive sizzle.

Volunteering nothing, O'Rourke waited for Jack to answer Woodson's soliloquy. Jack hesitated framing his thoughts, "Captain Woodson, the white man's on the move all over this planet. Our technology, airplanes, boats, and motorcars are taking us everywhere. Our curiosity about primitive peoples is unbounded. We're still looking under every rock and tree for oil, gold, anything that can be exploited. We're busy bringing God and the universal truth to everyone, everywhere. I guess it's our quest; our journey. Maybe it's the last frontier for white men. The last opportunity to escape the stench of our factories and motorcars. Maybe we're looking for the Garden of Eden. I don't really know why we're here. I'm just a patrol officer and I like being on the cutting edge of civilization. I'm sick of wars and empires and violence... but one way or another, civilization is coming to these people. I like these Papuans. Most of them are just like us; they love their wives, their families, their children. At heart, most Papuans are peaceful people and we're going to have to learn to get along with one another. I just want to make sure their first contact with us isn't a violent one."

"Peaceful people, my arse. These Kanakas are the most violent people on earth. They are probably the only people who devour each other for Christ sake. I've run into tribes up here who ate their dead parents because they loved them, and people who cracked their enemies' skulls and sucked out their brains, and people who roast their enemies or their own kind if they despised them enough. A Garden of Eden, you say? New Guinea is a hell, an inferno of heat, insects, snakes, disease, and cannibals. You aren't going to reform these people," Woodson warned. "They'll gnaw off your testicles and put your skull on a post outside their huts. You think these boys are civilized?" and he waved towards the crew. "They go along with you for the trade goods and a chance to take pot shots at their brethren with high powered rifles. You have to have a good reason to kill a native... self-defense or some other excuse. Not them; killing men is a sport for them. If you ask me and you didn't, I'd go back to Moresby and catch the first boat home," he said finishing his tirade.

"Why are you here then, Captain, if you feel so strongly about these people?" Jack challenged.

"Why, for the quid, what else? I make ten times more profit hauling cargo up here than I would running a lugger off Brisbane."

"You married a native woman, didn't you?" O'Rourke prodded, glancing knowingly at Jack.

"Well, a man needs a sheila from time to time," Woodson retorted defensively.

"What about your children? I hear you've spawned a few up and down the coast." Jack teased.

"None of your business, is it?" Woodson replied obviously smarting from the patrol officers' two-pronged attack.

"I also hear you've sent some of them down to Sydney to get educated," Jack continued.

"Well boy, you got me." Woodson shrugged his shoulders. "I have to do something for them, don't I? Maybe, someday this will be a country and they can live here and do some good."

"Then you care about this place?" Jack asked gently.

"Yes, I care," answered Woodson. "It's a fact. I don't want to see it all ruined," and he pointed to the sea and jungle beyond, "and I don't want to see or hear about you boys being killed on some fool government errand. If we stay along the coast and do some trading, that's OK. For the rest of it," and he pointed toward the towering island, "leave it alone. This is the last brave land. Maybe in a hundred years, when we're smarter we can try for the interior, but for now, we're ruining everything we touch! Trading guns and God for gold. It ain't right, boys but I'm through preaching. I ain't no missionary bringing the locals 'the Good News'." And with that, he stumbled off to his cabin, leaving O'Rourke and Jack alone to ponder his remarks.

"What's got his wind up?" O'Rourke muttered.

"His conscience," Jack replied. "He thinks we are pilot fish preparing the way for the conquest to come. He sees his trade goods as chains. Chains to steal the Papuan's freedom. He feels the missionaries separate the people here from their own basic impulses, and they do so, as you've seen, with remarkable success. I'm inclined to agree with him. You take a native's culture from him and you have to replace it with something. It's no use pulling him out of his society unless we equip him to take his place in ours. The captain doesn't see where redemption from heathenism is a very remarkable achievement, especially when the native's only get a tenth-rate dead-end education in return. That's why the Captain is sending his brood to Australia. The missionaries for the most part educate for religion... not for living in our world."

"Bugger that," O'Rourke answered. "Before we came along, the Papuans spent their days eating each other. You call that freedom? They are better off with chains. If I weren't a patrol officer, I'd be up here trading like Woodson or off in the gold fields. Judge Murray's law is the best thing for all concerned up here. It beats being croaked and stuffed into a cook pot."

O'Rourke, Jack thought, feels perfectly comfortable in this world; he accepts life as it comes, without complaint. All he wants is a level playing field. Woodson, on the other hand, considers white man superior to the Papuan only in that, armed with weapons and trade goods, he can inflict war and slavery on a grand scale.

"Tim, the Captain thinks we've done enough damage out here already," Jack said. "He would rather we leave the Papuans alone in their world, untainted by our rules."

"Not me," O'Rourke snorted. "I want to be the first one up there. I want to see the world the way it was, before it got civilized. I doubt if a few steel axes and some trade cloth is going to change things much. Not in my lifetime, anyway. I have trouble enough traveling my own road without getting locked up in anyone else's smoke and magic."

The men snuffed out their cigars and rolled out their sleeping mats. Jack listened to the gurgle and the sucking of the water against the cutter's bow. I see too much, he thought. I see too deep. I'm no reformer. I came up here to explore my own spirit, to dream. I guess I'm really here to find out why I'm here. Nothing to do but get on with it as Judge Murray would say.

With the Delta behind them, they entered the Daru lagoon around noontime the following day. Several blasts from conch shells, a boom of a garamut drum, and shrilling tin whistles from the police compound echoed through the village and announced the Valhalla's arrival.

Soon canoes full of stout natives raced across the lagoon to greet them. “Old Buguru,” Jack said to O'Rourke, pointing to a gargantuan man sitting in the middle of a long canoe. Forty years ago Buguru led a raiding party that not recognizing the noble impulse that brought them to Daru, had devoured two missionaries.

After surviving fifteen years in the Moresby stockade, Buguru returned to his village and became the soul of amicability. In the following years he helped priests build missions all over the Delta country and in the nearby foothills. Today he was a chief rightly loved by his people and deeply appreciated by the Delta District Commissioners. Buguru was no longer a name used to frighten naughty children into compliance.

Buguru hauled his massive frame aboard, tilting the cutter sideways and nearly capsizing the canoe below him. Purpled cicatrix scars from myriad knife and arrow wounds crisscrossed his sagging tattooed breasts making them look like desiccated breadfruit. An enormous gray beard that matched a mountain of frizzy hair was topped by a headband of cassowary feathers. Two large quills from the same bird punctured the septum of his large flattened nose and stretched a foot in either direction. His neck and shoulders were bedecked with strings of crocodile and shark teeth. A circle pendant made from a pig's tusk rested on his huge belly and a black palm wood club was attached to his wrist by a thong. His lower body and torso were wrapped in palm leaves which also covered his buttocks and genitals.

“Mother Cassowary!” chortled Somatu.

“Silence stupid boy! Buguru is a man,” Sgt. Manu rasped. Manu's appraisal was right on Jack thought, and he could not help but feel the aura of raw power that Buguru exuded. Every tooth that dangled from the morbid string around the chieftain's neck represented an enemy killed, captured, wounded, or eaten. His necklace bespoke of a lifetime of slaughter that had started in his childhood and continued as he helped the government pacify the district at the mouth of the Fly. An old man? Hardly. Buguru obviously still held sway over the peninsula.

Jack moved forward to welcome Buguru and was immediately clasped around the waist and lifted into the air by the chief's powerful arms. "What did you bring me?" shouted Buguru as he lowered Jack gently to the deck, still locked in his embrace.

"Tea, coffee, sugar, and tinned milk," Jack gasped as he freed himself from the giant's grasp and pointed to a stack of stores piled in the gangway.

"Ah! Tinned milk from a cow. How I love it! But why you not bring me a cow? I have never seen a cow. The only milk I ever tasted came from a woman's breast. It is sweet, but not so sweet as tinned milk," he laughed. "I have missed you much, Jack. You are my son. You are not like the Commissioner who sulks all day on his veranda and who only stirs to make busy work and trouble for my people," Buguru waved his club in the direction of the district settlement.

Native women ringed the shoreline, using the cutter's visit to break away from household drudgery. Several younger women, their lap-laps hoisted up to their thighs, were wading out into the water. Their arms, necks, and breasts were smeared with white clay in a vain effort to ward off flies and stinging insects. The mud also served to void the odor of mother's milk and to soften their nipples.

"The further from dis village the mud is found, de sweeter de smell," an Oroka carrier joked to the amusement of the others. Naked children, clamoring for attention and excitedly clutching their genitals, followed the women into the water. Older boys solemnly squatted on the edge of the embankment and watched curiously as the launch fired up its engine, sending a cloud of diesel smoke rolling over the assembled crowd. An old man coughed loudly and spat a gob of red betel phlegm into the sand.

A heavy-set man was puffing his way down a steep path that led to the water's edge. District Officer Jackson barked some orders to the constabulary men trailing behind him. Two policemen rushed forward and clambered aboard the launch at the edge of the jetty as DO Jackson paused, removed his cap, and wiped the sweat off his large florid pink forehead with a trade scarf.

The constable at the helm waited until the man in the bow heaved the anchor aboard, and then he guided the small craft toward the encircling reef. In minutes, the launch pulled alongside crashing its prow into the side of the Valhalla as the men in the canoes hastily paddled backwards to avoid capsizing. "Avast you misbegotten buggers!" Capt. Woodson screamed at the men in the launch. "You bloody twits will sink us all!"

Ignoring him, the constable sprang aboard the cutter and snapped a smart salute. "Welcome to Daru," he said proudly. "Kiap Jackson wishes you to come ashore immediately."

Jack returned the salute and said, "Tell the DO we'll be ashore as soon as we can. Mr. Woodson, where will you anchor?"

"Right here, and not a yard closer," Woodson replied. "There's a reef not ten yards from the beach. I don't want to get holed in this God forsaken place. It would take two months to get repaired and hauled out of here. I'm staying on the boat. And you'd better leave some police aboard or these buggers will steal us blind," he muttered to Jack and nodded at the natives waiting below in the canoes. "No women either," he motioned towards the crowd on the beach. "They're worse than the men."

"I will come to the village this afternoon," Jack said as he clasped Buguru's hand. "We will need many strong men." Buguru nodded and grabbed a case of tinned milk and without a word clambered into his waiting canoe. Jack and O'Rourke scrambled over the side and seated themselves in the launch. The canoe men easily beat the launch ashore and awaited them on the beach lining up silently behind Buguru.

Jack leaped out of the launch. O'Rourke was close behind. The DO grasped Jack by the hand firmly. “Good to see you again Jack. I presume you are O'Rourke?” Jackson said shaking O'Rourke's hand. “Welcome to Daru such as it is. Best we go to the Settlement House. It's too damn hot here.” They left Buguru passing out tins of milk to his favorite women while he waited for the rest of the canned goods to be brought ashore. Jackson turned and started up the hill. The rest of the party followed him up a narrow path that led to the DO’s compound.

Even though Jack was wearing shorts and a light shirt, he could feel the sweat trickle down his back. After the cooling breezes on the Valhalla, he was immediately aware of the suffocating, muggy heat that engulfed the island as it baked in the noonday sun.

The officers lunched on the veranda of the Settlement House. Burns-Philips Company fly paper streamers hung everywhere, entrapping a myriad of flying insects that broiled black in the sun and then oozed down and dropped onto the planks below.

One hause-boi ladled boiled bully beef, steaming hot rice, and baked yams onto their plates while another fanned the men with a palm frond or swished away flies with a whisk. “Boy!” DO Jackson shouted at the servant. “Get away from here with that fan. Dammit, you're making me nervous.” Jack was annoyed but kept his thoughts to himself. Why do white men, even patrol officers, order their hause-bois about and shout curses at them if they can't guess what's on our mind? Why do we call them boys when most of them are fathers with children of their own?

Jack rapidly lost interest in the fly-splashed food and was preparing to make his excuses when O'Rourke beat him to it. “Finished! I'll be off to the trading store.”

Jack nodded glumly as O'Rourke left to secure sago, coconuts, and sugar cane for the trek.

“You’ll want the canoes secured to the Valhalla,” the DO said. “I’ll see to it this afternoon.”

“Thanks,” Jack said. “I’ll see to the men.”

"Give the schoolhouse a visit when you've finished. Let me know what you think of that lot," the DO called after him. Jack nodded his assent and hurried down the track before the DO could decide to join him.

Word had already been sent to Buguru to inform the people that carriers were required by the government. Over a hundred volunteers were in front of the palm-thatched houses when Jack entered the village. The number of rows was increasing as more and more men joined their ranks. Only the young, the aged, the deformed, and the women were left in the houses. The men had been told that the pay was fifteen shillings a month, so they wanted to know the magnitude of the task that the Government was offering for such pay.

The men stood patiently while Jack explained the nature of the expedition, the large tract of country they would cross; he mentioned the hardships and the possibility that some of them might not return. At first, they started to waver, but when Jack told them that this was "government work" and that it was "work only for strong men" nearly every man stepped forward. They were all "strong men" or wished to be considered such by their people. All eyes watched as Jack moved among the men followed closely by a clerk, the village constable, and Buguru.

"This fellow looks fit enough," said Jack pointing with his swagger stick to a Constable's son. The clerk made a note in his record book as the local constable swelled with pride.

Jack moved to the next man in line and the clerk said glancing at his book, "This man has just become a father." Without a word, Jack continued down the row.

The sun was well past its zenith and still the selection went on. Jack stood in front of a man painted black from head to toe. "This man looks strong," he said.

"His wife died six month ago and he is still mourning," the clerk said.

"It's time he began government work," and Jack tapped him on the shoulder. The widower grinned as the clerk jotted down his name.

Altogether Jack selected ten men to add to the six prisoners from the gaol that Jackson had thrust on him. As a group, these Delta men were the strongest natives in Papua, though of the two groups, the Oroko men from Moresby will probably be the most difficult to handle, Jack thought.

The clerk gave each man a blanket, a loincloth, and a flannel shirt for the mountains and told them to report to the Valhalla before sunrise the next day.

In addition to the carriers, the patrol had acquired the services of five more constables to augment the Moresby squad under the direct command of Sgt. Manu. Together the carriers, constables, and patrol officers numbered 50 men. From the start he and O'Rourke had agreed that a small party was necessary to successfully cross such a large area of country. They also knew they would have to find villages, because they could not carry sufficient food to sustain themselves. As it was the carriers would have to carry 50-pound packs over difficult country, march on a handful of rice, and sleep under the most trying of conditions.

On his way to inspect the schoolhouse, Jack passed through the village. Clouds of dirty brown dust, stirred up by oxcarts carrying copra to the drying sheds, danced among the forest of house posts. On their porches women sat glumly chewing betel nut and pounding bark into tapa cloth. They scarcely looked up as he passed. He began humming and half-sang a patrol officers ditty he had picked up at Rabaul:

"Oh, I wish I were an acting ADO.
Oh, I wish I were an acting ADO.
If I were an acting ADO,
I'd get more pay than a poor PO.
Oh, I wish I were an acting ADO.
So it's hi, it's ho, it's fiddle dee dee,
That is what I'd like to be."

A five-foot fence encircled the entire school. It was made of long bamboo tubes placed horizontally on top of each other. They were kept in place by saplings pegged into the ground. This fence had been ordered by government officers to keep the pigs away from the schoolhouse.

Inside the fence on the windward side, a lone building stood facing in a north-south direction. As Jack stepped into the doorway, he could see at least fifty children in the room. Some were sitting cross-legged, hunched over crude slates in front of one of the teachers, while others sprawled over each other's warm, brown bodies behind him. Several of the younger children studied pictures in a worn book as the other teacher sat on the floor with a pupil's head in his lap picking off lice as he spoke. On the walls Jack could see biblical picture stories and an English alphabet chart which used images from a culture totally alien to these children.

A cockroach had eaten its way through the first picture labeled *apple*. A portrait of George V smiled benignly at the children. A small boy spotted Jack and in a clear shrill voice, piped out, "Good afternoon, Sir!" The student body leaped to attention, as did the schoolteachers. "Good afternoon, Sir," they chorused, slightly embarrassing Jack. "Carry on," he said and saluted back.

The senior teacher turned to the students, "Sit down," he commanded. They immediately obeyed, forcing the teachers to hopscotch through the tangled arms and legs to greet Jack. The first man clasped Jack's hand and pumped it vigorously. "I am the assistant teacher, Orabai, and this is Onai. He is a cadet from Moresby College. The children as you can see, are all ages and are in the first to fourth form," he announced proudly. "Would you be pleased to hear some recitation?"

"No, thank you," Jack said quickly. "Please continue."

The teacher looked disappointed, but turned to the class and said, "Return to your work at once. No one is to be naughty. Do you hear me?"

"Yes, sir," they chorused and pretended to look at their slates, but one by one, their heads raised up like flowers to peer curiously at Jack. He looked over their shoulders as they painstakingly shaped and reshaped the letters on slate boards trying vainly to match those in the copybook.

When the teachers excused the children for recess, Jack followed the class into the schoolyard. The older boys went down to the river where they supervised the nose cleaning of the younger children. Then they led them back to the schoolyard where they initiated a strange game. The boys held long willow wands in their hands... a three-foot piece of string was attached to the wand and a small oval-shaped piece of white cardboard dangled at the end of the string. They waved the wands in the air making lazy figure eights over their heads.

In a few moments clouds of small yellow, blue and white butterflies were circling around the eggs-shaped disks. When a butterfly landed on a disk and closed its wings, the boys would grasp it quickly in their fingers. Using small cassowary bones, they pinned the live butterflies atop their bushy hair.

Soon the yard was full of gamboling, laughing children who raced around in circles, flapping their arms, their bushy hair alive with fluttering butterflies. The older girls were giggling and smiling self-consciously at Jack as they pretended to be busy sweeping the school grounds with small hand brooms.

"I say the government teacher is taking a long time to arrive," Onai commented. The children are getting dirty again."

"That isn't surprising for Europeans," said Orabai, the oldest of the teachers. "In the years I've taught here, I've never seen a government person arrive before midday. You only have to visit the copra plantation or the Patrol Post to see what the people mean by 'European sleep'. The policemen, clerks, prisoners, and workers start at eight o'clock when the conch or bugle blows. But the white men usually arrive a little ahead of morning tea and it takes a long time for the teapots to run dry. Then after Big Tea, they nap through the afternoon," he told Jack as they walked across the wet schoolyard. "The plantation men gave us wood and nails to build the school. The government gives us books and pays my salary."

A poor place to construct a school, Jack noted. The owners of the copra plantation had allocated this parcel of land for a school because it wasn't needed for copra sheds. During the wet season the floods scoured the area of accumulated wrappings, human and animal excreta, and debris deposited during the dry season.

Huge breadfruit trees towered high above blocking most of the sunlight. The undergrowth around the classroom was so thick the village was not visible. Swarms of mosquitoes infested the dark shadows and bothered the children. There were no latrines. Jack was appalled by the putrid smells that permeated the grounds. The teachers and the students used the bush. Neither the teachers nor the villagers believed the white men's stories about tiny worms that would make them sick. Nobody had seen these worms of destruction including the native orderlies. The bush was kept clean by fat pigs whose bellies drug on the ground.

Two by two, the children happily marched back into the classroom and renewed their places on the mats. An evil-looking man with a gourd mask stuck his head through an open window. The children clutched their tablets and shrunk to the floor fearing to meet his gaze.

"Go away!" shouted the teachers and rushed towards the open window. The man pointed a cassowary bone at the teachers, and they shrunk back in horror. Spying the white man at the other end of the building, he leaped into the air and flapping his arms like a bantam rooster, crowed loudly. Then cackling like a hen, he fled across a meadow and disappeared into the bush.

"Who was that?" Jack snapped at Onai.

"That's Kaori," he replied, taken aback at the sharpness of Jack's tone. "He's a sorcerer; the worst of the lot. Everyone fears him in the village, even Buguru."

"Why don't you run him off?" asked Jack.

"Can't seem to catch him. He comes around most always at night, demanding food or gifts. Besides, you can't prove sorcery," Onai said defensively.

"I'll report this to DO Jackson for you. I'm sure he'll take some action."

"The DO not catch this man. He can disappear. No one can catch him."

"Perhaps," Jack said. "Good dai! Good dai students!"

"Good dai, Sir!" the children chorused.

Disgusted with himself for feeling slightly apprehensive, Jack walked slowly back toward the village. He noticed the MO and his native assistant on their way down from the police compound and quickly caught up with them. The assistant carried a bilum loaded with packages of medicines and syringes. "You're just in time for sick call," he said gleefully. "Care to assist?"

"Why not?" Jack said shrugging his shoulders. The MO withheld comment and continued to puff a pipe as they walked toward the main square of the village. "There was a strange chap hanging around the schoolhouse. The teachers call him Kaori. They seemed to fear him," Jack volunteered.

"Kaori's our local boogie-man. He tries to make trouble when he can. He resents me and my men and the teachers as well. Since we've come up here, he's lost a lot of power over the villagers. We can't condone sorcery, Jack. In fact, we lock them up if we catch them practicing their conjurer's tricks. The trouble is that in the natives' minds all my medicine is just another bag of tricks. They can't separate our "magic" from their magic. We've put an end to yaws and leprosy, but the truth is," he continued, "I've seen them heal people with their mumbo jumbo who I couldn't help. Call it empathy, call it mind-over-matter, but I've seen children with pneumonia get up and walk out of hospital, fully recovered after a sorcerer rubbed soil on their chests."

"Has Kaori ever been charged?" Jack asked.

"When I first opened the clinic, Kaori showed up and pointed a cassowary quill at one of my orderlies. The man fainted and fell into a trance. He began shaking, turned ash-colored and died. I couldn't do a thing to help him. Called it toxic suggestion in my report, but Canberra made me change it to a case of cerebral malaria. Maybe it was." He tapped out his pipe on a post. "Canberra's always right, you know. Look at any native orderly manual, all written in the King's English. They just can't recognize down there, the fact that pidgin and Motu aren't forms of broken English. They are true languages. We should be teaching Motu at the school. It would make communication easier for everyone if we did."

A great commotion followed the arrival of the patrol officer and the MO. Many villagers fearful of the MO's needle tried to flee at the last moment, but the Daru constables, the black dogs of the government, stood guard at the likely escape points. Pigs squealed as their owners dragged them over the fence and threw them out of the compound. Sleeping dogs, aroused from their torpor, snarled at each other; dogfights broke out everywhere and created swirls of dust adding to the cries and confusion. After they received their shots, the children tearfully buried their heads under their mothers' arms. The women took their turn and walked away ashamed and crying that the white men had seen their bottoms.

Then it was Buguru's turn. Under a weathered canvas hat, the pink face of the MO grinned mischievously at Buguru who was bent over a box that had been placed in the middle of the square. The orderly poked Buguru in the buttocks with his needle and Buguru yelled in consternation. "You scream louder than a pregnant woman," the MO's jowls shook back and forth as he laughed. Buguru scowled as he walked across the compound trying to muster what dignity he could while he massaged his buttock with one hand.

A que formed in front of the second assistant who made them swallow tiny yellow medicine balls which the village people said were made from the brains of dead people. A glum crowd gathered in front of the MO and he roared at them in pidgin: "Supposim you fella sockin talk belong Doctor Boy, me cookin no good shit-haus biling all! Orright! Supposim me cookin, alla man e must workim new falla!" (If you don't listen to the orderlies, I'll condemn your latrines, which are not good, to be burned down, and you'll have to build new ones!)

A loud wail came from the other side of the village. Someone was beating his wife. "Let him beat her," said one of the Daru constables at Jack's side. "If dis husband throws his wife out of de house and down onto de ground. Only den do I make an arrest," said the man.

The DO joined Jack in the square and they walked down to the river's edge where men were fashioning a lakotoi. This was no ordinary lakotoi; it was an evoka, a craft designed to sail long distances. As many as twenty men were busy milling several huge logs. It wasn't all work as they took turns hewing the logs and beating on drums. Small boys brought a supply of coconuts and betel nuts. When the evoka was finished, it would be over seventy feet long. Its masts would be thirty feet high and would host tall heart-shaped sails made of coconut matting. The beam was over twenty feet wide and the deck, hoisted above the twin logs, would house several families who would be off trading for kona shells several months at a time in the Western Islands. In the days before iron, it would have taken years to build, but even with iron adzes the village men still required several months to complete their task.

The two men followed a forest trail and emerged onto a promontory where the river met the sea. Patches of black wooly clouds were racing toward the headlands. They paused to watch a group of men busily prepare a hangi for a feast honoring those who were leaving in the morning and perhaps never returning. Cooking pig was men's work and Jack watched as they covered the hot coals and stones in the pit with wet banana leaves. The carcasses of several pigs split down the middle and were laid carefully on the leaves. Then another layer of leaves was added completely covering the pigs. The men added sugar cane and bananas to this next layer, and then more leaves, followed by vegetables, pineapples, and spinach. Alternating the foodstuff with layers of banana leaves, they finally filled the whole pit. They tossed the remainder of the hot coals and ashes carefully on top sealing in the entire meal. The food would steam and cook for several hours and then would be dug out for the evening's feast.

The rack of clouds had reached the tops of the tallest trees and seemed to draw the smaller clouds towards them. Not a patch of blue was left and the clouds seemed to form a huge funnel in which everything that breathed and moved in the village was trapped. Smoke from the kitchens filtered through the thatched roofs and formed large halos that hovered above the houses in the timeless air.

Somewhere in the distant skies to the north, lightning flashed like a beacon. It dimly illuminated the outline of a massive flowering flame tree that stood outside the Government House. The two men sprinted for shelter as the first huge drops of rain began splattering the dust. A lightning bolt shattered a mango tree on the edge of the compound; thunder crackled and deafened their ears. A cloud burst and rid itself of a million gallons of rain, dumping it precipitously on the plantation grounds. Native women scurried homeward, banana leaf umbrellas held over their heads while their naked breasts pranced up and down. Huddled in small groups, men waited stoically under the giant pandanus trees for the storm to pass. Eventually they gave up and ran toward the village to join the women and children in the smoke-filled huts. Promptly at six p.m. the rain stopped and the skies cleared.

Just after dark women brought them a basket of prawns cooked in coconut oil and packets of pork, spinach, and other vegetables from the hangi. The rest of the feast had been carried into the village. The choice bits of brains, snouts, noses, ears, and jowls were given to the older men. The backs and sides were shared by police and the carriers while the remaining hams, hocks, and shoulders were eaten by the village men. The women and children weren't offered a share of the pig meat; instead, they ate fish caught earlier in the day. After their meal was finished, Jack sat with the other white men in settler's chairs, his feet propped up on the porch rail. Smoke from their cigars created a blue haze that circled lazily overhead.

The men listened quietly to the drumming and chanting which was accentuated by the occasional wailing voice of a wife or mother already grieving for a husband or a son soon to be departing on the long dangerous trip into the unknown territory. Mundi, the house-boy, poured more tea, stirring in canned milk and sugar while Sandar, the other house-boy, used his whisk to shoo away the cloud of flies that hovered near the dining table.

“I wouldn't want to be in your shoes. I'd rather be here in this hell any day than on a patrol up in that God forsaken country. In fact, I'd rather be in a Brisbane pub drinking Four X pilsner than in this pesthole of liars and lazy rogues,” and he pointed his stogie towards the village. Jack noticed the house-boys' ears twitch as they exchanged knowing glances, yet pretended not to understand the white Masta's talk. Interesting, Jack thought, how the local officials, missionaries, and even patrol officers he knew talked over the natives' heads, acting as if they didn't exist.

“Well,” Jack said, “I'd rather be out there on patrol facing honest savages any day as opposed to being in a city. Our so-called civilization is full of liars and thieves and corrupt politicians.” He punctuated his remarks by flicking an ash off his cigar. “The Papuans that I've known are strong people. They love their families and they have proven helpful to us 'Outside Men'. If they lie, it's because they have to lie to protect themselves. We drum up a thousand petty rules that they can't comprehend and then send them to the stockade or put them in work parties if they don't obey. Most of the time our laws must seem pretty silly and useless to them.” Jack leaned forward in his chair.

“Of course they appreciate the kerosene lamps, the fish hooks, the steel machetes, and adzes. They really don't need our bibles, boats, or booze, and they aren't certain about our medicines. But they have shown a willingness to learn. Someday when kids, like the ones I met at the schoolhouse today, are grown, they are going to run this country. From what I've seen, Papua's going to be one helluva great country.” Mundi gave Jack a grateful look as he warmed his coffee with an extra dollop of brandy.

“Not in my time I wager,” Jackson replied. “And not in yours either if you persist in heading upriver on this damn fool patrol.”

“Time for bed,” O'Rourke said slamming the front legs of his chair down on the floor. He stood up, his tall body towering over the others. “Morning will come early,” and he strolled down to the sleeping veranda, opened the screen, and by the light of the kerosene lamp started unlacing his boots. DO Jackson grumbled a

“Good night” and disappeared into his sleeping quarters in the rear of the house. The boys quickly cleared the dishes from the table and stacked them in the kitchen to be washed in the morning. They quietly left and headed to the village leaving Jack alone with his thoughts. The burning coconut shells that had been tossed in the stove sent a pallid cloud of smoke across the porch keeping the whining mosquitoes at bay. The chirping of the crickets and the whirring wings of the cicadas could be clearly heard now.

Leaning back into the squatter's chair, Jack listened to the buzz and thrum of countless tiny wings and soft rustlings syncopated by secret calls from the jungle. His shoulders relaxed, his head nodded and fell forward, his chin rested on his chest. The cigar fell from his grasp as he dozed off; his body tilted to one side of the chair. Jack didn't see a set of luminous eyes peering at him from the jungle nor did he hear a sound as a quick hand grabbed the still smoldering cigar lying near his outstretched feet. He shifted his weight slightly but did not awaken when a dark figure pointed a cassowary bone towards his stomach and snapped it in tow. He didn't feel the bloodstained branches of bougainvillea waving in front of his face.

Awakening with a start, Jack stretched and then headed for his cot. Before we white men arrived these people lived in the Stone Age, but they were free, Jack thought as he undressed. They murder each other one at a time or a few at a time when they go raiding, while we more civilized men slaughter each other by the millions in our wars all around the globe. Who's civilized and who's the barbarian, he wondered as he wrapped himself in a blanket and netting, rather unsuccessfully trying to keep from being bled white by the blood sucking insects.

After a brief blessedly cooling rain, the thunderous roar of the bullfrogs kept him awake even though his body was quiet and his eyelids closed. With the village drums stopped, Jack could still hear the women wailing deeply.

Where's the real danger? Is it from savages running amuck or from white men lusting for power and territory? Or is it the nature of the universe itself that we need fear most? His mind finally stopped and he dozed off. He felt but didn't hear the Great Mother whisper, "When men talk or think too much, I do not hear them. I can only listen when you are silent. So be still. You are not who you think you are. You are capable of doing more than you dream of. You cannot see too deep or too much. Follow the light, not to me, but through me. What you search for is in yourself."

Jack awoke with the hot morning sun burning his face and body. Not bothering to lace his boots, he shuffled from the sleeping porch and gazed owl-like at the table on the veranda. An orange oilcloth had replaced the pale cloth of the day before. Ringed by fried bananas, paw-paws and mangoes filled the platter in the center of the table. A bowl of rice sprinkled with cinnamon and topped with pineapple segments sat at its side. An open tin of jam had an open tin of O'Forty milk as its neighbor. The scent of freshly baked scones and coffee wafted across the porch. The decaying corpses of flies and roaches from the evening before had been swept away. A breeze off the inlet brought the scent of brine keeping the village odors at bay.

"A good day for the race," cried a cheerful O'Rourke as he stepped out of the kitchen, coffee mug in hand to join the men on the porch.

"What race?" Jack asked.

"Why, the human race, of course," O'Rourke sallied.

With a groan Jack sat down at the table. "Are you always this bloody cheerful in the morning?"

"It depends," O'Rourke responded, "on whether I slept in a chair or in a bed. Now, if I've spent the night with a pretty woman, then I'm twice as cheerful."

"Well, you won't be spending many nights in the next few months in a bed or with a beautiful woman unless you run into some native debs," Jackson said as he slid into a chair. "So you may have your morning spats."

"Let's eat and get on our way," Jack growled. He gulped hastily from his tin coffee cup simultaneously searing his lips and throat. "Christ!" he howled, spilling coffee on his unkempt shirtfront, slightly scalding himself, as the house-boy sniggered. "Well, I'm awake now," Jack said. "Wide awake and raring to go."

The whole village came down to the pier to see them off. Old men muttered in their beards; the women wailed and cried. Small boys jumped up and down and grabbing their crotches, peed in the sand. Sand flies were buzzing around their heads indiscriminately inflicting painful bites on black and white alike. Only the white men seemed to notice or care. They brushed away the flies with one hand while shaking hands with the other.

Jack and O'Rourke stepped out of the launch and onto the Valhalla which quickly weighed anchor as the two police officers and the men waved their last farewells to the crowd assembled on the shore. The cutter moved out of the roadstead just as the tide was beginning to run out and headed across the shallows for the Tauru passage. Jack made an entry in his journal:

> *We left Daru at 10:45 a.m. on the first of January, 1935. The patrol has begun.*

PART TWO

THE FLY RIVER

The Valhalla moved across the Tauru passage. The Fly Estuary was like an inland sea. An archipelago of islets built up from river silt, mud, and mangroves dotted the shallow waters. The mists which hung like a screen between Daru and the estuary often barred the traveler's way, but today the mystic veil over the amazing river was less harsh than it appeared.

"I'd hate to be stranded on a mudflat here," O'Rourke muttered. "It doesn't look too safe to me," and he pointed out some estuarial crocodiles that were skimming away from the cutter, flashing their wet reptilian tails. A squall sent the porters and constabulary scurrying for cover and then they were through it into bright sunshine and calm. They left the tides of the sea and the tides of the jungle were ahead of them. A lime green canopy descended as they entered a long gloomy corridor.

"We are on the mighty Fly River, gentlemen," Woodson announced. "Some say that it pours as much water into the sea as the Amazon." The Valhalla, towing the heavily-laden canoes, progressed slowly upstream against a four-knot current. Then the tide turned and the small craft picked up speed rushing by the reed-lined banks.

When night fell, Woodson ordered the coxswain to tie up to the river's edge. There had been no mosquitoes during the day, but at sunset they descended with a vengeance. The men sat under mosquito nets that were not all that could be desired, and dutifully ate the first of their iron rations. Cookie brought out small charcoal pots and the porters fed them with coconut chips in an effort to dissuade the murderous bloodsuckers. Soon a pall of smoke drifted over the boat, providing some relief. "The Valhalla might be an old tub, but she brought us here, safe and sound, didn't she?" vouchsafed Woodson from the cutter's cockpit where the three men sat together under a canvas canopy. "Did you ever see a place like this before?" as he gestured to the jungle that closed around them.

"This whole stretch of river resembles a fairy land," O'Rourke replied. They were being rewarded by a wonderful view of fireflies flitting among the mangroves. The trees appeared as if lit by thousands of flashing miniature light bulbs flashing. The water reflected the fiery skyscape.

"It's truly awesome," Jack replied his voice muted by the sounds emanating from the river. Large frogs, small frogs, tree frogs, tenor frogs, basses, squealers, croakers, and whistlers; their mighty dissonance echoed through the mangrove swamps.

"Sounds like Saturday night in me old pub in Sydney," O'Rourke said, adding an imitation croak to the clamor around them.

They laughed and then Woodson said, "Pipe down or I'll feed you to the crocs," and he pointed to the yellow eyes and elongated snouts of a pair of reptiles that had slithered silently up the bank close to the mooring lines.

"Fair Dinkim! They are monsters," said O'Rourke. The carriers had spotted them as well and Jack was relieved when they drove them off by splashing their paddles. "Care for a swim before we hit the sack?" O'Rourke asked.

"No thanks, not tonight or any night," Jack replied. A gibbous moon rose silvering the ripples that swished across the mud banks adding to the dream-like scene. The men sat around the engine's low hood that served as a table smoking cigars.

Sergeant Manu was serving as the "smoke maker" for the constables. First he dried the tobacco with a burning ember held close above it; he then rolled the cigarette using a leaf in lieu of paper, which he inserted in a long bamboo holder. Placing the lighted end in his mouth, he exhaled, blowing the smoke out of the open end of the holder. When the smoke issued forcefully out of the reservoir holes, the pipe was passed to the constables. There were many "aahs" as they drew in each puff with a curious whistle of pursed lips. To the white men it seemed a round about way to enjoy the fragrant weed, but they didn't doubt the merits of a cool smoke.

“Two deep puffs and they will turn barmy and fall asleep,” remarked Captain Woodson.

“Three and they will suffocate themselves,” O'Rourke proclaimed. The constables smoked quietly and then as if on cue, they stretched out on their mats, pulled down the mosquito netting and sank into a torpid sleep.

Woodson and O'Rourke went below to the cabin leaving Jack alone to stand the first watch. He spread his mat on the deck and covered his body loosely with a mosquito net, aware of the vast overwhelming nature above him, the power and intensity of the stars. As he rolled onto his stomach, the ash from his cigar fell off and landed on the back of a small snail that was traveling across the deck under the light of those same stars. The snail shrugged off the ash as if it were an incident of small importance and meandered patiently onward in search of some leaf-like substance.

What if I have only a snails-eye view, not of everyday life, but of existence? Jack speculated. Here in the rain forest a man can't roll the universe into a theoretical ball. The life force is all around us. On the one hand it reminds us of the oneness of man with nature, and on the other hand, tells us that we are the intruders. Here nature dictates the territorial imperatives. There is no neutrality.

Stars of the fifth and even sixth magnitude seemed sharper as Jack surveyed the sky. His nostrils filled with the musky smell of leaves wet with low-lying river mist that mingled with the sweet, soft odor of decomposing leaves from the forest floor. The stupendous cacophony of the frogs merged with the shrill screeching of the insects and with the gurgling of the river. Jack's eyes closed. Sleep seemed to emanate from this district like a thin pulsating anesthetic, possessed of a definite healing power.

The Great Mother murmured, “There is more than this forest ... this planet ... even this universe you dream of. One day you will know that death is only an illusion, and you will be free to serve a higher power.”

When morning broke, the Valhalla was stranded in the center of a great mud bank with the river so diminished it didn't appear to be the same stream. “The tide must have fallen nearly twelve feet. It's good you found the channel,” Jack said pointing to the thin band of water that led to the main stream. “We have at least two fathoms here.”

“That’ll do,” replied Woodson.

After the carriers went ashore to build breakfast fires, Jack and O'Rourke went inland to shoot some fresh meat. The foliage of palm vines and great trees were covered with stag horn and orchids, the silence caused them speak in whispers. The cool of the green gloom was a welcome contrast to the already fierce sun beating down on the open riverbank. Countless birds concealed themselves in the dense foliage and though they could be heard, they were extremely difficult to shoot. When they made a kill, they were unable to locate the downed birds. Sometimes the barbed spines of the lawyer vine could be avoided but the mosquitoes could not. “A man could starve to death in here with food all around him,” O'Rourke complained.

The two men entered a clearing surrounded by a dark tangle of vines and branches. A shaft of light penetrated the forest and reached down to the earth below. A small structure stood in the center made of thousands of twigs and sticks. Grass topped its broad roof and lined the rigid interior walls. The lawn in front of the four-foot high structure was covered with pale pebbles, snail shells, dead beetles, berries and piles of cut flowers. “A bower bird's nest, but it looks like no one's home,” O'Rourke remarked as the men carefully stepped around the nest and onto a dim track and worked their way deeper into the glen.

“Look!” Jack said and pointed to a branch near the treetops. “It's a bird of paradise! Be quiet,” Jack urged, and both men stood still. To their amazement it popped a red berry in its mouth and began to display. The head and neck were pure yellow above a rich metallic green breast. Long plumed tufts of orange feathers sprang from each wing. The bird bent down, stretched, and raised its long plumes and extended them until they formed two golden fans, each striped with brilliant red at the base. The whole bird was overshadowed, its crouching body, yellow head and emerald green throat forming the foundation and setting for the golden glory that waved above.

"I'll be damned," O'Rourke said as the bird opened its beak to display a pale green lining. To their delight, a female landed on a perch high over their heads. The male danced excitedly further out on his perch, trying to entice the female, who perhaps noticing the men below, flew away. The rejected suitor rearranged some of his feathers and flew back into the treetops and resumed his patient vigil.

"That was a beaut show," O'Rourke said and applauded the performance. On the way back they stumbled into a mound of green ants and were bitten repeatedly. Both men began cursing as they flailed at the biting hordes with their bush hats. They retraced their steps to the river as quickly as they could, but the mud was exceptionally affectionate and clung to their feet like a determined lover. They rejoined the cutter and were pleased to discover that the porters had already prepared breakfast and had brought it aboard the Valhalla. "A spot of Negrito rum in your cocoa boys?" a cheerful Woodson called out.

"Not on your life," said O'Rourke. "What a vile brew that would be." Woodson shrugged and ordered the deck-boi to anchor in mid-stream. As they ate, the tide returned. In less than an hour's time, the riverbanks and shallows disappeared. Jack stared at the almost incomprehensible world in front of him.

The tidewater area was a fierce marine battlefield where a relentless war raged unceasingly, as was the luxuriant tropical jungle that stretched around them, each plant, and each tree, striving for a chance to live and bring forth its seed. The great trees served as hosts for countless parasitic growth which flourished so profusely they completely hid the form of the parent tree.

Everywhere mammoth trees staggered and bent under mighty burdens of vines that slowly strangled and smothered them to death. Amid the forests an equally profuse insect and animal life fought for survival in a universe seemingly ignored by a detached and indifferent God.

Sergeant Manu joined him, and as if he could read Jack's mind interjected, “If a man should die here, the Great Mother will grow roots in his palms.”

“We don't want to end up pushing up palm trees,” O'Rourke quipped.

“Then we'd best move on,” Jack said and set the day's marching orders.

The party was soon underway; the Valhalla moved out over the broad waters, led by the blaze of the morning equatorial sun. Myriads of horseflies and butterflies danced in front of them. Hornbills, Goura pigeons, and dazzling flocks of lush feathered parrots escaped the jungle rainbowing upwards into the sky.

“Parrots as small as wrens and pigeons bigger than turkeys. It's unreal,” O'Rourke exclaimed. Driftwood and occasionally whole trees floated past the Valhalla.

Double watches were posted throughout the day to prevent the cutter from being holed up or crushed by the floating debris. The lookouts kept a sharp eye out for natives, but so far they had not seen a single native or canoe. The only sign of human agency was distant smoke far inland from the river.

A lonely egret, pure white and disdainful, preceded the Valhalla up the river. It waited until the cutter drew near, then it slowly turned and began a rather awkward take-off. Rising into the air, it became an apogee of delight. Its long legs were folded under and using its broad wings, it sailed up over the water and landed a few hundred yards ahead to wait patiently for the cutter.

“A good omen, Kiap,” Somatu said. “Only good spirits live inside the white bird. The white bird flies ahead to tell the people we are coming. The black bird is an evil thing. When you see a black bird, you know bad things are coming behind you.” Somatu prophesied and went back to his task of repacking Jack's field kit.

Late in the afternoon, they turned due west into the face of the setting sun, leaving the egret behind when it turned and flew over the cutter and headed down river towards the estuary. The sky ahead was barred by banks of rose and magenta clouds, floating on a brilliant background of thalia-colored sky. Every moment the clouds changed, flaming and flaring like a fire, gradually fading out to greet the dark shade of night. In its turn, the river like a mighty gilded mirror reflected the sublime mutations. At intervals, it appeared as a vast lake of liquid opal, flushing, changing, and iridescent as the alternating scheme of the skies decreed.

Some of the trees seemed to be hung with ominous-looking black fruit. But the pendulous shapes were flying foxes clustered together in their thousands awaiting the setting of the sun. At dusk they arose in dark clouds to feast on the wild fruit trees.

"Shoot 'em, moriboa," Somatu appealed to a constable, pointing up to the bats swinging overhead.

"Be silent boy. We have white man's kai kai. We don't need a stinking fruit bat," He said to please the patrol officers.

The engine-boi anchored the cutter in the lee of a small island. The river was still six hundred yards wide at this point. O'Rourke ordered the men to break out the iron rations, and he permitted the cooks to light a small kerosene stove to boil tea. Somatu and Kanai passed out the tea. Jack could hear them complaining about the rations. "We could have fed on moriboa," the expression on Somatu's face clearly showed disgust for the white man's food from a box.

Night fell and swallowed their world. Silently the river glided around the island sanctuary, carrying its waters from far lands, pregnant with mystery and enchantment. The stars danced to light the world. As on the night before, the fireflies flew over their heads until the sky above resembled a miniature meteor shower.

The porters were all hunched down their backs against the ribs of the cargo deck as if they sensed the deep darkness was hiding headhunters or evil sorcerers. The jungle around them exhaled its sweet scented breath. They had left the mangrove stench far behind in the mouth of the estuary.

Goblin frogs began to chorus an anthem from the swamps and the crickets bassooned while the mosquitoes shrieked. The silhouette of the cutter lay motionless on the deep water and only the purling of the current against the bow stem told that the waters moved. The ship slept. She rested like a dream vessel on the waters of Lethe; Morpheus had taken the wheel. All the party slumbered except Jack and Somatu who kept the dogwatch, tormented by a horde of insects that descended on them during the night with a sound like surf breaking on a distant shore. Attracted by the light, they found their way into Jack's and Somatu's eyes, noses, ears, and mouths forcing them to douse their lanterns.

The gold-plated day revealed myriads of dead may flies. Their corpses littered the deck like a powder of snow. The engine of the cutter coughed and fired into action getting underway while the men washed themselves and the decks with buckets of water pulled from the river. The craft rounded another bend when suddenly a 50-foot canoe shot out of the reeds in front of them. It was propelled by twenty men whose long sweeps pulled it across their bow. They shouted and immediately a dozen more canoes came out of the reeds and surrounded the Valhalla. The nervous constables immediately grabbed their rifles, jacked shells into the chambers, and aimed them at the men in the canoes as had Capt. Woodson's ship's crew.

"Don't fire," Jack and O'Rourke shouted in unison. Both men realized a cloud of arrows launched at such close range would finish them off in an instant. The boatmen clearly wanted to trade. They kept repeating the call of "Sambio" and at the same time held up paradise plumes and decorated arrows. Jack had Cpl. Isi break out some red calico trade cloth and toss a few patches overboard to the upraised arms in the nearest canoes. The natives pointed to a village perched upstream on the river's edge and made signs urging them to follow.

Kere, the ship's engine-boi, had kept the cutter steadily pushing forward driving the canoes out of the way. These canoes were awkwardly built and sluggish compared to those made by the Delta men. Pushing ahead at four knots, the cutter easily gained on and passed them, arriving at the village well before them. Following Capt. Woodson's commands, Keri headed close inshore while Jack organized the trading party. O'Rourke took charge of the constables and made plans to defend the party if trouble developed. Everyone aboard noticed the natives as they paddled inshore had snatched up bundles of arrows hidden in the reeds, an altogether excusable act of precaution.

O'Rourke and the constables jumped ashore and formed a perimeter of defense, their rifles held at the ready; the porters lugged a case of trade goods onto the river bank. The villagers were loudly crying, “Sambio! Sambio!” and the dogs set up a blood curdling yell that sounded like anything but a welcome. By this time the canoes had come up and their occupants joined in the universal cry of “Sambio!” Some of the men on the high red bank began a fantastic song and dance to the accompaniment of a large drum and half-score of whirring bull roarers, while others rattled ominous-looking human skulls.

The villagers threw their bows and arrows on the ground as they approached. It was extremely brave of them, to come forward totally unarmed and without any knowledge of the character of the men on the expedition.

“First contact,” an inner voice warned Jack. “Be cautious. Show no fear. Take charge.”

He assured them of his friendly intentions by calling out “Sambio!” and patting the nearest native on the shoulder. The facial features of these people were amazingly Semitic. Indeed, they might have passed for bronzed Phoenicians and they possessed the same trading instincts. They piled smoked skulls, decorated arrows, and bird of paradise plumes on the ground as Jack laid out more calico cloth, steel axes, and knives to begin active trading.

Matches and the taste of salt and sugar alike astonished and pleased them; but what they wanted most were the empty tins the cooks had saved for trading purposes. The tribe lacked utensils of any sort beyond bamboo tubes, palm tree baskets, and string billums. There was no evidence of pottery although there was an abundance of clay in the area.

For a few tins, Jack purchased a bundle of arrows. For the same currency, he bought paddles, stone clubs, and other implements. Laying down a steel axe and some red cloth, Jack pointed to five human skulls and signed that he wanted them. The owner the skulls held up five fingers indicating he wanted five steel axes.

Captain Woodson startled the traders by pulling off his hairpiece and waving it high for all to see. Then using a bit of ledger-de-main, he removed his glass eye from its socket and handed the trophies to the astonished man who sucked his cheeks inward and made a whistle-like sound. "I keep a supply aboard the cutter," Woodson said in an aside to Jack. "These skulls will fetch a hundred quid apiece in Sydney."

The Captain pointed to the skulls and the man quickly nodded his agreement. Jack thought he could see sparkle in both men's eyes; the glass eye even seemed to twinkle. Such a bargain could not be refused. The shrewd old man said something to his followers, and they carried the axes back to the settlement's long house while Jack sent Somatu back to the cutter to store the skulls.

The trading went on for two hours -- steel knives for bone knives; tins for arrowheads; cloth for baskets; steel axes for stone axes; jam for arrows. Jack was keenly anxious of securing their primitive weapons and artifacts to send back to Daru and the village men were eager to possess the trade goods. After trading profitably, the warriors led their visitors with great show and hilarity to their village.

The village was comprised of several long flat-roofed dagus, each about 100 feet long and 35 feet wide with sides opening onto verandas and faced each other around a common square. Since there were no other structures in sight, it appeared the families and clans all lived inside these mammoth houses. Cooking fires were lit and smoke filled the rafters where couscous, tree kangaroos, and river rat carcasses were hanging on mask-like meat hooks along with ochre-colored skulls with cowry-shell eyes.

Jack presented an older man, presumably the headman who wore a wig made of cassowary plumes, with an axe and some red cloth. He tittered gleefully as he accepted them while the warriors beat sticks wildly on their newly obtained tin utensils. The young men were amiable characters and Jack determined that given time he could have established some lasting and trusting friendships, but the sly and savage expressions of several elders made him extremely cautious.

Ordering O'Rourke and the constables to cover him, Jack sat a small, broken skull on a bamboo stake about 100 yards from the village. The natives watched as he returned to the steps of the dagu. Nonchalantly he raised his rifle to his shoulder and fired. The bullet shattered the skull, effectively demonstrating the accuracy and power of his weapon. Many of the people jumped off the verandas and ran shrieking in terror. Then Jack pointed to a large palm tree and said to O'Rourke, "We need some coconuts." O'Rourke ordered the squad of constables to blast the coconuts out of the trees.

"Point taken, I'd say," said O'Rourke as more natives fled howling into the bush.

The carriers packed up the trade wares and souvenirs and started toward the cutter. They were soon surrounded by some less timid men who approached Jack and began patting him gently on his arms and back. Jack smiled and handed them some trade cloth. They left the clamoring tribesmen on the bank and climbed aboard the cutter which quickly cast off and headed up stream. The sound of drums and beating of tin cans grew fainter and fainter. Even after the sound of the drums died away, the cry "Sambio! Sambio!" rang in their ears.

"You have to understand boys," Woodson said as he kept a watchful eye on the river ahead, "you meet natives who have had some contact with white men, but haven't learned to respect his weapons and fighting ability, are more to be feared than new people seeing whites for the first time. On first contact, your average kanaka probably will be too much in awe of you to turn hostile. On your second contact, they will have sized you up, and begin to lust for all those steel axes and shiny baubles. On your third contact -- LOOK OUT!" and he clamped his jaws tightly together.

For the next few days the Valhalla pushed westward and northward up the Fly River past Lake Murray, past the junction where the Strickland and the Upper Fly unite their millions of gallons of water and send them onwards to the coast. The great tidal bore that inundated whole islands and river banks in its passing surge had been replaced by stronger and stronger currents. They had entered a more accessible zone of lake and timber country allowing hunting parties to go ashore. The constables shot game every day: pig, cassowary, wallaby, couscous, and pigeon. They also ate liberal rations of rice, supplemented by sago, coconut, and sugar cane. Life aboard the Valhalla was very pleasant at this stage.

At ten o'clock in the morning of the 20th of January, Jack ordered the party ashore to a small wooded islet in the middle of the Upper Fly. The Valhalla could go no farther, owing to whirlpools and rapids dead ahead. "This is the end of the line boys. As it is I'll need to use the cooking oil for fuel to get back to Daru," Woodson said tapping his pipe on the railing. All the stores and equipment were quickly landed and at three p.m., Jack and O'Rourke shook hands and waved goodbye to Capt. Woodson.

"Take care of yourselves," Woodson shouted.

"A piece of cake," O'Rourke bellowed back over the cheers of the carriers. A last sympathetic farewell sounded from the deck-boi's bugle. They watched silently as the Valhalla was swept downstream and soon was lost from sight.

The patrol was now completely cut off from civilization, but they had canoes and their stores. They had not met any natives in the lake country, but twice a raft had drifted past the Valhalla laden with bananas or sago. "Where there are trees," Sgt. Manu said pointing to the shoreline, "there are people everywhere. And among them will be headhunters," he added somberly.

"We haven't seen anyone for days," Jack challenged.

"Are there not pigs in the forest?" Sgt. Manu waved his arms northwestward. "They know we are coming. My Mother! There will be people like the sand."

One of the carriers queried, "What people are dey?"

"Maybe Chinamen?" said one of the policemen.

"What if dey are bad-tempered?" asked a Daru man in a querulous voice.

Corporal Isi answered with the greatest assurance, "Well, what? We are ten!" and he patted his rifle.

The carriers and the police spent the rest of the afternoon erecting a base camp and repacking their supplies. The immediate task was clear: the party would canoe up the Fly and search for a tributary into the highlands.

During the afternoon Jack and O'Rourke had taken an inventory of the supplies, and in the early evening they became absorbed in an endless computation of rations. "Will there be enough to see us through the mountains?" O'Rourke asked, "And down again to the coast? The trade goods will be of no use if there are no people up there. Do you think Manu's right... people like the sand?"

"Maybe," Jack replied. "We haven't seen much sand in this part of the river."

The two men sat silently watching darkness fall upon the river and brooded over their tins of coffee. O'Rourke broke the silence. He began reminiscing about his family in Australia, where he had eaten to his heart's content of home-cured bacon, fresh cream and jam, and where the cherries would now be bowing down the trees.

Jack's thoughts drifted to the green hills of Moresby that would now be alit with kerosene lamps and electric lights... to the Homestead where he grew up. On nights like this my mother would close the shutters, set lamps around the room and light the candles in the silver candelabra on the dining table. Jack could still smell the pale white and pink frangipani flowers she would float in a bowl of water. The Baron and Captain Larkin would play chess while they waited for the storm. The Baron would stare gloomily at the chessboard while the Captain sent adoring glances at Lady Emma. He treated the Baron cavalierly and Lady Em, as he liked to call her, as gallantly as he pleased. He enjoyed courting my mother right under the Baron's nose.

One evening the Captain said, “Baron, you look like you've just eaten a meal of bat dung. Checkmate!” he cried, and leaned back in his chair and glanced to see if Lady Emma was impressed. They were real characters, but real men. Every evening they would try to impress my mother with their world-shaping opinions and they seldom agreed on any subject.

A conversation overheard so long ago sprang into Jack's mind as he stared at the campfire. “The inarticulate masses of the Orient are only beginning to wake up, and one day, so will the people of New Guinea. We are only the mediums of destiny,” the Baron had said using his favorite ploy.

“Nonsense,” Captain Larkin had retorted. “If they do wake up, we will use force without a shred of compunction and put them back to sleep again, forever if necessary.”

“Not as easy as you make it sound,” replied the Baron. “You offer only a very small candle on a very dark night. Policemen, courts, trade goods, sanitation, irrigation districts, hybrid corn, even armies mean nothing to men who would prefer their freedom to covert slavery that comes with the European idea of progress and civilization.”

Capt. Ned dismissed the Baron's argument with a wave of his cigar. “We have the means, the power to go anywhere today, even to this backwater of the world. Civilization will have its day, here and everywhere else.”

“You're wrong,” the Baron refused to back down. “These people are territorial, and the truth is, they will find the energy to overcome anything we throw their way. You forget the most important element is man himself. They are of this place, and we are not. Once they come to truly know us, they will expel us from this part of the world."

"Baron, you make life too complex. Life isn't like a chess game with a fixed set of rules. You seize life by the throat and enjoy it to the full. It doesn't matter to me if I'm here or up island or in the China seas. I don't want any part of a world full of half-men bored with their lives. The world is my oyster, and I'll swallow it while I can. But not before I shuck out a pearl or two." When the arguments grew too heated, Lady Emma would smile sweetly at the two of them and offer them brandy for their coffee.

Why didn't she marry one of them? Jack wondered. I used to think it was because I was underfoot, but both of them were kind to me in their own way. I think they were both too extreme. The Baron was an isolate, trying to escape the institutionalized world, and the Captain was afraid of being tied down. So he chose a life on the open seas where he thought he could control his own destiny. They were more alike than they knew. They were both afraid of risking intimacy. My mother cared for them both. It didn't matter. In the end they died alone, true only to themselves.

Clouds rolled up to blot out the moonlight that filtered through the tops of the trees and lit the swirling waters of the Upper Fly. A clap of thunder sounded to the north, and a flash of light lit up the sky. The rain fell, making heavy noises on the leaves of the jungle and the canvas of the tents. It was a comfortable sound if one was under shelter and absorbed in his memories, Jack soon fell asleep.

Around two a.m. an excited Sgt. Manu rushed into their tent. "Kiap, the water comes!" he squawked in his rasping voice. The men scrambled out of their tents to discover that the flood waters were threatening their supplies. Wild contradictory cries of alarm filled the campsite. The fear of water, of a flood rising silently in the darkness, was causing the men to panic.

"Sgt. Manu, bring the men here to me! We've got to save the rice," Jack exclaimed to Tim, "We need to build a platform in the trees!" O'Rourke nodded and left to break out the axes.

In the dark the police and carriers scrambled through the rising waters, cutting bush timbers and dragging them to the high ground in the center of the island. They gathered bush rope, and working together, built a platform eight feet above the ground in a cluster of trees. While Jack and the carriers put the supplies on the platform, O'Rourke and the police were busy tearing down the camp and storing equipment in the canoes.

By dawn there was nothing to keep them on the island and the party jumped in the canoes and paddled upstream to find some dry ground. Looking back they could see the whole of the island and the surrounding riverbanks were under water.

"What a bloody disaster. It looks like Venice. Lucky we have gondolas," O'Rourke said as the canoe flotilla made its way up the flooded river.

The carriers talked ceaselessly as they paddled. "De black bird warned us to go home. Dis is not our country. We should go back." Jack heard one of the Daru men say. He noticed another paddler, one of the prisoners from Daru, nod his head in grim agreement. They paddled for another three or four miles and rounded a bend in the river when Jack heard an outcry in front of him. He could not immediately see what was happening. The lead canoe had accidentally swung out too far into the swift current and, in doing so, encountered a whirlpool. A deep whirling saucer, its vortex was six feet below the level of the river. Cpl. Dekadua, in the next canoe, saw the peril and shouted a warning... too late.

The endangered canoe spun like a toy in a bathtub, turned over. The men who had been thrown clear began swimming counter-clockwise and were thrown out of the whirlpool, except for one man who clung to the canoe as it swirled round and round. He was drug into the dark maw, screaming a warning. The other canoes closed quickly to rescue the survivors.

"Puk puk!" screamed the men in the second canoe and they pointed to a crocodile moving rapidly towards the men in the water. Jack called for his rifle, unlocked the safety, and began firing at the eyes of the crocodile as it approached the canoe. Sgt. Manu was also firing from the rear canoe. A cold chill went down

Jack's spine as Situnu, the constable's son from Daru, shrieked in agony. Jack watched in horror and shock as Situnu, clutched in the jaws of the crocodile, disappeared into a swirling eddy beneath the surface. A cloud of blood and mud rose to the surface.

Somatu jumped out of the canoe, a paddle in his hand and waded toward the spot where Situnu had disappeared. Somatu began to strike his paddle on the head and snout of another crocodile that surfaced in front of him. Sgt. Manu, clutching a long sharp-edged pole in his hands, leaped into the water near Somatu and savagely stabbed at the crocodile again and again. Jack steadied himself as best he could in the middle canoe and aimed his rifle, but he didn't dare fire for fear of hitting either man.

Sgt. Manu impaled the crocodile with his improvised spear and walked it shoreward, its tail flailing the red-stained water beneath his hips. As Sgt. Manu pushed the crocodile onto the sand bank, Jack fired puncturing its body with several bullets. O'Rourke jumped onto the sand bank as his canoe grounded and finished off the crocodile firing directly into the eyeballs. Sgt. Manu furiously jabbed it again and again, as Somatu scrambled shoreward. "Finis! Finis!" O'Rourke shouted at the Sergeant. "The damned thing is finished." Slowly rolling his head from side to side, Sgt. Manu backed away from the dead reptile keeping his spear pointed at his head.

Somatu stood alone in the shallow water with tears streaming down his face. He shouted his farewell, "Situnu! Situnu! You gone now." O'Rourke and Sgt. Manu gently led him from the river. The carriers and constables rescued the other swimmers. O'Rourke and Sgt. Manu climbed into the beached canoe dragging Somatu with them. The party headed slowly and cautiously upstream staying close to be bank until they had passed the vortex. Sgt. Manu sat cradling the still sobbing Somatu in his arms. The men from Daru were crying as well.

Whenever the paddlers spotted crocodiles, they started screaming, "Shoot 'em! Shoot 'em!" to the constables.

But O'Rourke warned them not to bother and the carriers scowled at him. "Too many crocs, not enough bullets," he said loudly enough for the men to hear.

"The Daru men don't care; they want revenge on the little people who live in those creatures," Sgt. Manu cried. The weary and saddened survivors pushed forward, and late in the afternoon landed on a high bank under a cliff. While the carriers unloaded the canoes and set up tents and cooking fires, the police scattered across a sand bank and unearthed hundreds of turtle eggs; a food greatly relished by Papuans. A few policemen went into the nearby forest to obtain meat and discovered some faint hunting tracks. Sgt. Manu investigated the trails and soon reported that the party was in the territory of people who wander the forest. "Little People," he said as held his hands above his waist. "They have no gardens and they sleep under the bamboo. We must avoid them. They will fire arrows very quickly. It is their country," he warned direly.

That evening the carriers moved away from the Kiap's fire and pitched their tents on the highest point above the river bank. The policemen soon followed suit and were busy setting up their tents midway between the officers' and the carriers'. "Why are they moving away?" O'Rourke enjoined Sgt. Manu.

"They don't want to sleep near the Kiaps. Everyone know that the white men snore at night. Snoring attracts crocodiles and pythons." Sgt. Manu cackled as he left to join the other Papuans on the high bank. That night their already troubled sleep was interrupted by a gigantic boom as a huge boulder crashed down from the cliffs above and rolled through the camp at the spot where the police tents had been pitched. It ground to a stop after crushing several boxes of trade goods and some bags of the precious rice. The avalanche was no accident. It was accompanied by whistling and squealing yells from the cliffs above the camp. Jack and O'Rourke leaped off their cots just before a hail of arrows struck the tents penetrating the canvas walls. The aroused constables fired a volley over the cliff and for a while, all was quiet.

They surveyed the wreckage briefly with their torches. “We can't do much about this until daylight. Best we try and get some rest.” Jack said. “Sgt. Manu, tell the porters to go back to their bivouacs. Then post a constable at each end of the camp.”

“Yes, Kiap,” the Sergeant left barking orders as Jack and O'Rourke returned to their tent. They moved their cots to the center of the tent before lying down.

“Good Night, sweet prince,” O'Rourke jested as he pulled an arrow from his pillow and tossed it on the ground. “I'd hate to end up looking like an over-stuffed pin cushion.”

“No worries,” Jack said. “These boys would turn your skull into a mantle piece. That is after they skewed you over a barbecue.”

“Now that's a thought to tuck in Mother O'Rourke's boy,” The two officers lay on their cots, staring into the darkness.

An hour later they heard a call from above the camp and the air was again filled with bamboo arrows. One carrier was pierced in the buttocks and screamed. Sgt. Manu grabbed the offending reed, jerking it out before the man could protest any more. “Smooth points,” he said showing Jack the arrow. “No barbs or it would have torn out his bottom!”

M.O. Tenoso dressed the carrier's wound with an antiphlogistic plaster while the other men squatted behind trees fearing another attack. Soon they heard the voice again. This time it came from the south. The police fired several volleys immediately in the direction of the hidden voice. There were no more attacks and they slept fitfully waiting for dawn.

Sgt. Manu had the porters up and hard at work before the sun peeped over the horizon. Fires were lit and the men settled down on their haunches to devour breakfast, the last of the sago and sugar cane. Tins of hot tea were passed back and forth. Nothing was seen of last night's raiders but arrow shafts dotted the ground around the camp. The toppled boulder had made a mess of the two storage tents. “Sgt. Manu, see what can be salvaged from this,” Jack ordered.

O'Rourke took Cpl. Isi and two other policemen for protection left immediately with the Oroko men to recover the cache of stores they had left downstream. Under Sgt. Manu's direction, the Daru men began repacking provisions for the canoe trip upstream. Meanwhile, Jack took three Daru men, all good swimmers, to try and recover equipment from the overturned canoe. Jack stood guard, keeping an eye out for any crocodiles that might emerge from the reeds while the men nervously dove over the side of the canoe and searched the bottom of the river for the lost supplies. They were unable to locate any of the expedition's scientific instruments which included prismatic compasses, an aneroid barometer, a sextant, a chronographic watch, and a Leica camera.

The work party made quick work of the salvage job and they were relieved to be safe once again on the riverbank. “No likum puk-puks,” one of Daru men muttered. Jack and Sgt. Manu examined the gear that had been smashed by the boulder the night before. Crushed billy cans and kerosene lamps were lined up for his inspection.

“The things no good. Fuel go finis,” Sgt. Manu said pointing to the flattened tins.

Jack nodded. “At least the tomahawks and calico cloth haven't been damaged.”

“The Kiap food go finis,” Sgt. Manu said, looking ruefully at Jack, and pointing to the mixture of mud, sugar, coffee, and tea oozing its way across the low escarpment. A column of ants was already busy scurrying off with the remains of the stores. Their black bodies bridged a puddle of spilled O'Forty tinned milk.

“No worries, Sergeant. We will eat what the men eat. That way I will know their strength,” Jack said cheerfully.

Sgt. Manu nodded his approval. “It is much better that way Kiap. Also not so much to carry,” and he grinned at Jack for the first time. “The Daru men are talking about home. They say a bad thing is following us. It is best we leave river soon. Alone in the mountains they will be too afraid to turn back.”

"Good point, Sergeant. We'll be under way as soon as Kiap O'Rourke returns with the stores." Both men looked up as a flying fox sailed eerily across the campgrounds and careened into the limestone cliff behind the camp. It slid sickeningly down the face of the cliff to its death below. The carriers stopped working and stared anxiously at each other.

The uneasy silence was broken by a yodel that issued from the cliffs above. A cloud of arrows vibrated through the air and rained down splattering at their feet. As the men scattered for cover, a constable staggered and fell to the ground an arrow piercing his throat. A carrier standing in front of Jack howled as an arrow pierced his forehead. He plopped face down into the mud, one hand clutched around the arrow shaft. The constables began firing randomly at the unseen enemy above the cliffs. Jack knelt beside the carrier and glanced at the blood bubbling from the man's throat. The carrier's body trembled under his hand. His eyeballs rolled violently as the man vainly tried to rise to his feet, pumping bright blood over the sand. Then he shuddered violently and struggled no more. A wave of nausea overcame Jack and he vomited violently, the bile filling his nose.

A terrific din of high-pitched falsetto calls came from the densely timbered spur opposite the camp. A band of little men raced out of the forest in a tangled group and began firing arrows. Some were whooping and jumping up and down as they launched their shafts. Jack pulled his revolver, dropped it clumsily on the ground, and recovering it, began to fire directly at the warriors. Several of the constables began firing as the pygmies fled back into the forest. Another yodel echoed, this time from the north, followed by a crackle of shots, as a squad pf whooping policemen led by Sgt. Manu raced toward the green wall of jungle. A muted scream from somewhere deep in the shaded glen sent parrots flapping out of a mango tree.

The battle was over as suddenly as it began. The face of the enemy, an indistinct shadow glimpsed, only half-seen, had disappeared into an illusion of twilight and leaves. Jack glanced through the wisps of smoke that laced through the camp. He could see the useless vestiges of something that had irrevocably ceased to exist. Three carriers were dead and two others were painfully wounded, arrows protruded from arms and legs. While other carriers firmly held the wounded, Tenoso, the medical orderly, went to their aid and calmly broke off the arrow shafts and drew them from the men's bodies.

Sergeant Manu ordered two constables to stand guard at both ends of the camp. He barked commands and soon another group of constables were scrambling up the treacherous path that led to the top of the cliffs. In a few minutes, they had reached the high ground and Constable Dekadua hollered to the Sergeant that they were all alone. The pygmy warriors had abandoned their vantage point. Jack and Sgt. Manu moved among the agitated carriers to reassure them. Drumbeats were echoing from the jungle to the north and south of them. “We must leave this cursed place, Kiap,” Sgt. Manu entreated.

“We can't go until O'Rourke returns and we’ve taken care of the wounded men. Tell the constables to fire on anything that moves,” Jack replied. Sgt. Manu left to instruct the constables at each end of the camp. When he returned Jack ordered him to take a detail across the river and bury the bodies of the fallen carriers. “Don't bury them where those little bastards can find them,” Jack commanded.

Neither man needed reminding that the pygmies were head hunters and probably carrion eaters. The sun beat down mercilessly on the now very subdued and humbled group of men. Green blowflies attracted by the blood spills were hovering around the camp. O'Rourke and the Oroko carriers returned around three o'clock and were devastated by the news of the attack. The late afternoon meal was broken several times by men wailing farewell songs. A breeze from nowhere began to rustle the leaves, making dry sinister noises, like the scrapings of insect wings. The air darkened sending purple clouds billowing across the jungle and settling on their world like a lid.

A ball of Saint Elmo's fire swept down the river towards them, and then whooshed off into the forest, where the wind cut a swath before it. The carriers clutched each other but although their mouths formed words, the sounds were trapped in their throats. The men fled into tents that creaked and tossed in the gale like the topgallants of an old sailing ship. Trees corkscrewed into the ground, loosing a frenzy of leaves that plastered the campground. A dimple of a cloudburst lashed through the camp flattening everything before it. A horde of fruit bats followed like giant black gnats, causing the frightened sentries to abandon their posts and to race back into the camp.

"Ghosts!" they cried and the carriers rolled their eyes and moaned loudly. Some of the Daru men ran towards the beached canoes hoping to flee this fearful place but Sgt. Manu blocked their path.

"Stop!" he roared. "You stupid children. There are no invisible men. Were your fathers cockroaches? Are you witless women to run from the wind?" The Daru men hesitated, their panic subsiding as Sgt. Manu reviled them in their own language. Turning his attention to the policemen, "Back to your posts, you sons of gnats," he commanded waving his swagger stick in their faces. "Do you want the Kiaps to regard us as cowardly men, fit only to sit in the huts of old women?" and he waved his baton in the direction of O'Rourke and Reed who assumed looks of bland disinterest, allowing Sgt. Manu to handle the disorder in camp. "Clean up the campsite," he pointed to a group of men struggling to regain their self-control. "Recover the tents," he ordered, "and rebuild those fires."

Seeing the ferocious scowl on Sgt. Manu's face, the men turned sullenly back toward the campsite and began the task of restoring order. Sgt. Manu moved among the carriers, scolding and chiding them into activity. "Sons of gnats, bring me firewood!" and a few porters scurried off to escape his wrath. "Put those tents up and peg them down," he rasped at a group of men who were still standing indecisively by the canoes. "Move, I tell you!" and he slapped his swagger stick against his thigh for emphasis. “Cookie, bring the Kiaps their tea,” he snapped at the crestfallen cook who felt the reproach in his voice.

In short order, the tents were in place and the cooks were serving tea and hard biscuits. Still Sgt. Manu moved among the carriers and the policemen. His jokes and jeers evoked a smile here and a snicker there from the men, but for the most part the carriers sulked among themselves, particularly the Daru men. Around 10 p.m. Sgt. Manu posted constables north and south of the camp. Jack and O'Rourke sat in front of their tent. “An early start tomorrow, Sergeant. It will be best to leave before we have more trouble. You did well today. Are you sure the men are all misbegotten sons of gnats?” Jack inquired teasingly.

“They are all good men, Kiap, but they truly believe something comes after us.”

“What do you think, Sergeant?” O'Rourke asked quietly.

“I think there are no ghosts following us but something that damn sorcerer Kaori has sent to do us harm. I catch him when we return and put a finis to this nonsense,” Sgt. Manu vowed. “Tonight I will stand first watch,” Manu saluted the officers and went to his own tent near the constabulary men.

The yellow glow of the tilley lamps reflected softly off the rifle stocks of the men posted at each end of the camp. Jack let go of the accumulated tension in his arms and legs. “A rough start,” O'Rourke said quietly. Jack nodded and then he allowed himself to drift into sleep unaware of the eyes glaring in the darkness that followed his every move.

Shortly before dawn, Jack awoke to find Sgt. Manu shining a weak torch in his face. “Kiap, de Daru men, they gone!” he shouted. Jack sprang instantly out of his camp chair; he glanced toward the beached canoes. Two canoes were missing. “They all gone, Kiap. They take the wounded men too!”

“When did they leave? Who saw them go?”

“No one saw them leave but it did not happen while the dog was in the sky.”

Jack glanced at his watch. No more than two hours ago, he thought. O'Rourke popped fully dressed out of the tent, buckling on his pistol belt as he strode towards Jack and Sgt. Manu. "They can't have gotten very far. I'll take some of the constables and bring them back," he said confidently.

"You'll never catch them. They won't stop until they reach Daru. Even if you manage to bring them back, they will just desert again at the first chance." Jack turned to Sgt. Manu, "Why do you think they left?"

The Sergeant paused a moment, thinking before he spoke. "I think the Daru men believe the white men do not care for them; that the white men only care about crossing the mountains."

"What do you think, Sergeant?" Jack asked quietly.

"I think Daru men are weak-legged women not like Motu men. There is no bad thing that follows us, but if we go back to Daru, I will put an arrow in that Kaori anyway. He make this trouble," Sgt. Manu finished.

The two patrol officers stood at the river's edge surveying the canoes. "Sod it! They took the best canoes and the best iron pots," Jack exclaimed.

"Fewer men, fewer mouths to feed. We won't have to pack that gear over the mountains. No records to keep. Just our journals. The constables can carry supplies as well as the carriers. They have stronger legs. We'll make a fair go of it," O'Rourke laughed.

"We'll give it another week then," Jack said carefully. "If we find a river heading northeast, we'll go on. If not, we turn back to Daru. Agreed?"

"Agreed," said O'Rourke. "I never liked the misbegotten sons of gnats anyway," and both men smiled at Sgt. Manu's look of chagrin. They left Sgt. Manu to supervise the loading of the canoes as a slate gray band of clouds began to turn pink in the early dawn.

"It's a mad country. Let's get the hell out of here," O'Rourke said. The canoes were filled to the gunwales with gear. One canoe had a canvas shelter rigged over the top to keep the sun off of the patrol officers. Sgt. Manu assigned four carriers and four policemen to each canoe. As soon as the canoes were fully loaded with men and supplies, he ordered them to move upstream.

Sergeant Manu joined Jack and O'Rourke in the last canoe, and the porters and constables paddled energetically to catch up with the other craft that were already strung out over a half-mile of the river. Their smaller and lighter canoe cut through the water like a knife as the men dipped their paddles in unison.

Corporal Isi called from the bow of the canoe, "Can de men have their tobacco?"

"Not now, Corporal" Jack responded. "It will make them talk too much and I want them to paddle. They must earn the tobacco."

The men dug in deeper and soon they had drawn even with the lead canoe, the paddlers only pausing to clap coconut shells together as they swept past. Except for the rustle in the water, the men mostly paddled in silence, changing places frequently to ease the strain in their shoulders and arms.

Around ten a.m. they stopped for "Big Tea". "The men need food. They can't paddle on empty stomachs," Jack told O'Rourke. "Let them smoke after they eat," he said to Sgt. Manu. "They need the energy the tobacco provides."

"The Kiap knows how to lead men," observed Sgt. Manu to the porters as he passed out sticks of tobacco. Their eyes sparkled and they began teasing the paddlers in the slower canoes. When the meal was finished, the men cut pandanus fronds for shade.

By late afternoon, the sun had lost much of its intensity, the wind had subsided into a light breeze, and most of the men were becoming talkative as they pulled on their paddles less earnestly. Paddling had become a more or less pleasant pastime for the men. Overhead birds mostly honey catchers, crisscrossed the stream and hornbills were feeding in the lagoons.

"Pull in there Sgt. Manu," Jack ordered indicating a likely clearing on the far bank of the river. A few thatched- roofed houses dotted the clearing, but they appeared uninhabited. After beaching their canoes, the men stretched and surveyed the empty dagus. They knew very well that people used all sorts of magic to prevent others from using their abandoned homes. Not wishing to offend the owners, the party made provisions to sleep outside the compound.

Somatu brought Jack and O'Rourke a pot of coffee and returned to prepare their food. Jack swirled his coffee in his mug. The bush, the fatigue, the mosquitoes, the deadly snakes, Situnu's horrible death, the unwarranted deaths from the pygmy attack, and then the desertion of the Daru carriers, all were troubling his thoughts. “I've got to be more careful,” he mumbled to himself.

“What are you muttering about?” O'Rourke asked.

“Nothing,” Jack replied and slapped a sand fly.

“Too early in the patrol to be talking to yourself. I've been on worse treks than this one. It's never easy in the beginning, but we'll be right. Count on it,” O'Rourke said puffing on his pipe. “But I'd rather be in a pub in King's Cross.”

Sergeant Manu approached the men, “How many cups of rice for the men, Kiap?” making his role of mediator between the officers and the porters clear.

“Extra rations for everyone, Sergeant and add sago and sugar cane. We'll use it while it lasts. Canoeing is hard work and when we move inland the carriers will need all their strength.” At this stage of the journey, Jack wasn't too worried about rations since they still had sago and coconuts to supplement the rice. “Give them plenty of tea and sugar to wash down the sago.”

“Yes, Sir, Kiap!” Sgt. Manu said cheerfully and returned to the cooking fires. He supervised the cooks as they carefully added extra rice and then chilies which added a touch of red to the food. Each man presented his banana leaf for a share of the rice and his tin cup for sugary tea. It was a peaceful camp. There were fewer mosquitoes and after Sgt. Manu posted guards, everyone fell quickly to sleep, exhausted by the previous day's events. Jack dreams were full of visions of drowning men.

Morning came quickly and after a hasty breakfast of rice, tea, and sugar, they pushed off again, hoping to gain an hour or two's march on the punishing sun.

Late in the morning they passed the mouth of a river. After examining it, Jack decided it was too small for their purpose; they would have to find a larger ingress to the mountain barrier. As the party advanced, the river became more choked with island and rock barriers, and the current became more difficult to negotiate. The men poled in places where it was possible, and grabbed low overhanging branches to pull the canoes upstream.

The further they advanced, the further they were from the mosquitoes, the low marshy country, the lagoons, and the large sago areas. The country was changing. High sandstone banks covered with tall timbers and dense luxuriant foliage began to close in on them. Casuarinas trees appeared and on the small islands wild figs were plentiful. Rounding a larger island, they spotted a pile of driftwood neatly stacked on a sandpit. "A likely campsite," O'Rourke suggested and they went ashore to examine their find. Nearby the porters discovered a tree that had been felled by a stone adze. "People who cut down trees also build gardens," added O'Rourke hopefully.

The men made a huge bonfire out of the driftwood in addition to the cooking fires. For the first time, Jack and O'Rourke joined with the carriers for the evening meal. Jack sat watching the police secure the canoes from the floods that still came daily; Somatu came up silently beside him, and pointed to the canoes separately, as though they were living things. He said, "One... Two...Three...Four."

"Who taught you that?" Jack asked.

"Kande," he answered offhandedly.

"What else did Kande teach you?"

Somatu gave a beautiful round of distorted profanity ending with a string of son-of-beeches and returned triumphantly to his cook stove.

Later that evening as Jack and O'Rourke sat before the fire drinking their coffee, Somatu visited them. "Why do the men of Papua engage in headhunting?" Jack asked Somatu, hoping to find the answer that always escaped him.

"It is because of God," Somatu said.

"Which God?" O'Rourke exclaimed.

"There is only one God," Somatu responded. "He is the God of Iunagazim and all the coconut people. He is old... not a new god. No one knows his name. He looks after the sago, the birds, the pigs, and the cassowaries, and protects unborn children." Somatu went on to relate how headhunting was because of God: "In the time before children, God killed Somali, the god of the Bushmen and the bad-talk people. God planted Somali's head in a garden and from it grew the first coconut. That is why we only take heads from the Bushmen... because they are of Somali, and it pleases God to see their heads. We never take the heads of coconut people."

"The pygmies are not Somali's people?" Jack asked.

"No, but they are bad-talk people."

"Have you ever eaten human flesh, Somatu?" Jack asked directing his eyes toward the bonfire.

"I was born with the taste in my mouth," and Somatu quietly left the fire to go to his place beside Kande in the sleeping tent, leaving the officers with something to think about.

The next day the party entered a northerly stretch of the river and in the clear morning air, they could see a range of mountains fifteen to twenty miles ahead of them. Jack pointed out a mountain dome, five to six thousand feet in height, between the glistening water and the green dew-drenched forest. It rose between two tabletop mountains of lesser elevation. "The headwaters of the Fly must be somewhere up there."

"And the Strickland must start over in that direction," O'Rourke said pointing to the east at a mass of high peaks and domes, ten to eleven thousand feet in height, that spread their length eastward. They paddled on for another mile, keeping the mountains in view and were just coming to another bend when the constable in front spotted the mouth of a deep river about seventy yards in width and it appeared to come down from the northeast. The carriers paddled excitedly toward it, and propelled the canoes out of the main stream into a back water between high sandstone banks.

"This is it," Jack cried aloud. "This is our road to the highlands. Sgt. Manu, take us in there," he ordered, and the police and carriers dug in with their paddles and turned up the river. The composition of this new river was different than that of the Fly. The banks were closer on either side, the current was stronger, and the water was clearer. The scrub hens called, the Waikiki flitted through the treetops, the cockatoos were more numerous, and the hornbills rose noisily from their resting places as though they were angry at their presence.

The sun rose higher and higher turning the day into a sweltering steam bath of moist heat under the shadows of the forest. Crocodiles slid into the river, sometimes only a few yards from them, but the police did not fire for fear of disturbing any primitive people with such an unnatural noise. They had been traveling for about six hours, always looking for signs of human habitation, when they came unexpectedly upon a bamboo raft tied to the southern bank. It had not been used that day, for no tracks led away from it.

A mile further upstream they discovered another raft. Jack stepped ashore with Sgt. Manu and Somatu and climbed to the top of the bank where they found a faint track. Fresh human footprints showed clearly on the muddy path. The men followed it silently for a few minutes. Then they heard the sound of human voices and the thumps of sago making.

Sgt. Manu advanced cautiously to the edge of the sago clearing, and peering for some time into it, returned and whispered to Jack, "There are three armed men and some women there." Jack started forward. Sgt. Manu, grabbed him by the arm and held him, "You will get an arrow," and he made a peculiar whooshing noise with his mouth.

"I want to make friends with these people," Jack said in a hushed voice. "Perhaps they know of a trail to the mountains." Jack crept to the edge of the clearing with Sergeant Manu following closely. Somatu trailed further behind, keeping under cover at the edge of the sago. Jack cautiously surveyed the peaceful and primitive scene.

Not thirty feet away were a number of women and young girls making sago. They were singing and talking, and occasionally sighed tiredly as they whipped the water-soaked pith with long canes. Three men stood nearby, apparently on guard, for they all held bows. The men were dressed with a covering of bark cloth quite unlike the pygmy nomads they had met along the Fly. The women and girls wore short grass sporrans.

Jack hesitated; his first impulse was to leave presents and go away, trusting the natives to understand the act. However, when he looked again and saw how peaceful they seemed, he decided to make friends with them, then and there. He signaled to Somatu to hand him the trade goods and nudging Sgt. Manu to cover him, Jack stepped into the clearing holding a bright red cloth and a shiny steel knife overhead and called to the people in a friendly tone.

One of the girls yelled and bolted, but the older women stood amazed, while the three men stepped forward a few paces, arrows already fitted to their bows. Encouraged, Jack stepped forward, holding the cloth and knife in one hand and opening the palm of his left in a friendly gesture. He felt certain they would come to him, but there was a crashing sound to his left. The spell was broken. The women bolted and the men wheeled and pulled their bows in that direction.

Somatu cried out and the men fired their arrows. Jack felt a tug on his bush hat as it flew off his head. Shots rang out on his right as Sgt. Manu fired over their heads. The bowmen immediately fled, shouting excitedly as they retreated into the forest.

"Where's Somatu?" Jack yelled. Both men turned and quickly retraced their steps. In his eagerness, Somatu had followed Jack into the clearing, but in doing so, had fallen into a sago soak... his yelp scaring the natives out of their amazement. Somatu was standing embedded nearly to his waist in mud with two terrible-looking bone-tipped arrows close by.

"You stupid boy," shouted Sgt. Manu. "Now what have you done?"

Barely containing his disappointment, Jack consoled both men, "It's alright, Sergeant. It is my fault. I should have taken your advice. Somatu could have been killed."

"So could you, Kiap," Sgt. Manu said as he handed Jack's hat over to him; another bone-tipped arrow was lodged in the band. Jack took the proffered cap from Sgt. Manu, and looked it over carefully.

With a deep chuckle Jack said, "How will I explain this souvenir to O'Rourke?" and even Sgt. Manu began to grin. Together they pulled Somatu out of the sago bog. "Not one word to O'Rourke," Jack ordered as the three mud-covered figures marched out of the forest and down to the canoes.

O'Rourke eyeballed the arrow protruding out of Jack's bush hat and the barely-concealed smiles on the three faces and shrugged his shoulders as if to say, "Who's asking?"

They camped that evening on the southern bank opposite and slightly downstream from the dagus. The nomads watched silently as they prepared camp. The spectacle of men clearing an area in so short a time and erecting shelters must have amazed them. Jack wondered where they came from and how long they had lived there with no knowledge of civilization and very little knowledge of the myriad of peoples living along the river or elsewhere in Papua.

A steaming kerosene tin of cooked rice stood a few yards from the fire, while on the ground, in sixteen places, the carriers had set their plates for the meal. These plates were an oddly assorted lot, ranging from pieces of bark and large leaves to empty biscuit tins.

Somatu, attempting to impress Jack with his abilities as a cook, began to count the places for the food in English. He reached "tarteen" skipping two numerals as he did so; then he went back to ten, paused and jumped to thirteen again, jumped to "tickteen" and found the number of places correct. Somatu used a flat stick to dump large slabs of over-cooked rice out of the tin onto the various plates. Once around, then twice and the rice was finished.

Jack detected a small Matterhorn among the others. "Whose plate?" Jack asked.

"Mine," Somatu said, smiling shyly. The carriers squatted on their haunches and began their meal laughing and chiding one another.

"Not much different than dinner at Baxters, isn't it?" O'Rourke said, looking over Jack's shoulder. "We'd better get used to it, Jack. If we don't find food in the mountains, a handful of rice will look pretty good."

They walked out to the sand spit, where Kande was preparing a meal for the policemen. A kerosene tin was suspended over the fire. Jack looked into it and saw a score of white balls. "Crocodile eggs," Kande explained, then added quickly, "They're not very good Kiap; the baby crocodile is ready to come out."

"Ugh!" O'Rourke grunted and they went to their own fire where Somatu was busy preparing their meal: rice mixed with the last of the dried raisins. On the way back, Jack picked up a shellback of a turtle and examined it by the firelight. A human design had been drawn on the back and painted red and black. A piece of string was attached to it. A child's toy, like my horse on wheels, Jack thought.

A dog swam across the river and wandered into their camp. Somatu offered it some rice and after it finished, Jack tied a piece of red cloth around its neck, and released it with a pat, hoping it would carry the peace offering back to the settlement. A terrific din of high-pitched, falsetto calls sounded like the croaking of a thousand frogs came from the densely timbered spur across the river and unnerved the dog that ran yowling and yipping into the forest. The cry only lasted for a minute or so. The men answered back howling madly at the top of their lungs, and a sudden silence ensued which lasted for over an hour. The natives called out three more times and each time the carriers hollered back. Then there was a silence during which Jack assumed the river people must be holding a conference.

When the dog reappeared, Somatu befriended it and later in the evening, he took it into the tent he shared with Cpl. Dekadua and Kande. The Corporal disappeared into the tent and a few minutes later, he drove an agitated Somatu outside, telling him to keep himself and his flea-infested dog away from the police tent.

A worried Somatu plopped his kit beside the carriers and they too urged him to go away. "Sleep beside the fires," they jeered. "You are a flea." Somatu complained aloud to no one in particular about "bad-talk" men reminding the officers of the previous night's conversation.

"No worries," Sgt. Manu said as if he could read their thoughts, "that flea will not bite these dogs," and he strode off to his tent.

The next morning they discovered that the settlement across the river had been abandoned. O'Rourke went over with canoe full of policemen and left some bits of calico and a knife on a stump and returned quickly. "No one's home," he shouted.

Moving upriver, they encountered a series of shoals and rapids. The first was really a small cataract, but the canoes had to be unloaded and hauled up with ropes. Then the men had to return and portage the supplies forward. The porters did most of the work while the police stood guard at each end. The first cataract had a drop of six to eight feet in fifty yards, but above the drop line the river became a calm and placid stream again.

With the morning sun shining fitfully through the thick mist that hung low over the water, it did not seem at all like Papua; the still waters, the hills and banks with their dense foliage, the towering trees that leaped skyward, the flowering D'Albertis.... all combined to make a picture of quiet beauty.

After paddling for about two miles, they came to another ledge of rapids. They managed to portage the canoes and again entered calmer waters. They continued this new pattern for the next fifty miles... a ledge of rapids followed by calm water. On the second day, a crowd of nomads, including women, came down to the bank of the river to light fires and watch the canoes being loaded. They ran away as Jack and O'Rourke approached them waving red cloth.

"It's obvious they want to be friendly; they haven't fired arrows at us," Jack said. "It's pathetic we have no way to speak to them."

"They're too timid," O'Rourke suggested. "But they can tell that we mean them no harm."

"It's your white skins, Kiap," Somatu, who had become Jack's shadow, said. "They fear you are spirits."

"Someday I want to come back here and establish a patrol post. If we stay long enough, they could get used to us and one day, we could develop a relationship with them," Jack said.

"Why bother?" O'Rourke replied. "There's no trace of gold here," indicating the pools in front of the rapids. "You can't get the timber down river from here and there's not enough land for plantations," indicating the steep canyon walls. "It would be better to head inland."

The always-practical O'Rourke, Jack thought. Why isn't it enough to just be friendly and learn from each other? Why is the quest for God, gold, glory, and territory always our motivation for discovery? Maybe these people are the lucky ones. If we find nothing here of value, they may have another fifty years of freedom before we overrun them. As they advanced up the river, Jack waved to a small group of people huddling around the trade items he had left on the shore. The men hooted loudly and a few women waved timidly.

Late in the afternoon of the third day, they had just managed to portage over a wide ledge and were resting on a bed of rocks that overlooked the shoals when they heard something like a cannon shot coming from somewhere up river. Then more explosive cracks echoed off the canyon walls. "My Mother," exclaimed Cpl. Isi. "What gave birth to dis ting?"

The carriers stood around open-mouthed. They were upset; no Malays or Europeans could be in front of them. It was something to which they could not attempt to give an explanation. "Bumbuken," Somatu said.

"What's that?" Jack asked.

"It is the spirit of the Great Mother." A noise like thunder clapped down the river; the ground shook and broke under their feet with a violent jolt. Jack and the others who were standing on the rock ledge were tossed headlong into the water. Jack crawled forward on his hands and knees and was astonished to see the tall trees on the shore sway and snap like matchsticks and fall into the river. The earth jerked in convulsive movements. The mountains seemed to get up and walk.

"Guria! Guria!" shouted the terrified men.

An earthquake, Jack thought. Now he knew what the sharp sounds had been. Jack stood up in a partial crouch; hands spread before him, and waited out a series of diminishing shocks and tremblers. Moments later, a wall of water swept down the river, turning over the canoes and spilling the contents into the water.

When the shock waves ceased, Jack and the men dashed into the water to retrieve their supplies. They quickly recovered the goods and stacked them high on the rock ledge. "Whew! I've been in quakes before," O'Rourke exclaimed excitedly. "I was in on the one in Rabaul when Matupi erupted, but this was worse."

They surveyed the damage. "The flour is finished," O'Rourke said pointing towards the gooey mess that trickled down the sides of the rocks.

"We've lost some rice," Jack noted. "Have the cooks repack what's left into dry packs."

"My tobacco's soaked," O'Rourke said wryly as he spread some on a rock in an effort to dry it out. "We have the trade goods and the ammo. But we've lost two canoes," and he indicated the broken hulls crushed between a pair of boulders.

"Kiap! The river. Look at the river," Sgt. Manu cried. "It go finis." As the men looked upriver, they saw that the river had slowed down to a trickle barely flowing over the shoals. Upstream they could see that a landslide was blocking the river.

"Now that will be a helluva of a nut to crack," O'Rourke prophesied.

That night they stuffed themselves with rice that had been soaked. “Use it or lose it,” Jack instructed the cooks. The porters avoided Somatu's company. His crime was naming the Great Mother and thus bringing bad luck on them all. They took every opportunity to make him the butt of their lewd jokes; someone hid his swag that contained empty bottles and tins he had been hoarding.

Somatu pretended to be unaffected and calmly ignored all indignities and insults. In fact, to show his contempt for the Orokos, he ate his rice in front of them, and smoked his tobacco rolled in a piece of paper like that of the white men. That night Somatu slept close to the Kiap's fire and avoided bedding down near the Orokos.

In the morning, O'Rourke, accompanied by Cpl. Dekadua and two other constables, went forward up the river to explore the landslide. They returned in a couple of hours with the news. “The river is blocked for miles. It's too far to portage the canoes. Besides, I don't know if there's deep water beyond the blockage,” O'Rourke said. “There's a small stream about two miles ahead that's coming down from the northeast. It may be our best bet. I had Cpl. Dekadua shinny up a tree. Tell the Kiap what you saw.”

Cpl. Dekadua was proud of his tree climbing ability and liked to show off whenever he had a chance. Dekadua puffed his chest out proudly, “Two mountains, Kiap -- very high and a long ridge dat way,” and from north to east, he swept his arm in a wide arc.

“Probably the limestone ridge. The highlands are beyond that ridge,” O'Rourke commented.

“Could be,” mused Jack, “and if that's so, somewhere on the western end will be the Purari.” Everyone waited while Jack made up his mind. “Sergeant, have the men prepare the packs. We're moving inland.”

“Yes, sir,” answered the Sergeant and he began barking orders. Two hours later, the police and the carriers stood ready for inspection. The constables were the most heavily-laden. Each man, in addition to his BSA 303 rifle and bandolier containing twenty rounds of service ammunition, was to carry a swag containing a flannel shirt; 100 rounds of ammunition; a month's supply of tobacco and matches; an axe; a 16-inch scrub knife; and a 10-pound packet of rice.

Twelve of the porters carried 40 pounds of rice wrapped in weather-proof painted canvas rucksacks on their backs, as well as a swag containing a blanket, a flannel shirt, a supply of tobacco, and a spare loin cloth. Each carried a tomahawk and knife in his belt. M.O. Tenoso carried the medical supplies including medicinal rum and another porter, the tea and coffee. Two men were assigned to carry the Kiap's rifles and ammo as well as their personal effects, spare clothing and boots. Another carrier was laden with the trade tomahawks and knives. Cpl. Isi and Dekadua carried spare red calico cloth and salt instead of a packet of rice. Somatu and Kande were put in charge of the kerosene, cook stoves, and buckets.

Sgt. Manu carried only a shotgun and a light pack as he would be moving often up and down the march line. The two patrol officers carried their shotguns and pistols and spare ammo, tobacco, notepads and compasses. The tents would be slung on poles and carried by two men. At every rest stop the tents would be given to fresh carriers. In the wet country, the double load would be cruelly hard on the bearers, especially in the steep terrain that lay ahead.

Sgt. Manu handed each man a day's ration of hard biscuits for emergencies which they stuffed into their swags. Then the men filled their canteens with fresh water. “We are ready, Kiap,” said Sgt. Manu saluting Jack crisply. Jack nodded and set the order of the march.

Jack and six policemen would march in the van. Three police would march in the middle, and O'Rourke and the remaining constables would bring up the rear, keeping an eye out for stragglers. “We march for fifty minutes and then rest for ten. At each stop, check your feet for sores or injuries,” Jack told the men. “Sergeant, take the lead,” and Sgt. Manu started up a trail that ran near to the stream, heading northeast.

It began pouring rain as the police marched into the forest. The party followed a thin trail that led to the top of the ledge, 1500 feet higher up, slipping and sliding and cursing the mud all the way. Then it was down into a ravine, and up to the top of the great ridge again -- all in a downpour. “A bloody vertical swamp,” O'Rourke complained.

That evening they discovered a cliff overhanging a deep ravine that sheltered them from the rain. Without bothering to strike the tents or light a fire, they made a hasty meal of left-over cold rice from the night before and wrapping themselves in blankets were soon fast asleep.

Jack and O'Rourke smoked quietly. Jack had been unable to smoke on the trail; he couldn't seem to manage to hike, and keep a pipe lit as the others did. “We'll change the marching order tomorrow,” Jack said to O'Rourke, his voice echoing in the cleft. Getting no reply, he glanced at O'Rourke, who was already fast asleep. Jack covered him with his blanket and touching Sgt. Manu said, “I'll take the first watch and Isi the second. You must be alert for the third watch. If there is any danger, it will come then.”

“Goodnight, Kiap,” and Sgt. Manu left and took a position in the front of the overhang, where he finished his pipe before laying down, one hand grasping his shot gun and holding it across his chest. The next morning, the men ate some hard tack and filled their canteens before leaving the rock ledge.

It rained all that day and the next. The party saw no signs of human habitation as they slid down the face of one ravine and clawed their way to the top of the next ridge. Ridge followed ridge and ravine followed ravine, but each time they had gained more elevation and were inching their way closer to the highlands.

The carriers had donned their flannel shirts. Most carried pandanus leaves over their heads if they had a free hand. Late in the afternoon, they followed a rivulet that led up to a ridge, which in turn lead them into a open clearing. To the south they could see a waterfall cascade 1000 feet below them, where it fed a river, a long silver ribbon, racing through the jungle 3000 feet further below.

The vanguard was waiting for them on the farthest edge of the clearing, and Sgt. Manu called for the Kiap. Jack moved forward and the Sergeant pointed out what appeared to be giant bird nests in the trees overhead. Jack peered up into the trees, and he could make out a collection of unusual huts built on tree posts forty feet above the forest floor. The trees had been topped off and platform houses had been erected on the stumps.

There was no movement, no sign of life in the aerie above or on the ground below. Jack had a premonition that they were being watched. "What do you make of it Sergeant?" Before Manu could reply, a goblin-like figure stepped out of the mist. The apparition was dressed in black and wore a black cape made of fruit bat wings, which effectively camouflaged him when he stood on the edge of the dark forest, surrounded by the cloud-like vapor. A foot-long gourd covered his genitals; a hammer-shaped knob was attached at the tip.

"Good God! Would you look at that?" O'Rourke said coming up from behind and breaking the eerie silence. The shrouded figure in front of them struck his gourd making a clicking sound with his fingers, and several other men dressed in black capes moved out of the mists. The constables jammed shells into their rifles and rolled their eyes towards Jack and back at the forest man.

"Sambio!" cried Jack and pulling a piece of calico cloth out of his jacket waved it overhead. He broke open his shotgun and handed it to Somatu who was standing at his side, and walked a few yards forward and laid the cloth on a tree stump. Turning his back, he returned calmly to his place beside O'Rourke.

The caped men remained motionless, except for rapidly clicking their gourds. Then one of them ran forward and grabbed the cloth and returned it to the shrouded figures who examined the cloth and began rapidly clicking their gourds. The leader of the group suddenly fell on the ground and began rubbing his face and his thighs with the cloth. Standing up and taking two arrows from his quiver, he broke them in two and threw them on the ground. He then placed his quiver behind a rock and urged his followers to do the same. Soon all the men had dumped their bows and arrows behind trees and boulders. They began laughing and prancing, leaping up and down, and clicking their gourds with their fingers. The carriers started laughing and soon were whooping and hollering back at the caped men.

Corporal Isi called out a warning over the din. "Be careful men of Oroko. These fruit bats do not wish to fight you. They are going to fornicate you." His comment, accompanied with an obscene gesture, reduced the carriers to hysterics and some fell to the ground howling with laughter.

Click. Click. Click. Click went the gourds as the caped men looked on in wonder. "Clickety click," shouted Corporal Isi. "Which of you has the bride price?" and the men howled again.

"Fasim lip, stupid man," shouted Sgt. Manu, but he was smiling. The Sergeant stepped out into the clearing and spread some salt from a bag onto a stump. The cloaked men gathered around it and with some on their fingers, tasted the salt and then smiled their approval. The black-caped men pointed to the village and shouted, "Tambio! Tambio!" and with gestures encouraged the party to follow them to the compound.

The patrol followed close behind the dancing, strutting warriors. "Can you believe this place?" O'Rourke asked pointing skyward at the structures overhead. Ladders led to an upper platform about 20 feet above the ground, from there more ladders led upward into the tree nest-like houses some 40 feet higher up in the trees.

"Ai Ai Ai Ai," shrilled the guides and suddenly excited nearly naked women and children started to fall out of the sky. They didn't use the ladders, but instead, slid down long bamboo poles like firemen reporting to their fire trucks and soon they surrounded the party touching the policemen.

The headman invited Jack to visit a hut. "I'm not sure about this," Jack said as he started to climb a ladder.

"No worries. If you break your dick, these fellows seem to have plenty of splints," O'Rourke grinned encouragingly.

Jack made it up the two spidery cane ladders and managed to crawl through a small trap door into the hut. A fireplace made of small stones sat in the middle of the floor. An ochre-covered skull with shell eyes hung grimly from a post in the middle of the room. At that height the hut was cool and free of mosquitoes.

From this aerie, Jack had a splendid view of the country. In the distance, he could see the mountaintops that Cpl. Dekadua had described and the long limestone ridge. We're on track, he thought. They can't be more than a day's march away. But the tree houses weren't built to provide a view but rather for defense. His hosts showed him that the ladders and poles were not fixed in the ground and could be pulled up when the last man got safely home. Piles of rounded rocks, obviously intended for defense, were stacked along the walls of the room. Bows and bamboo arrows hung from the roof beams along with bits of smoked couscous and dried food stuffs. Firewood was stacked in the corners, and mats were rolled and laid in neat piles at one end of the hut.

"Ingenious," Jack said to himself. These men could withstand quite a siege, he thought. The huts occupied so many of the trees that an enemy couldn't succeed even if he tried to burn them out. From their overlapping vantage points, they can protect their flanks.

The black men squatted and smoked as they showed Jack their primitive tools: adzes, digging sticks, cassowary awls, and fishhooks. Jack took one puff from a gourd full of smoke as they passed it to him. He examined the tobacco leaves. They were good quality, but the men smoked it green. One puff of the rancid stuff was enough. Jack coughed, staggered and nearly stepped into the open trapdoor. It was 40-feet to the ground and making an alarmed face he pointed downward. A man took the gourd from his grasp and fell on his side laughing.

Leaning out the open window, Jack fixed the position of the mountain range to the northeast with his compass. He allowed the headman to examine his compass as he and his comrades exclaimed in wonder at the needle that floated, the black tip always pointing northward. Using an old conjurer's trick, Jack had the headman hold a steel tomahawk in front of his chest. Jack turned around slowly, showing the men that the needle always pointed north. Then he swung the small box close to the steel ax and the magnetic needle swung dramatically in the opposite direction. The headman gasped in surprise and then Jack took the ax from him and handing it to another man, allowed the arrow in the box to follow. The natives were amazed. Jack put the box back inside his rucksack and pulling out a match, he held it high in the air for all to see.

Then Jack casually flicked the match-head with his thumbnail and a small flame lit the darkened hut. The men wanted nothing to do with this magic and they fled screaming out of the doors and windows and leaped onto the fireman's poles, hurling themselves to the ground. Jack pulled a harmonica from his pack, placed it in his lips, and smiling to himself, cautiously grasped a pole and leaped downward making the harmonica wheeze as he slid rapidly to the ground where he landed laughing at O'Rourke's feet.

"Have you gone mad?" O'Rourke asked and pointed to the somber group of natives who were now keeping their distance from the white sorcerer.

"Fair dinkum, mate," Jack cried and began playing Mother Macree on the harmonica while he danced a jig to the amusement of the carriers and children who gaped open-mouthed at the white-skinned dancing spirit. A boy held out his hand, his eyes pleading with Jack for permission to touch the instrument. Jack held the harmonica up for him to see and then he blew a few notes, touching the high and low end of the scale. He showed the boy how to plug a hole and change the pitch. He held out the harmonica and the boy grabbed it and ran a few steps away from the white magician. He blew into the mouth organ and sucked air through it making discordant sounds. The crowd shouted their approval, encouraging the youngster to make more sounds. Soon all the boys were racing around the compound, one blowing the harmonica and the others playing tag to get a turn.

Somatu produced a harmonica from his swag and demonstrated its use to one of the young men, who quickly imitated him and began making sounds. Some men of the tribe climbed up to their huts and came back with mouth harps made from reeds, and they twanged their instruments loudly adding to the discordant sounds made by the harmonicas. The women joined in the festivities and soon had a bonfire going. They brought out string bags of yams and the carriers helped the men prepare them for roasting. Jack had a porter light their two tilley lamps and hang them in nearby trees adding a depth of light that spread into the forest. The men and women of Tabamo, which O'Rourke had learned was the name of the village, were fascinated. This was the first man-made light that they had ever seen. The village men staged a dance, a wild dance for the party accompanied by flutes, drums, and their own mouth harps. They danced around the bonfires, their bat capes waving madly, casting eerie shadows in the firelight.

"These are very friendly vampires," commented O'Rourke and he began singing:

> "A young PO I met on jungle patrol
> His saksak house was one heck of a hole.
> When he felt blue and everything did go
> wrong
> He cheered his heart by just singing this
> song:
> *Kumul** in the tree top
> *Kapual*** on the beebop
> *Kindam**** in the sea
> I knew that I had never and I didn't think I'd ever
> See a *lulai* sitting a *tul tul* tree."
> (*bird of paradise **possum ***crayfish)

"So they are," and Jack grabbed O'Rourke by the arm forcing him to dance another impromptu Irish Jig causing the villagers and carriers to burst out in laughter to the utter chagrin of Sgt. Manu.

"These Kiaps are mad. We must return to the Headquarters soon," he said loudly, but no one, especially the police, paid any attention.

The patrol was off early the next morning, led by an advance party of Tabamo men. Jack and O'Rourke had learned from the chieftain, by using sign language and drawing maps in the mud, that the village was called Tabamo. The region they just crossed was called Wau, a bad place. The river was called Wai-Wau. To the north, indeed, was the limestone wall. It was called Fene, and according to the chieftain, beyond it was a river called Fene-Wau.

"If he can be trusted," Jack said, "and if the river runs somewhat southeast, possibly it will lead us to the Purari. Or the Kikori," Jack speculated. "The real problem is food. If we don't find food and a lot of it in the next two weeks, we'll be in trouble. Rice rations aren't enough. The men are complaining already about hunger, so far it's still a healthy hunger. We're out of sugar cane and sago. There's none of it growing here. Even if we do find villages, the people can't supply a party as large as ours. We can only trade, and hopefully, find sufficient game to meet our needs along the way," Jack paused. "The other alternative is to turn back. We have enough rice to get back to the river.... but then what? Even if the canoes are still there, it's a long way to Daru. We might make it in a pinch, but you saw the country. What do you think?"

"I say we go forward," O'Rourke answered. "We wanted an adventure and I guess this is a chance of a lifetime. It can't be more than 300 miles or so to the Purari. That is if we don't backtrack 1000 miles finding it, and then no more than a hop, skip, and a jump down the Purari River... a piece of cake."

Led by excited young Tambrians, the party made an easy six- mile trek in the morning, following a ridgeline that led southeastward. From a clearing at the top Jack and O'Rourke could see a limestone wall towering up to 6,000-7,000 feet and stretching unbroken from horizon to horizon. A formidable barrier.

"There's no way around," Jack observed. "We'll have to cut across somewhere. It might as well be there," and he pointed to a gap that seemed to be a thousand feet lower than the rest of the ridge.

The village chieftain joined them, "Dmumba," nodding his head and pointed, "Fene-wau," he made a sign for river by cupping his hand and waving it slowly.

"I'll lead Tim; you cover the stragglers," O'Rourke nodded and walked back to the rear of the column. "Sgt. Manu take the point," Jack commanded.

"Yes, Sir!" Sgt. Manu answered and started downward leading the constables toward a broad valley far below the ridge. The pathway, as usual, was a mire of slippery clay, often blocked by ant-infested logs and rushing streams, which slowed their progress. The patrolmen and their guides proceeded single-file down the narrow track, zigzagging like goats, crossing over roaring rivulets on slimy moss covered logs. Again and again, the carriers and villagers fell off the logs, incurring cuts, bruises and sprains in the process.

On an especially slippery log, Jack's oiled boots slid out from under him and he landed in the water below, painfully wrenching a knee. Badly shaken, he stood on the far bank, while a policeman cut him a walking stick. I have to be more careful, he thought. These men are counting on me to bring them out of here safely. I can't help them if I'm a cripple. Using the stick as a staff, Jack hobbled slowly down the track. Near the base of the ridge, the caravan encountered its first suspension bridge, a clumsy affair made of vine-rope and bits of bamboo, all strung awkwardly together. The carriers refused to cross until the policemen unstrapped their packs and made repairs with the help of the villagers.

Two hours later, the policemen, like spiders crossing a web, made their way over the bridge, leaving the carriers no choice but to go on or be left behind in that bleak spot. Their guides abandoned them here. “Tam Fui,” the chief said and clicked his genital gourd at the same time, making a rasping sound as he gnashed his teeth.

“Whatever it is, it doesn't sound good,” O'Rourke responded. He shouldered his rifle, leaving his hands free for the crawl across the bridge.

“Friend,” Jack said, staring directly into the chief's face, as he handed him a steel ax.

“Friend,” a tear formed in the chief's eye and rolled down his cheek. Halfway across the treacherous bridge, Jack turned firmly grasping the vine rail and waved with his free hand. “Friend,” cried the chief and even from there Jack could hear the sound of their gourds.

PART THREE

THE ROOF OF THE WORLD

A cold afternoon rain swept down from the limestone barrier as they picked their way across a treeless track of gravel, stumps, and bushes. The party endured hours of wet, sodden misery in silence until Jack called a halt at the base of a cliff. “Far enough. We'll camp here.”

The carriers struck the tents and quickly moved inside the shelters to eat a double ration of cold rice with a dollop of oily tinned meat on top. There were no fires that night to warm them; the wood in the area was in short supply, and what few scattered pieces they found were rotted and wet.

“We have about a week's tea left,” O'Rourke said, “unless we ration it. The tinned meat is about finished and the flour is rotten.” The wind howled through sieve-like holes and tore at the mildewed edges of the tent. “We might as well ditch the tents; they are about finished. It will lighten our loads a bit going up that damn ridge,” and he gestured towards the barrier with his thumb.

“Rice, tea, blankets, cook pots, rope, trade goods, and ammo. That's it,” said Jack glancing up from a list he was making on a notepad. “One carrier for the maps, journals, and our personal gear. The rest carry the essentials.”

“Why bother to keep records? They will all go into some clerk's pigeon hole, never to see the light of day.”

“We'll know. Someday we'll want to look back. Besides, one day some fools might try to follow our footsteps.”

“Speaking of footsteps how's your knee, Jack?”

“A bit crook, but it'll be right,” Jack alibied.

O'Rourke propped his feet on the kerosene stove. “You know Jack somewhere tonight men are sitting in easy chairs, in a nice comfortable bar, and having good food for the asking. What would you have if you were there?”

“Well, that's food for thought,” Jack said teasingly, “but it's not very nourishing,” and turned his attention back to his notepad.

"While you're ticking things off your list, you can tick off these rotten government tents the commissary lent us," as he pushed a hand through one of the slimy sides, letting in even more wind and rain. They fell asleep as rain dripped from the wet seams and formed pools of water by their heads.

The next morning was sunny as they started up a goat-track that looked promising. The carriers and police were strung out behind Jack over the zigzag trail that lead to the top of the barrier. Sgt. Manu and Cpl. Isi were at the point, a mere quarter of a mile ahead of him. "Are they going slowly on my account?" he asked himself. "Or, am I keeping up with them?" Jack continued talking aloud to himself as he struggled up the track.

"Broken Bottle Country," Sgt. Manu called the barrier, referring to the razor sharp limestone edges that lined their path. They reached the top of the crest shortly before noon. Jack called a halt and the party rested in their tracks while the MO moved from man to man, treating their cuts and lacerations.

They moved onto the plateau in the early afternoon. Sgt. Manu and the policemen were in the van. Jack walked in the middle of the carriers, and O'Rourke brought up the rear watching for stragglers. Sgt. Manu found it impossible to cut a straight course northward, for in dodging the craters, he was forced to turn in all possible directions. Every elevation looked like a spur of some divide; but at close quarters it turned out to be only the rim of more craters. They walked up narrow and silent corridors of rock, sometimes hearing the rumble of an underground river, often cutting past deep caves where they could see the drip falling from stalactites.

By nightfall, the exhausted patrol took shelter under the edge of a rock overhang. A cold rain dripped on their canvas bags and they gratefully drank the pooled water and filled their canteens from the overflow. Most of the men were too exhausted to eat.

All the next morning they struggled across the craters, gripped in the perpetual fog that lived on the plateau. "Ghost country," Isi muttered. All the carriers looked forsaken for they feared spirits. This was like no country they had ever seen.

By afternoon, the cold drizzling rain returned making their lives miserable. Jack called a merciful halt on one of the few level spaces they had encountered and allowed the party to regroup. O'Rourke climbed up through the branches of a lonesome tree trying to get a glimpse of the country ahead. "Spot anything?" Jack cried.

"Nothing. I can't see a damn thing through this mist," O'Rourke hollered back. Jack and the MO dressed the wounds of two carriers who had slid deep into one of the many pits and badly gashed their legs.

Somewhere behind them, Jack heard a cry of anguish as a straggling carrier fell into a crater. He made his way to the rear and found several carriers gathered around the rim. Cpl. Dekadua uncoiled a rope from his pack and handed one end to Jack and the MO. He fastened the other end to his waist and slid over the edge, carefully picking his way down to the man stranded far below.

"Pull, Kiap, pull," they heard Dekadua shout and moving backwards, they heaved and hauled on the rope.

Soon Cpl. Dekadua's head came over the top of the rim. He was dragging Nadnua behind him. "Taubada," he yelled as both men toppled over the edge. Jack looked down into the bottomless pit and saw a huge python wriggling across the broken shards easing itself away from the lip.

"How big was it, Dekadua?" the MO asked.

"Big enough to growl with de noise of a cassowary," the Corporal panted.

"We will camp here," Jack said. "Give the men an extra ration of rice," he instructed the cook. The men fell asleep as soon as they had eaten. Most of the carriers didn't even bother to remove their packs. They used them to keep their bodies off the cold, hard ground.

"Upward and onward," O'Rourke moaned the next morning as they struggled over even more difficult terrain. The craters were so numerous the patrol could no longer cut around them. They had to lower themselves down one side of a crater and wait at the bottom while a policeman scaled his way up the other side on his hands and knees. Then he tossed down a rope for the more heavily-laden men as they clawed their way to the top. There was no room to sit on the rim, so they had to descend quickly into the next crater, often dislodging surprised and irritated pythons. They huddled at the bottom getting a respite from the wind and rain before they pushed upward again. By now the party was nearing exhaustion.

"My damn gums are bleeding," O'Rourke announced, baring his mouth open with his fingers.

"So are mine," said Jack.

"Scurvy," O'Rourke said shifting his position on the side of rock where they rested.

"Even the police are griping; they are saying I will never find our way out of here."

"So I've heard," O'Rourke said gently. "Can you?"

"Can I?" Jack asked. "Keep the men here. Have the MO lance their boils and abscesses again. After you've rested, follow me straight north. I'll leave a trail of calico or bloody diarrhea," he laughed. Together Somatu and Jack started across the next ridge, blazing a trail for the patrol to follow.

"Listen, Kiap," Somatu said. "Moribou. Moribou." Somewhere down below them, Jack could hear the squeaking of hundreds of bats. "There is a big cave there. Let's go down, Kiap," Somatu begged. "When we strike camp, the policemen will be cutting timber, the greedy Orokos will find it, and there will be no moribou for us."

"You'll get your share," Jack assured him, and they moved forward. Every now and again, Somatu looked back and muttered to himself. "Far enough," Jack said after they crossed a dozen more craters, and the two men turned back.

Jack and Somatu clambered back to the crater where they had spotted the bat cave. "Sons of Bush Dogs!" Somatu growled in Motu. Then he turned to Jack, "Kiap, the carriers -- they are down there, and the camp is not made." O'Rourke joined them.

"It's true enough. Neither Sgt. Manu nor I could stop them. I threatened them, but nothing could keep them from going down there once they heard the squeals."

"Nothing short of assault and battery would have stopped them, Tim. Let's have a look." Somatu followed Jack down the path the starving carriers had made to the cave. They were all there, behaving like hysterical madmen. The carriers inside the cave were throwing rocks at the bats clinging by the hundreds to the limestone ceiling, while the policemen at the entrance were knocking down the bats with long sticks as they tried to fly to safety.

Sgt. Manu directed his torch onto the ceiling creating a scene from Dante's Inferno as he played his light first on the walls and then on the men busy bashing the bats' heads onto nearby stalagmites. Blood and guts oozed everywhere and the frightened squeals of the bats echoed in the cavern. The men were howling insanely. "Moribou, Kiap, moribou," they all shouted when they saw Jack enter the cave.

Jack trained his torch on their faces. The life spark had returned to the eyes of the starving dispirited men. "Carry on," he said and handed the torch to Somatu and crawled back up to O'Rourke's perch. "I didn't have the heart to stop them," Jack said.

"God, what a stench!" O'Rourke pinched his nose and held it closed with two fingers and nodded.

That evening the carriers marched around the campfire, tearing off joints of half-cooked bats and shoveling them into their mouths. "Bloody hell! Look at them." O'Rourke said.

Somatu, a bat in each hand, offered them to the Kiaps. "Not bad," said O'Rourke. "Tastes like a fishy kind of chicken. Once you get past the smell," he said jamming some bat flesh into his mouth. "It could end up on the menu at Baxters." Jack's stomach warred with his nostrils and he smiled weakly as he swallowed a small chunk. "As Bat Wings or Bat Pudding?"

In the morning as they marched out of camp, Cpl. Isi pretended to click his imaginary gourd as he led his fat-bellied charges past a scowling Sgt. Manu. “They are a happy lot all right,” O'Rourke grimaced, “but they all smell like flying foxes.”

He belched and swung a clumsy fist at Jack who faked a gasp, grabbed at his nose and turned away from the offender. “You have bat breath.”

“Piss off,” O'Rourke chuckled.

The sun was shining and Jack and two constables forged ahead of the main party. The rock crevices and craters were gradually disappearing. None too soon, thought Jack, for they were running out of food and their boots and clothing were in shreds. They crossed a small basin covered with alpine forest and hiked over the divide.

“Dis is safe country. Bottle glass go finis.” Cpl. Dekadua announced. Jack merely nodded. The fog was behind them now and they began to stride forward with a kind of pleasing recklessness. They hurried down a gentle sloping spur heading northward and paused beneath a large, slanting tree.

“Let's take a look,” Jack followed the two policemen high into the branches.

Cpl. Dekadua called excitedly, “Come quickly and see!” Jack's joy was unbounded. Through the rifts in the rain-clouds far ahead, he could see stretches of beautiful rolling country with evidence of a population. A broad river system drained the region.

“It must be the Kikori!” Jack announced.

“Almost like my name,” constable Koriki exclaimed. “Dis is a good sign.” This new land meant life versus death by starvation. When the clouds obscured their view, the three men knew that for just a moment, the curtain had been lifted to show them the promise land.

O'Rourke came along leading a tired-looking, foot-weary party, but when the constables in the tree shouted, “People and food” and pointed to the northeast, the weary looks changed to hopeful grins. Cpl. Isi clicked his imaginary gourd and shouted to the constables, “Can you see any women? My gourd is excited!”

The men began laughing as the party's buffoon strutted around pretending to stroke his gourd and singing a lewd police ditty,

"Lead us down the mountain, Sgt. Manu," Jack shouted as he quickly descended the tree. With renewed vigor, the party moved down the spur, making good progress to the river below.

"I'd hate to have been here when this happened," O'Rourke said as they passed over a huge landslide. An avalanche had leveled the forest like so much matchwood. Late that afternoon, Jack halted the party on the bank of the river. "We'll make camp here."

Sgt. Manu gave instructions to the work details and then reported to Jack. "Kaivamore is missing. No one has seen him." Sgt. Manu hesitated and then said, "He was pretending to be sick, but he was no more tired than the other men."

"Thank you, Sergeant," Jack replied tersely. "Send Cpl. Koriki back with two policemen to look for him and have them bring him straight to me."

"Yes, Kiap," Sgt. Manu left and gave the necessary order to the three policemen, who went back to search for the missing man.

"I do not like this place, Kiap," Somatu said standing at his side. "These stones talk."

"What do they say, Somatu?"

"They say we should not stay here but move to that place," and Somatu pointed to a ridge further downstream. Jack surveyed the heights above them. He listened to the stillness.

"Sgt. Manu, move the camp beyond that ridge."

"Yes, Kiap," he said as the porters grumbled and stared stonily at Somatu.

Early in the evening, a "halloo" echoed from the top of the mountain. Soon the policemen could be seen bundling the truant carrier roughly across the face of the landslide. A terrific detonation sounded through the glen. Everyone glanced fearfully upward at the men who were struggling across the face. The mountain moved and a huge slide of rock thundered down with such force they could hear the great boulders crashing together on the riverbed a thousand feet below them. The deafening roar was followed by a deafening silence as the men stood staring transfixed at the cloud of dust in front of them, not daring to speak. Kansu began to wail. “Kaivamore is gone,” and the wailing spread through the camp.

Search parties crawled across the rubble through the night and again early in the morning looking for survivors but found no sign of the missing men.

The men stood at attention as Cpl. Isi played a mournful tune on his bugle and the constables fired a volley into the mountain.

“Who knows who their mothers were,” Kande cried. But no one spoke. The saddened party shouldered their loads and moved down the track.

“What's next?” Jack asked O'Rourke. “I sent the policemen back to recover one straggler, and now four men are dead. How many more will die before we reach home?”

“I don't have a crystal ball. But that landslide was an act of God. The blame doesn't fall on your shoulders.”

“We are lucky that Somatu warned me. Sgt. Manu says that he listens to the birds, the clouds, and the stones; but the Oroko men believe he brings on these disasters by speaking their names. Maybe in my report, I should blame it on the mountain,” Jack said with a shrug. He then turned to Sgt. Manu, “Follow the river, Sergeant,” and Manu and three constables moved to the front.

Jack and O'Rourke had decided that the thundering river beneath them must be the Ryan since it ran from north to south. They followed it during the morning until they encountered a major tributary leading in from the northeast. The waters of this river were chalky white, heavily discolored by limestone. For a reference point, Jack decided to name it the White River. While he charted it into his notebook, the policemen felled a large Norfolk pine to bridge the river shortly above its conjunction with the Ryan.

They clambered their way up the Ryan Gorge for a mile or so, looking for a path to the summit of the limestone cliffs.

"Mother of all mothers," Sgt. Manu exclaimed as he led the vanguard around the face of a cliff.

When Jack and the main party rounded the bend, they stared open-mouthed at the cliff walls. Three parallel ledges ran the length of the cliffs for nearly a quarter of a mile, until they curved around a bend. Perched precariously on the ledges were row after row of yellow-white skeletons; some were still in a cadaverous state, their skulls stained an ocherous red. Bits of colored rags sticking to their rib cages, fluttered in the cold wind that swept down the canyon from the north.

A sharp crack broke the strange silence as a skeleton toppled from its perch onto a ledge below sending three more cadavers crashing downward, adding to the heaps of vertebrae and hollow-eyed skulls piled on the floor of the gorge. The wind blew more strongly and one by one more skeletons fell cascading into the abyss. The dried bones crackled and tinkled musically as they splintered apart on the rocks, sending up a shower of bleached knucklebones.

The porters screamed and throwing off their packs, raced back down the canyon. O'Rourke called, "Halt!" to no effect and for emphasis, he fired a shot which echoed down the corridor. The porters didn't even slow down and O'Rourke and Jack had no choice but to march the policemen back to the White River crossing where the porters were hiding in the trees.

Sgt. Manu spoke loudly in Motu for all the Orokos to hear. "You sons of bush dogs! You have eaten Judge Murray's kai-kai. You die, you think we bury you?" and he pointed to the policemen.

"No fear," the answer came from Cpl. Dekadua. "We throw you into a cave; de place where you were born."

"Are your heads made of stone?" Sgt. Manu continued. "How often must I tell you, there are no such things as ghosts?" Sgt. Manu broke off his harangue. "What you want me to do with these boys who wish for their mothers' legs?" he asked Jack. The carriers rolled their eyes toward Jack, hoping for a reprieve.

"Take them back and retrieve the packs; then follow us up there," Jack said pointing to a trail that led to the top of the plateau. "We will try to find a way to the Purari from there." At the mention of the Purari, the carriers' faces lit up with hope.

The patrol straggled up a narrow trail to the plateau and waited there for Sgt. Manu and the "skeery" porters to rejoin them. For the next three hours, in spite of the pain in his knee, Jack led the men at almost a quick-march pace through a pine forest, partly to restore a sense of discipline and partly to relieve his anxiety that their panicky flight could have led to another disaster. By the time they reached a clearing, the carriers were spent men. The weeks of incessant toil and the short rations were now telling on them severely.

"You've made your point, Jack. If we go easy, we will go farther. The carriers will obey orders, but they are beat," O'Rourke said.

"I take your point," Jack puffed. "Let's take a look-see. I want to know what's in front of us." While the men rested, O'Rourke and Jack pushed on to a spot where a tall tree had fallen providing a break in the forest. They stood spellbound looking at a scene of wild and lonely splendor.

"God, would you believe it?" O'Rourke said. "It's the Garden of Eden."

"It had better be, for we are in one sorry condition. We could use some time in God's country." Below on the opposite side of the Ryan, a large blue lake lay on a divide while the Ryan itself could be seen emerging from a deep gorge about two miles to the north. Beyond that as far as the eye could see, lay rolling timbered slopes and grasslands of a huge valley system. Cultivated soil-broken squares marched up every slope creating an enormous geometric grid. White columns of smoke rose into the air revealing the dagus of the people of this land.

"Have you even seen anything more beautiful?" Jack said in hushed tones to O'Rourke.

"Never. Never in my life. There's nothing in Queensland, or all of Australia to compare with this. It's a wonderland."

"I've dreamed all my life of finding something like this. "It's Shangri-La." They watched as the setting sun sparkled off the heights of a mighty mountain chain that stood behind the green cultivated fields.

Jack thought about the other patrol officers -- Woodward, Saunders, Rentoul, Flint, and Ryan -- and imagined what they would have given to see this sight of this vast land. They had explored the country as far as the Erewa, and they had heard of big populations to the northward, but here was something that went beyond all their expectations. Jack knew a debt of gratitude was due them and the other "Outside Men" of the Papuan Service. For this remarkable discovery was built on the lessons learned from the earlier expeditions.

"What kind of people has created something like this?" O'Rourke asked. "It looks like a colony of Chinese has come here. Whoever they are, they are not the same people we know on the coast."

Soon the carriers and the police joined the officers and they too gazed in amazement at this wonderland. "My Mother," said Sgt. Manu, "people like the sand."

"Just as you predicted, Sergeant. We will make camp here. Give the men an extra half-ration of rice. Tomorrow we will go meet these sandmen of yours," Jack added.

"Yes, Sir!" Sgt. Manu grinned.

"There are two distinct territories up here," O'Rourke maintained. "There's definitely a division between the two. The patterns of cultivation are different. We have some hard walking to do before we even reach the first territory."

"I'm satisfied there must be a million or more people up here," Jack said. "We will be the first white men to come here. I'm sure of that. Our first contact must be a friendly one. We can't shoot our way through that many people, anyway."

"We might not be able to shoot our way through," O'Rourke said, "but what if they give us no choice?"

"We can only do our best, but we must get home and report what we've found up here!" The officers crawled into their dirty blankets and slept peacefully for the first time in days.

The following morning the party worked its way down from the top of the plateau. By noon they had reached the floor of a small valley, broad and flat, and enclosed by 2000-foot sandstone cliffs. They came across a faint track, but it soon faded away. In the van, O'Rourke and Jack waited for Sgt. Manu and the carriers to catch up. Jack sent Dekadua and Agoti to search ahead for tracks. The silent, Northern constable, was a strange contrast to the talkative but likeable Dekadua.

"No one could ambush those two," O'Rourke laughed as the curious pair melted into the bush. In a few minutes, they could hear the usual argument over the best way to go. They must have separated;

"Where you go?" Dekadua's voice drifted out of the forest. No answer. A little later, they heard Dekadua's shout again, "You find road?"

This time Agoti answered, "Come dis way." Soon both men returned to report that they had located a large track that led to the northeast. When the last of the carriers and police caught up, they moved out to explore the newly discovered tracks. The pathway was a wide one and it led up a slight spur with prints showing on its entire length. Obviously there were natives in front of them, and they apparently knew strangers were coming their way. Broken and bunched branches blocked the track.

"My Mother," laughed Dekadua and he pointed to a cleft stick. Inserted in the fork was a piece of freshly cooked meat, already covered with ants, and a broken human finger bone.

"What do you make of it, Corporal?"

"I tink dey telling us dat if we come down dis trail, dey will cook and eat us. Kaip."

"Corporal, you and Agoti take the point. O'Rourke, take the rear and Sgt. Manu, take three men and stay in the middle of the carriers. Cpl. Isi and I will cover. Somatu, stay close to me; have my rifle at the ready." Somatu nodded. "Move out" and he waved the two scouts forward.

They soon emerged from the forest onto some gardens that sprawled up the side of the spur. Three large but poorly constructed thatched dagus flanked the gardens; sounds from within told them they were occupied. There were no guards about and no one could be seen walking in the open.

"Curious," said O'Rourke. "I wonder if they thought their sign would be enough to keep us away."

The vanguard approached the first dwelling and Cpl. Dekadua called out, "Sambio!" A small girl ran out to investigate but slipped back inside when she saw them. Three men came out, weapons in their hands, while others could be seen assisting heavily laden women scurrying out the back with their belongings. As the policemen approached the huts, the villagers bolted. Nothing could stay them. They were all terrified, men as well as women and children. So Jack decided to take a risk and catch one of them.

"Cpl. Isi, seize that woman." Jack pointed to an old woman whose arms were loaded down with pots. Cpl. Isi ran forward and reached out to grab her, but the terrorized old women broke a pot over his head knocking him down to his knees. The men laughed loudly as Isi grabbed her by the feet as she tried to squirm away. Cpl. Dekadua took her arm, lifted her up and led her gently back to the dagu.

"Old mother! What fear? We not kill you." Cpl. Isi patted her on the shoulder and placed her netted bag over her shoulder. Sgt. Manu and the constables circled her and tried to demonstrate their friendly intentions while her relatives frantically called out from the forest.

The woman, wan-faced and trembling wouldn't look at Jack or O'Rourke, nor would she accept their presents. O'Rourke showed her a tomahawk, demonstrated its use, and signed he had more to give for food. Slowly, the woman realized the strange men meant her no harm, but she pointed to the trees and signed anxiously that she wanted to join her relatives. O'Rourke led her out of the compound and walked her slowly to a garden. The old woman stooped over and dug up a potato with her long fingers and handed it to him with a nervous smile. He let her go with a friendly pat on the shoulder. She ran up the track into the forest, to the waiting men who had never ceased calling for her.

The patrol camped on the edge of the village between the forest and the gardens. They listened to the natives yodeling excitedly and they watched the people tilling fields far below, disappearing into the forest. Soon a group of men could be seen near to top of a nearby ravine. They seemed to be trying to decide what do about the strange spirits who had invaded their homeland.

"These people are headhunters, Kiap." Sgt. Manu pointed to blackened skulls mounted on poles on each corner of the dagus. "The skulls have holes in the tops, Kiap. Those holes were made with clubs."

"Will they fight Sgt. Manu or will they leave us alone?" Jack asked.

"I don't think they will fight, Kiap. We are in their village now. Out in the open it would be another thing."

Towards sunset, six young men, all unarmed, slowly approached the camp. As they came, they stooped to pick up potato vines, and pointing to their abdomens, kept calling "Tomo. Tomo" and indicated that the party might take as many potatoes as they wanted. These men were soon followed by several more men who Cpl. Dekadua met halfway and coaxed them into camp. These men were short in stature, clean and light skinned, and had girlish mops of brown hair adorned with parrot feathers. The constables were cautious, because some of the men had bone daggers tucked in their grass sporans.

They avoided looking directly at Jack and O'Rourke until O'Rourke patted one of them on the shoulder and handed him a tomahawk. A few of the men pointed to the garden and signed that the party could eat to their hearts' content.

Twice Jack offered beads and cloth as payment for the food, but each time they waved them away. "They don't seem to be interested in our trade goods," O'Rourke said.

A new arrival strode into the compound. He was a splendid figure, darker than his fellow men, with a black pointed beard, a cassowary quill through his nose and a carefully coiffed and flower-decked mop of hair. As he strode into the compound, the younger natives made way for him.

"This is what?" Cpl. Isi asked jokingly.

"It must be de village policemani," Dekadua suggested.

"True, dis man has no clothes, but maybe his woman is washin dem," Cpl. Isi sniggered.

"Look at his beard," another constable added.

"We should call dis man Besoso," said Dekadua pointing at the man's beard. Besoso appeared to be a serious person. When he came to a halt in front of Jack and O'Rourke, he looked them up and down critically. Besoso jerked his head at Jack questioningly and pointed at him and then towards the limestone barrier. Jack pointed towards the barrier and nodded his head up and down. Besoso then pointed a finger to his ear and nodded his head, then pointed a finger to his eyes, and closed them which to Jack meant that Besoso had heard about but had not seen the barrier.

Besoso looked over the trade goods and equipment spread on the ground. Jack picked up an ax and knife offered them to Besoso who rejected them with lofty disdain. He signed that the patrol should pick up the axes and knives and pointing towards the south, he indicated they should go back the way they came.

Jack pointed in the direction that the patrol intended to take across the valley and then to all his men and then pointed again westward. Besoso thought this over for a minute. Then pointed to his men, and stooped over and picked up some dirt with one hand. He pointed to the east and spilled the dirt slowly onto the ground.

"He's telling us that there are men like the sand in the direction we want to go," said Sgt. Manu.

"Na bobi. Na bobi," Besoso said shaking his head. As if to change the subject, he pointed to some hornbill beaks peeping out the top of a policeman's swag. The beaks belonged to Dekadua, but Jack handed them to Besoso, promising to repay the Corporal. Jack put a mirror on top of the potato vines and signed that the mirror was a gift for the food.

One of the men picked it up, turned it over several times, looking first into the mirror and then at the backside. He held it up over his head examining his reflection from several angles while he kept grunting, "Aa. Aa. Aa."

Besoso grunted something and the man held up the mirror for Besoso. Besoso looked into the mirror and jumped back upon seeing his face. He bid the man to hold it at such and such a length; no, it must be right in front; now at the ground; now ten feet away. Jack was beginning to think the man's vanity would overcome his hostility. Then like a big bully, Besoso demanded the mirror, but the villager who clearly wanted the glass, put it behind his back, obviously intending to keep possession. Besoso grunted sullenly and turned away. Suddenly he lifted a club up from his side and bashed in the man's skull. With a shriek, the victim toppled to the ground, his brains spewing onto the gravel at their feet.

The party stood momentarily frozen in horror as Besoso stepped over the man's body and calmly picked up the looking glass. Jack's voice broke, "Get that man out of here." Sgt. Manu and Cpl. Dekadua grabbed Besoso, only too pleased to carry out the duty.

"You think Judge Murray's police are school bois?" they shouted at Besoso in Motu and they both drew their lower lips into their mouths to give added expression to their cheeky words.

Without waiting, the two constables picked up handfuls of rocks and pelted him down the trail in a most undignified manner. Besoso's people understood the gesture and began laughing, but no one wailed for the dead man. In fact, they paid no attention whatsoever to the corpse.

"Bloody hell," O'Rourke said.

"Move out!" Jack ordered.

The party picked up their loads and moved to an open ridge several hundred yards up the track to a site that overlooked the village and gardens. Jack posted extra guards and they went to sleep in the rain, knowing they were being watched from the forest.

The next morning the men prepared a meal of potatoes and spinach while the villagers yodeled from the forest and the police yodeled back. Cpl Isi, stroked his imaginary gourd and shouted, "These policemani don't fight until they eat their kai-kai."

"Be still, stupid man," Sgt. Manu said. "We want no trouble with these men."

Cpl. Dekadua and Constable Agoti climbed a tall tree at the edge of the clearing but could not find a track leading to the east or northeast from the campsite; therefore, the only route to the rolling slopes above the Ryan Gorge lay over the northern rim of the canyon, and Jack decided to follow it.

As the party moved off in that direction, natives in a cultivated field some distance along their path tried to wave them back. They began to yodel and rush to and fro when the vanguard ignored them as they marched into the area. Twenty men armed with bows and arrows moved out of a stand of trees and stood along the edge of the track.

Some of the natives feigning friendliness urged the party on its way but made no effort to guide them up the track. The bully Besoso was not with them. Jack looked ahead along the path. A creek ran across it and a steep bank 100 feet high ran alongside the wide streambed.

"A beautiful trap," Jack commented.

"This could be it," O'Rourke confirmed. Some of the constables noticed armed men moving into concealment on the opposite rim. To prevent a more serious situation, Jack fired a shot over the men who were obviously preparing an ambush. They removed themselves with surprising speed.

"Disarm these men," Jack commanded and the constables aimed their weapons at the natives behind them.

The men fell to the ground shouting, "Augwa-fobei" while the constables quickly relieved them of their weapons.

"Break their bows," Jack ordered and the constables snapped several bows across their knees and tossed them to the ground. "Go back," Jack cried pointing his rifle down the track and he fired over their heads. The men leaped to their feet and ran howling back down the track.

"Move out," Jack shouted to Cpl. Dekadua and Constable Agoti and they started forward. "Take five yard intervals," he instructed the carriers. "O'Rourke, take five constables and bring up the rear. I'm moving to the front. Keep your eyes peeled." O'Rourke nodded his understanding and fell in behind the carriers.

The patrol moved on, passing a half-hidden farmhouse. The people came out and stared as they passed. They climbed a grassy knoll, and there waiting brazenly a few yards off the track, was the bombastic Besoso, his chest still heaving with exertion from his run from the place of ambush to this new point of contact. Jack stared sternly at the chieftain. Besoso's arrogant manner was gone; now he waved in a friendly manner, pointing to the track they were following.

"Augua fobei," he said in a mild voice.

Intuitively the policemen distrusted this man's intentions, especially since he had brought so many armed men with him. They knew he was a man to be watched. "Sgt. Manu, take him prisoner and handcuff him," Jack ordered. Constable Agoti and Cpl. Dekadua jumped forward and grasped Besoso from behind before he could flee. Sgt. Manu pulled a set of handcuffs from his belt and clasped them firmly on Besoso's wrists.

"Move those men out of the way," Jack continued, and the forward group of constables started towards the confused young warriors on the path ahead. "Fix bayonets," Jack commanded and the police pulled the wicked-looking bayonets from their scabbards and attached them to their rifles. The police moved forward and brushed aside any men who had not moved off the track quickly enough. One warrior hesitated too long and Constable Agoti hit him on the shoulder with the butt of his rifle, knocking him to the ground. The man reached for his bone knife, but Agoti pushed his bayonet hard against his chest, making it clear to the man that if he persisted, he would die.

The warrior grimaced as Agoti kicked the bone knife beyond his reach and moved on toward the next man who turned and fled. Sgt. Manu hauled the squealing Besoso down the track.

The bully kept trilling, "Augua-fobei. Augua-fobei," but Sgt. Manu ignored him. Jack yelled at the confused natives and pointed back to their village.

"Constables, fire a round over their heads," Jack commanded, and the police began firing in the general direction of the men who retreated down the track. The patrol kept Besoso with them until they reached a ledge on the northern rim of the canyon.

"Turn him loose," Jack ordered. Sgt. Manu unlocked the handcuffs and with an unceremonious shove, pushed Besoso down the trail. The rear-guard laughed, jeered, and forced Besoso down a small gauntlet line. "Let him be," Jack called to them. The men hesitated and looked up at Jack standing alone above him on the ridge. In a flash Besoso pulled a small bone dagger from beneath his grass sporran and plunged it deep into Kande's stomach. He spun away from the police and dashed down a shallow creek bed.

A bare 100 yards away, he turned and holding the bloody knife over his head, shouted a battle cry, "Aag. Aag." Besoso never heard the bullet that silenced his voice forever. His face twisted into a look of astonishment as he fell forward onto his knees and toppled over. His hands made a queer fluttering movement. His fingers were convulsively plucking and clutching at the cold, earthy roots. The carriers looked apprehensively at the smoke curling skyward from Jack's rifle, and then back at Besoso's crumpled body, face down in the grass.

Jack sank back onto the ledge, his head down. Below him O'Rourke cradled the wounded cook's head in his arms. Kande's mouth opened and shut, crying for water. But when O'Rourke offered him a swallow from his canteen, Kande refused to drink.

A bitter scowl etched itself across O'Rourke's face as he realized he was unable to help. They heard Kande gasp, "My mother," as he turned ashen and trembled in O'Rourke's arms. A low gasp escaped from the lips of the dying man, and with it his spirit passed into the clouds.

"I'll never trust one of those cunning bastards again," O'Rourke exclaimed, still clutching Kande in his arms. "May they all rot in hell," and he laid the dead man's head gently on the ground and stood up slowly.

"It's my fault, Tim. I met arrogance with arrogance. We lost a good man for nothing. We can't shoot our way across this country. This is their territory. Besoso only threw a gauntlet in our faces. It will take years, if not forever, to undo the damage."

"The bastard committed two murders, Jack. As far as I'm concerned, his death was an inspired suicide. Life is meaningless to these people. You had no choice. If you hadn't shot him, he would have been back in an hour with the whole tribe."

"Maybe, but there has to be another way ..." Jack's voice faded.

The burial party fired a salvo over Kande's unmarked grave. Its echo disturbed a mountain bird of paradise. They heard its cry, "Wah-wah-wah wok-wok-wok," as it sailed over the canyon rim.

"Lead the way, Sergeant," and Jack turned toward the trail. The unhappy-looking men began to shuffle forward, crossing over the rusty stains on the rusty grass. Jack noticed they had assumed the shape of Australia, or is that my imagination, he wondered.

The carriers had been weakened from the weeks of incessant toil. One was crippled with an abscess on the knee caused by a limestone cut. The police appeared haggard and trail weary. Jack ventured a glance at O'Rourke -- a red beard and moustache covered his normally clean-shaven face, hiding the pallor beneath. His clothes were ragged and torn and part of the brim of his bush hat was missing. "You don't look so hot yourself," said O'Rourke reading Jack's thoughts as he passed on his way to the front of the line.

The party followed a track over a saddle, crawled down the other side into a park-like area of pine, hibiscus, and crotons where they met a woman leading a pig on a rope. She stood to the side of the trail and gladly accepted two strings of beads from O'Rourke and went on her way, quite fearless. She showed the beads to the police and carriers as they courteously made way for her.

The patrol's spirits lifted as they entered this new valley. It was pleasant here. Each cultivated area contained a squarely built dagu that was thatched with grass. Strong, long-legged women with wooden spades were busy tilling the ground, paused and looked up curiously and then renewed their labor. Some unarmed youthful inhabitants raced out and greeted the patrol in a most friendly manner. Jack offered them a steel ax, but they shook their heads and smilingly tapped their own beautiful axes of green stone.

This new race of people were fairly tall, slim in stature, light-skinned, and had large mops of brown hair, cropped like naval admirals' caps, which they had adorned with flowers and parrot feathers. A few men wore necklaces of parrot beaks.

The party sat down to a ration of cold rice by the side of the road -- a real road. A friendly old man with a bark hat fastened by pins to the top of his graying mop of hair and his cheeks adorned with fluffy side-whiskers came to speak with them. He had the appearance of a gentleman and in a civilized area he might have been taken for a squire or a country doctor. He was quite affable and sat between Jack and O'Rourke, smiling and nodding his head, and drawing in his breath between his teeth. Jack handed him a string of beads and he offered Jack a draw out of his bamboo pipe; Jack held out a looking glass.

"Aiza Aiza," the old man kept exclaiming as he saw his face in the glass. First, he rubbed his fluffy side-whiskers. Then he laughed. Then he frowned at himself. Then joy lit up his whole face. Finally, being sure that looking glass was a present, he carefully placed it in his bag. The old man waved his hand across the whole valley.

"I think we just bought the farm," O'Rourke said as the quaint character affectionately tugged O'Rourke's beard.
He gently tugged O'Rourke's beard again and looked up into the officer's face with a childish, lovable expression that seemed to say, "What a beautiful man you are!"

"Be careful, mate," Jack laughed. "I might have to come up with a bride price for you."

"Bugger off," O'Rourke grumbled but he was obviously enjoying his moment with the Dickensonian gentleman. While they talked, a hundred or so light-skinned natives -- men, women, and children -- surrounded the party. The old man, apparently someone of authority, was telling them that the outsiders had come down from the sky for every now and then he would point to their clothes, axes, and equipment and then point to the clouds overhead. But someone must have doubted his authority, for he turned around to answer some question and when he looked back at the officers there was a thoughtful expression on his face. From somewhere in his net bag, he produced a small piece of sugar cane and in sign language explained after a great deal of trouble, that this was the sugar cane grown on earth, but what did they have for sugar cane "on top"?

"A tough question," O'Rourke said glancing at Jack.

The old man looked intently at Jack who sat thoughtfully and then quietly told Somatu, "Bring me some of the sugar." Somatu returned in a few moments and handed Jack a sugar tin.

The crowd watched as he ceremoniously opened the tin and poured a small spoonful into the palm of the old man's hand. Jack took a few grains and put them in his mouth and exclaimed "Aij! Aij!" and smiled.

The old man looked at the white grains, then at Jack sharply. "Eat it," Jack urged him. With nods of approval from his followers, the old man started licking the sugar from his hand and he began making sucking noises with his mouth. He licked it all off his palm, enjoying every grain. The silence was intense as the people waited for the verdict. An ingenuous smile spread across the old man's face. He faced the crowd and spoke rapidly.

"There's no doubt about it. He's telling them it's the real MacKay," O'Rourke said. The people gasped with astonishment and started to whisper excitedly among themselves. Jack questioned the old man about the country, pointing to the territory around them.

The old man got up slowly and with a wave of his arm that embraced every mountain slope in sight, told him this valley system was the "Tarifuroro."

Drawing a little map in the soil with his finger and pouring some water on it from his canteen, Jack pointed out the main course of the Ryan and asked whether it, too, was the "Tarifuroro".

"Aija, aija," the old man nodded his head in assent. Jack drew another line, this time running eastward and he looked at him questioningly. Again the old man nodded understanding, "Waga Furari," he answered. Unknowingly, the old chap had told them of the Purari.

The next day they marched across the valley system, gradually moving higher and higher. As they climbed toward the eastern mountains, they hiked along wide tracks past dagus, cultivated fields and parklands. Since meeting the old man by the roadside, they had been provided with guides, eager to show them the way. At the end of each farm section, one set of guides would leave them with tearful farewells, only to be replaced by cheerful newcomers.

It was beautiful country and extremely fertile. Even the police talked about what excellent maize, sugar cane and taro would grow here. The track passed under an arch of long wooden slabs pointed at the ends like picket fences and they climbed up a slope to the most attractive area they had seen. Both sides of the track were neatly bordered with pieces of white limestone and planted ornamental shrubs and flowers. Long contour ditches drained the cultivated fields. Beyond the homesteads a fine grove of casuarinas had been planted. Each garden had its clump of bamboo, graceful as a green fountain, and its cluster of red and green coleus.

These people did not live in villages at all. They were homesteaders; each dagu sat in the center of a garden. Their guides led them into a small park of casuarinas trees. They asked the men to sit and rest. They gave the men leaf tobacco to smoke and sugar cane to quench their thirst. Then they pulled panpipes from their net bags and played tunes from a forgotten age for the patrol's amusement and pleasure.

"These drainage ditches took a lot of ingenuity and engineering. They bury their dead and split timber for buildings. They have excellent husbandry skills. Look at these terraces where they've planted asparagus and spinach ... and the pigs! They are properly penned. Who taught them how to do this?" Jack asked O'Rourke.

"It must have been the Egyptians. Have you noticed these men all roll their beards in those papyrus-like reeds? And their hats could have been worn by Iknaton himself," O'Rourke said, pointing to the conical double-cornered hat that covered their guide's hair.

"Black pharaohs?" Jack mused. "Or could they be Phoenicians?"

"These people are not Papuans as we know them, Jack. They have none of their habits," O'Rourke concluded. The men continued to survey the countryside. Orange, green, black and chocolate squares of land interfaced with each other. Some squares were burned black, and the pigs which had been turned loose to feed on the stubble were being managed by young boys and old men. They studied a tall peak off in the northwest about twenty-five miles distant. The high cone-shaped mountain was the highest they had seen in all Papua, a glorious monument with a snow-capped summit that seemed to glisten with pride. "Let's call it Mount Jubilee," O'Rourke exclaimed, "in honor of King George's silver anniversary."

"Mount Jubilee it is," and Jack reached for his notepad.

"Tarifuroro," said one of their guides who had noted the officers' interest in the mountain.

After gazing thoughtfully over the fertile valley, Jack made an entry in his journal.

> *"I've only been here a few hours and I'm already renaming their mountains. Tarifuroro would be the better choice."*

The muted sound of feet marching in unison broke his train of thought. A cloud of dust broke over the hill fronting the mountain, slightly obscuring his vision. "What have we here?" O'Rourke asked, glancing at the guides. With a nervous smile, Kedo, one of the guides, patted his hand on the ground, urging O'Rourke to sit down beside him.

"Not on your life," said O'Rourke as he reached for his rifle. The marching cadence grew louder and a large party of wondrously dressed warriors appeared out of the dust cloud. They were big men, well over six feet tall, broad-shouldered and powerful-legged, with highly polished and oiled skin. The tops of their heads were adorned with crowns of bird of paradise plumes. Reds, blues and yellows adorned their two-foot-tall bonnets. Their faces were lacquered a shiny bright yellow, contrasting with eyes etched in deep ebony black, each mouth painted a brilliant red or shiny black.

Each facial mask was unique and artfully designed. Some wore ochre on one side of their face, adding only a few black or white marks for effect on the other side. Others had created a half yellow mask on one side and half brilliant red on the other, or had painted their foreheads yellow and their cheeks red.

Each man carried a black palm spear with hand-carved ornate tips which they shook as they marched boldly forward. Cued by a warrior with bright green cheeks and black circles around his eyes, the men turned and flanked each side of the road making way for an imposing figure dressed in a cape and headdress made of bright red bird of paradise plumes.

A heavily armed cadre of warriors, trailing behind the feathered figure, began to chant, "Uu-waah, uu-waah," slowly at first, in a deep guttural tone. The tempo changed rapidly and ended in a high-toned crescendo. "Waah-waah-waah." The leader stopped in mid-stride, raised his spear, one powerful leg thrust through his skirt of cassowary feathers, and then he leaped high in the air, burying his spear into the ground in front of him. The warriors broke ranks, spears raised high, voices trilling, "yeep-yeep-yeep," and raced toward the patrolmen.

Jack reached for his rifle and stood beside O'Rourke. He heard the clicking of rifle bolts as the policemen stood to. "Kado. Kado," their guides whispered, and pointed to the log benches. Their eyes begged the men to sit.

Moving back cautiously to the bench, Jack sat gingerly on the edge, his rifle in his hand. "Keep still," he said softly, "but be ready to fire." The policemen sat down uneasily, opening the breeches of their weapons and sliding home a cartridge.

The howling mob closed within twenty yards of the seated men, scowling menacingly, then stopped in their tracks and drove their spears into the ground with a thunderous crash, creating a thicket of spears in front of the officers. They raced back to rejoin their leader, who was rapidly approaching with long strides. The chieftain stopped ten feet in front of Jack, who stood up to greet this powerful figure.

"Who the hell is this guy?" O'Rourke whispered. The giant made a fist and struck himself in the chest.

"Furaro!" he thundered in answer to O'Rourke's whisper. "Tara Furaro," he pointed to his men. Jack drew himself to attention and saluted smartly. He was pleased that the police had stood to attention behind him without receiving a command.

"Patrol officers Reed and O'Rourke at your service, Sir." He stepped forward and offered Furaro his hand. The chieftain studied Jack calmly for a moment, then confidently following Jack's gesture, slowly extended his powerful hand and intuitively grasped Jack's hand in his own.

The giant took Jack by the arm and pointed his spear toward the center of the park, and with his eyes, encouraged Jack to follow him. Jack and the chieftain strode side by side down a shaded lane, followed closely by the police and the carriers who were being jostled down the lane engulfed by a swarm of natives.

"If there is going to be a feast, I hope we're not it," O'Rourke murmured. The lane traversed a shaded parkland where flowing bushes had been planted with great care. They entered a clearing where row upon row of stone terraces had been built into a hillside. "Good lord, there must be ten thousand people here," O'Rourke exclaimed.

The chieftain and his personal bodyguard gave them no chance to examine the crowd as he marched them dramatically to the top of a wide series of steps that led to a large stone-covered platform at the base of the amphitheater. The crowd began singing, yodeling and waving madly as the chieftain walked to the head of the stairs. Without looking back, he led his personal entourage and the Papuan men up the staircase to a set of benches placed on a raised dais.

The entire patrol was standing on the dais in full view of the crowd. The honor guard moved to positions directly behind them. The patrol officers listened as Furaro spoke to his people, in a sing-song cadence, at first rapidly and then more slowly. He stopped speaking abruptly and gathered his breath, then began his trance-like singsong rhythm again while the onlookers sat in silence.

Finally he said something, pointed dramatically at the patrol, and the crowd broke out in a wild applause. The men pounded their spears on the ground, and the women yodeled in high-pitched falsetto voices. He made a gesture which Jack could not see, and the crowd howled with laughter. Then he turned, and with a smile, joined Jack and his men on the dais.

"A hell of an introduction," said O'Rourke in Jack's ear.

"Shut up," Jack said, and punched O'Rourke in the ribs.

To the west of the amphitheater a pillar of smoke rose from a hundred cooking pits. Soon, small but nubile girls with thatch sporrans and ringlets of orchids around their wrists and ankles carried in huge mounds of pork, spinach, asparagus, yams and bananas piled high on leaf platters. The food was spread in front of the patrol party.

"Tiset," Furaro commanded and motioned to the men to eat. Another wave of young girls brought them water sweetened with sugar cane in long bamboo tubes.

"This is tucker fit for a king," O'Rourke said.

"Or starving men," and Jack indicated the carriers who were noisily gulping down the meal. Jack studied the chieftain while they ate. Furaro's light-skinned oiled body gleamed in the sunlight. He had thin lips, an aquiline nose, arching eyebrows and wide-set brown eyes. He could be a Roman centurion, Jack thought. Who are these people? Where did they come from?

The chieftain finished his meal, and a young girl brought him a bamboo tube of water which he fastidiously used to rinse his hands and face. A man behind him offered him a straw whisk and he wiped his hands on it thoroughly. He stood up and clapped his hands together.

A hauntingly beautiful sound made from some type of flute or panpipe filled the air. The piper seemed to come from nowhere. He walked across the top of the amphitheater, very slowly, against a backdrop of bright sunlight and purple mountains, almost in silhouette, his glistening headband of green-beetle wings edged in sun-fire, playing his long slim flute. Native dancers flocked to the edge of the amphitheater and marched past the dais as if it were a parade-reviewing stand.

Nearly a hundred young small breasted women, their hips encased in grass sporrans and chanting an odd sounding harmony that began with an almost mooing note, paraded by bending their knees as they walked. They were followed closely by a group of prancing, black-painted men who were shaking their spears.

"The women are pretending to be cassowaries," Jack said, "and the men are the hunters."

"Those sheilas make the best looking cassowaries I've ever seen," O'Rourke quipped.

"You best keep your eye on the hunters, not the birds," Jack replied.

The king stood and shouted something that sounded like approval. A company of solemn-looking warriors with wig-like hair passed, marching and chanting in unison. They carried twelve-foot long spears, for thrusting not throwing. The fur of an animal was wrapped around the base of three ornamentally carved prongs. The men were strong-featured and broad-shouldered.

Colorful foot-long bird of paradise quills pierced their nostrils. A cadre of gray-haired men followed them, some with heavy paunches, who wore colorful woven mats made of orchid stems draped over their shoulders.

A legion of young men with ponderous leafed hats and bark cloaks, all armed with long bows and quivers of arrows, stopped in front of the dais. The king barked a command, "Setut." The men turned in unison and notched arrows in their bows. "Nevet," and the legion launched a cloud of arrows that landed far beyond the cooking pits. The leader pounded his spear on the ground, and the Greek-like archers marched out of the arena. Formation after formation filed by each distinctly armed and adorned, until finally the chieftain's bodyguard passed, each man hopping to a quick step comparable to the drills taught at the police academy.

"What a finale. Want to shoot your way through this mob?" Jack asked O'Rourke. The parade area had cleared when Jack tapped Manu on the shoulder. "Prepare the policemen for a parade drill."

"Yes, Kiap," and his face beamed. "Policemani, fall in," he shouted, and he magically produced his swagger stick. Jack felt a surge of pride as his tattered band of men "fell to" in front of the dais. Furaro looked on with great curiosity as the men stood to attention, fixed bayonets and presented arms. Jack returned their salute, and the men marched as if they had been drilling daily on a parade ground, not struggling for survival. They quick-marched, right turned, rear turned, left turned, passed rifles in precision to Sgt. Manu's commands. Finally they turned in front of the king and rendered the Queen Anne salute.

Furaro was obviously impressed with the maneuvers. He stepped off the dais and embraced Sgt. Manu lifting him off his feet. Setting him down he plainly asked to see Sgt. Manu's whistle, and putting it in his mouth, blew a shrill blast. Sgt. Manu ordered a parade rest, and the delighted chieftain blew it again, and the men snapped to attention. Then Furaro hugged Manu again.

"Somatu, bring me the trade kit," and Somatu picked up a swag bag and handed it to Jack. As Jack opened the kit, Furaro greeted a beautiful woman dressed in a furry couscous halter and short skirt of red bird of paradise plumes. A conical hat made of matching plumes sat elegantly on her head. A mischievous smile lit up her face and eyes. If not Furaro's mate, she was obviously a favorite, for he embraced her and invited her to sit beside him and examine the treasures Jack was spreading before them. A tall, lithe young man whose features matched Furaro's stood behind the woman.

"Maibu," said the chieftain, pointing at the youth and hitting his chest with his fist. "Nantu," he said, and raised the woman's arm higher for all the men to see.

"A family man, and obviously a very proud father," O'Rourke said aloud. "This man treats his family and his people regally. His mannerisms are those of a king and his family act as if they are royalty."

The queen made a sly little movement with her feet and danced between the officers and the king. She rolled her shoulders and turned her head back to the king with a laugh, managing at the same moment to give a quick wink at the two men. "God, she's a flirt," said the flustered O'Rourke. "She's a bloody flirt."

"Take no notice, O'Rourke," warned Jack. "We don't want to mess around with his majesty's harem." Jack spread out the trade articles and stared at them thoughtfully. First he selected a steel, keen-bladed tomahawk, tested the blade with his thumb to show its sharpness, and handed it to the chieftain, who took it nonchalantly and hefted it in his hand. He called to one of his retinue, and the man disappeared and returned with a large stick of wood. He handed it to the king, who stood it on end, and with an amazing show of agility and strength, raised the tomahawk and split the wood down the middle.

The king then sat down and whistled. O'Rourke sent Jack an amused look. "I've never heard a Papuan whistle like a white man."

"Wonders never cease," Jack said. He took the tomahawk from the chief and handed it to Sgt. Agoti. Jack pointed to one of the honor guard's shields. The king nodded, and the man handed

Jack the shield. Agoti and Jack moved twenty paces or so apart. Agoti's back was turned and he hefted the tomahawk by the handle.

"Now!" Jack commanded. Agoti whirled, and the tomahawk whished through the air, embedding its head deeply into the shield. The king didn't stir but his queen gave a surprised squeal. Jack wrenched the blade from the shield and returned it to the king who regarded the instrument with respect. He could see Furaro analyzing the instrument: a new weapon; a superior weapon.

Sgt. Manu broke out the steel axes, and in minutes two carriers split a thick log in half, chips flying everywhere. Jack had his men lay the axes at the king's feet. He then picked up some steel knives and gave them to the guards for their inspection. He touched the point of one to his fingers and easily drew blood. The men handled the blades carefully, testing the points against their palms and whistling to themselves.

Jack selected a long hunter's knife and demonstrated how the blade could be fitted in and out of the handle. He cut a string bag in half and using the serrated edge, he sawed a small branch in half. Seeing interest in the young man's eyes, he handed it to the king's son, who looked to his father for approval. Furaro nodded, and the young man grabbed the knife from Jack's hand. He opened it quickly and cut the string bag to shreds. Smiling broadly, he closed the blade and shoved it into his girdle.

When Jack handed the queen a looking glass, she pulled back astounded by her reflection. She showed it to the king, who was more composed, but nonetheless examined the back of the mirror to see how this magic was done. The queen walked down the row of guards and showed them their made-up faces.

"They think the mirror is some kind of magic," O'Rourke observed.

"For them it is. They are seeing the creative power of their own imagination for the first time. I wish I had such a mirror," Jack said quietly. He picked up a framed photograph of King George and pointed to the king's bodyguard and to the people sitting in the amphitheater. “Furaro,” he said and clapped his chest with his fist. Then Jack pointed his finger at the carriers and police, and then to himself, and thumped his chest and said, “King George,” and pointed to the picture and handed it to the chieftain.

Furaro studied the picture carefully. He seemed to be uncertain as to how the picture was created. Jack pulled a pad out of his pack and the royal pair looked on curiously as he sketched a butterfly, and then drew a sketch of the royal lady, very quickly and accurately. Then he went over to one of the guards whose face was painted red and yellow. He rubbed off some of the red ochre and daubed it on the drawing, and he put yellow ochre on the butterfly. A touch of black from the corner of the man's eyes added outlines to the headdress. He put some dots and lines on the butterfly.

The king was a quick study artist. Surprisingly, he pointed simultaneously to the drawing and to the painting. “King George,” he said, and saluted the painting.

“This is one bright boy,” O'Rourke said impressed.

“They're all bright boys. Look at them. They all get it.”

Next Jack produced a gold medal of King George attached to a pale blue ribbon. He showed the bas relief to the king and pointed to the portrait. The king studied the two and nodded his understanding. Jack draped the medallion over the man's heavy head and shoulders and stepped back and saluted Furaro.

The king rose to his feet and stared hard at Jack. He touched Jack's shoulder, touched his teeth, and smiled. The bodyguards formed a phalanx around him and his family. They marched off through the park as the people filed out of the arena, leaving the men alone for the first time in several days.

“Whew,” said O'Rourke. “You pulled it off, Jack. The old boy's impressed.” In a few minutes the young bowmen who had paraded earlier joined them. These new guides led them to a cluster of huts that had obviously been prepared for them. The floors were made of bamboo and sprung lightly under their feet as they entered the room. There were piles of sleeping mats in the corners. Netted bags full of steamed yams hung from the doorposts, and bamboo tubes of cane water were stacked in the middle of the floor.

One of their guides pillowed his head on his hands, a sign that they were to sleep here. The carriers and policemen covered themselves with their ragged blankets and prepared to sleep. Jack instructed Agoti and two alternates to stand watches during the night and stepped outside to join Sgt. Manu and O'Rourke who were standing by a small fire ring. It was a bright, moonlit night. All around the camp they could hear bamboo panpipes. The flute-like sounds rising and falling in rhythm were accompanied by resonant thumps on the garumut and the beat of kundu drums. He had never heard anything like it. “It's damn well...almost symphonic,” O'Rourke ventured. They listened for a while until Jack called to one of their guides and signaled by pillowing his hands that they needed to sleep now. Even a concert of panpipes can go on too long. He doubled the guard for the night -- the mood could easily change from peaceful harmony to savage attack. Jack fell asleep staring out at the points of light bobbing in the darkness as the pipers wended their way homeward.

Shortly after sunrise, three maidens brought the party pandanus nuts for their breakfast. The girls giggled as they squatted on the floor of the hut and chopped the meat into edible portions, giving Jack and O'Rourke an opportunity to scrutinize them. They were quite comely, with an almost Asiatic-Polynesian cast to their features. Each girl's makeup was unique. They had painted colorful, almost costume-like masks around their eyes and noses. One girl had a red mask, punctuated on the borders with white dots. Her lips were painted with the same bright red shiny ochre.

The second girl had big eyes that were highlighted by a bright blue mask that extended downward and covered her nose. Her lips were painted jet black which contrasted beautifully with her brilliantly white teeth when she smiled.

The last girl's mask had created a smile of white ochre that accented her almond-shaped eyes. She was the oldest of the trio and she sat cross-legged in front of O'Rourke and handed him pandanus nutmeats while the other girls served the police and carriers.

"It looks like you've made a friend for life," quipped Jack.

"She's a comely wench," O'Rourke replied. "Back home men would take notice of these sheilas, to say nothing of the king's wife."

"That one's a real beauty and dangerous too. Best we keep our distance here."

"No worries, Jack. I want to get home in one piece."

"Have you noticed everyone's teeth up here?" Jack asked. "No betel nut stains. No jaw or mouth disease. No gaping holes. Even the old men have straight teeth. It seems they don't use sugar cane to the extent the lowlanders do. The food is better up here, more balanced." Jack opened his journal and surveyed the hall where they were sitting. All the belongings, wall coverings and roof supports were stained with elaborate designs. Numerous carvings on boards, some deeply embossed, others mere scratchings, revealed the faces of men, birds and animals, done in an impressionistic style. Bright colors, red, yellow, black and white, made from clays and charcoal brought them to life.

The art here, Jack mused, was perhaps the beginning of all art. It had as its birth man painting his face and his body, perhaps to look more ferocious to his enemies in war. The primitive warrior set out to look as unnatural and fearsome as possible, often using white ochre because it's the opposite of black skin.

The artist began by painting a portion of his body or face white. He painted white circles around his eyes, perhaps his nose. He then decorated his body and navel, paying particular attention to the navel, which is the central spot of the body. To heighten the effect of the white paint, he made his black skin more deeply black with more paint. But a monotone can be dull, and the artist looked for more colors. Reds and yellows were easily available from the earth's oxides and clays, so these were added as each man chose his particular decorations.

"Their body paint is gorgeous. Have you ever seen anything like it, O'Rourke?"

"The colors and designs are awesome, Jack. They are walking Picassos."

"Those coffins," Jack pointed to a pile of wooden boxes stacked neatly at the far end of the park, "are high art. Look at the woodcarvings and the storyboards. Two circles cut into a head represent a man's face. Add circles for breasts and you have the beginnings of a whole body. Show action or movement with a paddle, bow or spear, and you began to tell a story."

"I remember once in Rabaul," O'Rourke said, "when a sculptor showed me some figures with pigtails. I thought his ancestors had long hair, but he told me that in the past, the first white men who visited them came from tall ships and wore pigtails. That's what he was carving, the history of their contact with 18th century seamen."

"I wonder what figures they will carve for us. Pale-skinned ghosts with long red beards, I suppose,"

Sgt. Manu joined them. "What of today?" he asked.

"We'll wait here for the moment, Sergeant. If nothing develops in the next hour, we'll move on to the east... with our guides' permission. Have the men prepare to move out." While the men packed, O'Rourke and Jack stood in front of the thatched hut smoking. The Sergeant's question was answered when the constable on guard called and said, "Men are coming."

Three light-skinned young men accompanying Maibu, the chieftain's son, were approaching the hut on a track that led up from the valley. Maibu, very self-possessed, entered the compound and greeted the officers. He wore a cane belt, a pendant pigs-tooth necklace, possum-fur armlets, and a coronet of green phosphorescent green beetles shards. On his head he had a cluster of black cassowary plumes with a bright orange wing of bird of paradise feathers which projected from his headband and framed each cheek. He pushed his right foot into the ground, and pointing to the imprint, snapped his finger and thumb and waved his arm in the direction of the footprint. “Kado. Kado,” he said pointing to the party.

“I think he wants us to follow him.” O'Rourke grinned. Sgt. Manu ordered the men to assemble, and they marched out of the park single file, police in the point, middle and rear. Jack and O'Rourke, accompanied by Maibu, followed the three guides in the van. Maibu led them upward from the source of a creek and eastward across a tableland of grass and light forest. Late in the afternoon they reached an extensive cultivation.

A bamboo rest house was being constructed for them by a dozen men. They put down their bundles of pit-pit thatching and brought lengths of sugarcane and gave them to the carriers -- a gesture of peace and welcome. “Airu - Airu,” they chanted. An old man was standing there with a green bamboo tube six-feet long and three inches wide, with the internodes punched out. He came forward and presented it to Jack who nodded his thanks.

“Have a drink,” Jack said and passed the heavy tube, filled with water, to O'Rourke.

The old man appeared to be suffering from asthma. He asked Jack to cure him, and he handed Jack a leaf package of cooked spinach. Placing his finger to his ear, he nodded his head in a knowing manner and pointed to Jack and then to the sky, clearly showing he expected treatment. Jack gave him a little sugar with a few drops of kerosene. The man took it and jumped to his feet, smiling, signaling that he was cured already. The villagers prepared a meal of pig, spinach and yams for the men, and then returned to their village.

Toward nightfall Maibu came and sat with Jack and O'Rourke. He made a thin cigarette with his tobacco rolled in a dried leaf and inserted in the end of a bamboo pipe. As he smoked, he looked at the men with friendly, thoughtful eyes. He patted his abdomen and asked if they had eaten enough. He smiled when the officers nodded yes. Maibu stood up and pointed to a homestead and indicated he would spend the night and return when the sun was up, and lead them on to the Waga-Furari.

After he and the guides had gone, O'Rourke asked, "What do you suppose he thinks of us? What fairies and magic does he believe in?"

"I don't know, but it's a good thing these people are friendly," Jack responded. "If they chose to, they could destroy us in a moment's notice. One thing for certain, they believe in kindness, and it was our good luck that we met that old man up at the head of the valley."

Maibu returned in the morning and led them into a heavily populated valley. He was a favorite with every member of the party, not only because he had given the men pig and food, but also because, as Cpl. Dekadua said, "He was a good man who knew how to treat men."

Little boys as likable as they were numerous came to hold their fingers, or to crack gatora nuts between their teeth for them when they sat down to rest. When they saw Jack or O'Rourke looking at the wild flowers, they ran and picked them for the officers. "How free and happy they all seem," O'Rourke said.

"I know," Jack responded. "But why shouldn't they be? They have all the food and clothing they need, and obviously a leader who knows how to care for and protect his people. It makes you think of the 'poor Papuans' on the coast, or worse, the slum children of our own cities. They have nothing to compare with this country."

As they followed Maibu and the guides across the tableland, Jack spotted a track that led toward a pair of mountains. He turned up the track, indicating he wanted to explore it. But Maibu moved in front of him, stamped his foot in vexation, and indicated in an irritated tone that if the expedition turned that way, it would go alone.

The explorer in Jack was disappointed. They were not going to get a guided tour of the region. It was becoming clear that in spite of the friendliness of their guides, Maibu had been instructed to speed the patrol on its way. Maibu tugged Jack's arm and pointed to the east and indicated that he would lead them to a place where they would get plenty to eat. Jack stepped back on the track and signed he would follow the guides eastward.

Maibu led the caravan down into a beautiful glen with a half-dozen farms. The party was resting by a small stream that ran through one of the cultivations when an old man came along, calling, "Hamena. Hamena." A group of natives trailed close behind him.

Maibu turned to the man and said, "Nuni naipa," signing that the old man was related to him. Women walked freely among them. None of them seemed to fear the patrol officers or constables. The carriers helped the local men strip poles and gather grass to make an overnight shelter. Maibu joined the officers and the old man and they sat down by the stream to rest and smoke their tobacco. Although friendly, Maibu would never use their matches to light his pipe. He preferred his own fire, and he certainly didn't take long to produce it. A thin hard stick, split at the end with an opening held apart by a small stone, would come out of his bilum. He would hold the stick with his feet, and taking a length of stripped bamboo, and using it like a rope around a drill, would cause the shavings, in the opening of the cleft of the stick to catch fire. The whole process took only a matter of seconds to accomplish. Maibu lit his pipe, pointed to his little red ash and then to Jack's box of matches. "Hado," he chirped, as if saying, "This is my match. Those are yours."

That evening they feasted on pigs and yams and spinach while Maibu's people looked on with remarkably restrained curiosity.

Maibu came to them at daybreak the next morning and placed some pandanus nuts on the ground. Somatu cut them into chunks and laid them in the open fire along with finger-sized green plantans. The roasted nuts had a flavorful, if somewhat woody taste, which was easily made more palatable by chewing a wad of sugarcane.

"Aiju. Aiju," Maibu said when they had finished their meal. He explained that the Wagi Furari was a long way off and that the patrol would have new guides. He waved goodbye and disappeared into the mists.

"I will never forget that beautiful young man," Jack said.

"And I will never forget his beautiful young sisters," O'Rourke responded.

The next morning they climbed from the glen to the tableland ahead. Groves of pandanus trees had been planted in parks to provide a food source. Here they were introduced to another chief, and some of his people, all of whom kept chanting the friendly greeting of "Hamena" as they moved among the patrolmen. These were of a different type than the men of the upper valley. They were darker skinned with thicker lips and kinky hair. Hundreds of people followed them and all were very friendly.

In fact, they were getting fearlessly friendly. O'Rourke was especially wondrous to them because he had red hair. They wanted strands of the patrol officer's hair, holding out their hands and pointing to his head and yelling, "Mda, Mda."

O'Rourke cut off a lock of hair and gave it to one man, who delightedly and carefully wrapped it in a leaf. Wanting more, the rest surged forward, clamoring. O'Rourke gave ground, tripped and went down under a struggling mass of people, snatching and pulling at his hair until the constables came in and broke up the scrum.

"Who gave you the haircut?" Jack asked when he came up on the mob.

"I did. I cut half of it off and gave it to them. Then they wanted the rest. A man can't get any peace," he said as he climbed onto the track.

They traveled eastward all that day. They met men and boys at every point in the track, and passed through large cultivated areas and parklands but the soil here was poorer and the inhabitants of this region were dirtier and more unkempt than the light-skinned people they had left behind.

The party came to a wide river spanned by a major bridge of a type they had not seen before in Papua. It was held in position between two timbered pylons erected on either bank. Enormous rock piles supported the pylons that had been hand-hewed from pandanus trees. Two warriors on the opposite side of the river manned a tall lookout tower that looked like it had been made by storks. Dry poles, topped with blackened skulls, stood on either side of the bridge.

"Wagi, wagi," said their guides, and clicked their teeth ominously." Looks like good times are here again," snapped O'Rourke. A tall yellow-faced member of Furaro's imperial guard, flanked by a dozen of the black-painted bowmen was waiting for them in front of the bridge. He stepped solemnly forward, and opening a box made of dried leaves, offered Jack a miniature likeness of the king carved on a black hard nut. Attached to it was a lock of light colored hair.

Jack unpinned his metal patrol officer's badge and handed it to the bearer. "For Furaro," he said pointing westward.

The guardsman took the badge, shouted "Furaro," and thumped his chest. The king's emissary and his bowmen turned and marched back toward the Tarifuraro Valley. Their guides called to the men in the towers and they waved the party forward.

"The coast is clear, I guess," O'Rourke said. The men marched side by side across the remarkable bridge that spanned a foaming stream.

"It must be the Kikari," Jack said.

"No doubt. The Purari can't be too far to the east," O'Rourke responded.

"You hope," said Jack, and O'Rourke clenched his teeth on his pipe grimly. They climbed up a slope to the east and examined the country ahead . Below the timberline was a vast sea of grass and a small track led through the grass.

"Wagu, wagu," the guides cried, and they could see that "wagu, wagu" meant grassland. The guides shouted "Hamena," the friendly greeting, and turned and left the party standing alone on the track.

"Maibu and Furari," shouted the police and carriers, and the guides turned and waved once more.

They had left the people of the Happy Valley far behind them, below and many miles to the west. This new section they were crossing was a black and cold country, with mists continually rolling down from a new mountain to the northeast and across the tableland. There was rain by late afternoon -- not a brisk, purifying downpour, but a dark tedious drizzle which funneled down their collars, turning even the light-hearted Cpl. Isi into a bad-humored churl who cursed anyone who stumbled across his path.

The health and morale of the party, in spite of the brief respite in the Happy Valley was far from good. The howling, sleeve tugging, arm grabbing and jostling encounters with the friendly but overly curious Furaro people had at times become oppressive. Though they didn't know their language, they could intuit that the Furaro's were saying, "Look, he raises his hand. He sits down. He eats. See what he did then?" The policemen had shown great restraint and patience lending a willing eye and ear to what everyone wished to show and to tell them. However, this also contributed to their overall fatigue.

Many of the carriers and policemen had developed seeping sores and abscesses. In addition, most of the men, including Jack and O'Rourke, were showing signs of fever and dysentery. The patrol was making erratic progress down a small gully between two hills that gave them some protection from the bone-chilling wind and mists when Jack called a halt. "Enough. We need to rest. Sgt. Manu, we will camp here." The weary men tossed their string bags of potatoes and spinach down and sank wearily to the ground.

"Come, you lazy men. We need wood," Sgt. Manu prodded a few men to their feet and they followed him reluctantly up to a clump of trees at the base of the hill. It was colder here at night than it had been in the lower valleys, and the men moved their rag-covered bodies closer to the fires. Wind-blown sparks flew skyward and reflected onto undulating clouds crossing low overhead. Now and then a coracle cirque of a moon peeked out, projecting a streak of moonlight onto the hills, creating an eerie world of sliding shadows and fluctuating shapes.

Wrapping himself more tightly in the remnant of a mat he'd carried with him for the past few days, Jack shivered from the cold. Up here in the valleys, Jack thought, even the trees, grass and rocks seem to be alive, speaking their own thoughts dimly. It is unfortunate that we humans can't hear their voices clearly. We have lost our connection with the life force. We're like flies that have found themselves suddenly unstuck from flypaper. For a brief moment we're free. Then we forget how our own voracious self-importance trapped us in the first place, and we get stuck again. We must somehow turn away from the trivia of our lives and recognize the "otherness" of the universe. We can't reason our way out; life is too complex for that. We must trust our instincts.

A commotion at the policemen's campfire pulled Jack out of his reverie. Somatu was chasing Cpl. Isi around the fire ring, waving a fiery grass broom.

"I am God. I'm going to destroy the world," Somatu shouted with demonic glee. Sgt. Manu tripped Somatu as he ran by. Somatu plunged to the ground amidst a shower of sparks and sprang quickly to his knees, shouting "I am on fire. I am on fire. I am the God of fire," and he howled at the moon. Sgt. Manu rapped him on the head with a stick, causing Somatu to howl again.

"What the hell?" O'Rourke yelped.

"Let Manu handle this," Jack cautioned O'Rourke.

"Be silent, stupid man. Be careful what you speak. You do not know who you are," Sgt. Manu scolded. Somatu crawled slowly back to the fire and rejoined the laughing men sitting in a circle.

"Be still and I will tell about God and the Great Mother." Sgt. Manu stood up and walked to one side of the fire where the men had grown silent. He pointed to the moon and the sky above him.

"A long time ago, the Great God made all you can see. He made the sun, the earth, the sky. But there was nothing else here. Then the Great Mother left her home in the moon and came to this place. From her womb came the people, and she brought air and water and made all living tings. This land is wonderful. Life easy for the people. There was plenty to eat, and they are very happy."

"Then one day God came back and he jealous over what the Great Mother made, and he pushed the first people out of this land. He put the poisonous and evil things everywhere, like the tai pai. He caused women to know pain when they have babies, and men had to work hard to fill their bellies with sago.

"One day a strong man, a coconut man, I think," and Sgt. Manu looked across the fire at Somatu, "became angry, and he led the people into a battle with God, and they kicked him out of this place forever. The Great Mother felt sorrow for what happened and she began to cry. Her tears came and came until the waters rolled all around the land and made us safe from God. He cannot walk on the water. He can make earth quiver. He can send evil tings in the wind. He can make fires crack open the earth.

"But that is all he can do. The Great Mother can put us to sleep and she can wake us up. She can warn us of danger from evil tings and that is all she can do. All the rest we must do!"

The men sat quietly staring into the fire. No man looked at his neighbor. Even the loquacious Isi was silent. O'Rourke fumbled for a moment in his jacket and produced a pack of navy-cut cigarettes. "Been saving them for a rainy day," he smiled self-consciously. "Time to join the boys for a smoke."

The men moved aside and made a place within the circle for the Kiaps. The men smiled appreciatively as the packet was passed from man to man. No one spoke. Each man was content to smoke his cigarette and to think his own thoughts.

Jack felt an absurd sense of joy that these almost savage, scarcely literate policemen had carefully preserved their narrative of the origin of men. Are they really illiterate? What does that mean, Jack wondered. Sgt. Manu is wiser than I'll ever be. How arrogant of me to consider any tribal people primitive or illiterate. The men had reminded him once again that the consciousness of men is free, a thousand times more than what's normally realized. And it thrilled him. No doubt it was the Neolithic hunters, men like these Papuans, sitting around a campfire, who had first discovered that reciting a legend could induce the feeling of freedom and unity of mankind.

One by one the men snuffed out their cigarettes, each preserving a stub of tobacco in his tin for another day. O'Rourke returned to the campfire while Jack and Sgt. Manu posted the watches.

On their way back, Sgt. Manu said softly to Jack, “You are different than most white men. I told the men you care for us and that I saw you speak with de Great Mother. They know she will show you the way back. Good night, Kiap.” Sgt. Manu walked off into the darkness to his post above the fire circles.

“What was that all about?” O'Rourke asked as Jack walked back into their campsite.

“Sgt. Manu is convinced the Great Mother will show me the way home.”

“Ask her to locate an air strip for us while you're at it. I'd rather not walk out myself,” and O'Rourke turned over and promptly fell asleep.

An airstrip? Out here? That would bring an end to this world almost immediately, Jack thought. Civilization delivered to their doorsteps. A winged, conquering God triumphs again. Jack dragged his shivering body closer to O'Rourke for warmth. Finding little there, he rolled over and said, “I'll make a plan tomorrow,” and fell asleep facing the stars that were beginning to crowd the now cloudless sky.

After enduring an intensely cold night, they broke camp at sunrise. A narrow track led through dew-drenched climbing bamboos and moss-covered trees. About a mile east of the campsite they emerged onto grass and tree fern country with the track leading them up through a narrow gap at about 11,000 feet to the base of the yet-unnamed mountain. The long thin line of carriers and policemen was stretched widely apart and the van was nearly a half-mile from the men in the rear of the column. They walked through fields of daisies, buttercups and Christmas bells flowering in the short grasses on the slopes.

Gazing back to the southwest, it seemed as if they were walking across the top of New Guinea. An enormous area of country spread out behind them. Mount Jubilee stood prominently in the west. The great Tarifuraro valley was hidden below the tablelands they had just crossed, while far up in the northwest, they caught a glimpse of the top peaks of the mountains beyond the limestone barrier.

The banks in a dry streambed provided some protection from the cold wind. Jack's lips felt numb, and as he touched them, he discovered a leech. He tore it off and flung it to the ground. "Ugh," he cried, and tore another off the tip of his tongue. He glanced down and saw blood oozing out of the top of his boots. He frantically ripped them off; his boots were filled with blood. "Don't rip them off," he called to the carriers, who in their frenzy were tearing at the more visible bloodsuckers that had clamped on their bodies with vice-like grips.

Lighting his last cheroot, Jack applied the tip to loosen the grip of the stubborn creatures. The leeches lay on every blade of grass and every bush and tree, waiting for the unwary passerby. They entered through the eyelets of their boots, clung to their lips and eyelids, and found their way into the men's crotches and armpits.

"Leeches. Bloody leeches," cried O'Rourke as he scrambled down the riverbed and undid his trousers. He discovered a dozen leeches around his crotch; he borrowed Jack's cheroot and began pulling off the blood-gorged worms as rapidly as he dared. "The damned government ought to issue rubbers," he swore, as he plucked off another slimy offender.

"Let's get out of this country," O'Rourke cried. "I'd rather stumble up this streambed than go out in that damn grass again."

Rain clouds obscured their view for some distance ahead. They crossed the gap and dropped gently eastward, still trekking through grass and tree fern country. They chose to follow dry streambeds whenever they could. Driven by the intense cold, Jack had the men make for a patch of timber about two miles down the track, the only possible camping place if the party was to survive the night. The winds blew bitter cold, turning the rain into sleet that lashed their faces. The carriers strung out, stumbling forward across the half-frozen plateau.

"A rotten country for men from the lowlands to traverse," Jack said to Sgt. Manu in the lead.

"We must reach the river soon, Kiap. These boys cannot manage much of this evil country."

They entered the timber patch and were erecting lean-tos when O'Rourke staggered into the camp, dragging a spent carrier with him. Both men collapsed on the ground. "There are more carriers back there. Too weak to make it in," he uttered.

Constable Borege carried in another of the exhausted men on his shoulders, but the others were still behind. "Dey need help, Kiap," he pleaded.

Jack was hard pressed to persuade the Orokos to go back with Cpl. Dekadua and bring the unfortunate men into camp. "Carry them in," he said to Dekadua. "Don't waste time trying to walk them back."

The remaining men began to gather wood and build fires. Cpl. Dekadua and the policemen returned with two nearly dead men. "De Orokos ran away," Dekadua cried. "Dere are two more men out dere. We could not carry dem."

The Oroko carriers, one by one, snuck back into camp and huddled by the fire, warming their frozen bodies. Each seemed to think he was the sole survivor.

"You men," Jack ordered the Orokos, "go with the Sergeant and bring in the stragglers."

But they shook their heads sullenly, refusing to go. They could see nothing but death out on the cold grassland, and they were spent men themselves.

"God help you, old sport," O'Rourke said, and pointed to Jack's badly wrenched knee. Jack began putting on his boots and puttees.

A black heavy sleet was falling and the cold was intense, even in the shelter. Dekadua was finished. Another ten minutes out on the frozen grassland and they would have had to carry him in, too. Dekadua told him that Hakea was still alive. They had brought him a good distance, but had left him covered with a mat.

Jack went back along the track, accompanied by Sgt. Manu and Somatu, who volunteered. About a half-mile from the timber they found Hakea, half frozen, but still alive. "Take him back, Sergeant. We will go after the others," Jack shouted as he helped Somatu load the carrier onto a makeshift litter they had brought with them. They continued down the track and met Agoti packing a man across his shoulders.

"Lolopa is back there," Agoti shouted. He staggered forward, back doubled over in the howling wind. A few minutes later, they found Lolopa. Jack tried to force some rum down the man's mouth. But he spat it out and bit the top of the bottle. When Jack and Somatu started to carry him, he struggled against them.

"He is mad, Kiap," said Somatu. "Leave him and go back to the fire. He is already dead, and you will die, too." Jack said nothing, but pulled the carrier to his feet.

The two men carried and half-dragged the Lolopa over the cold and wind-swept pass. Two more policemen showed up to assist them and they moved quickly into the shelter with its blazing fire. But Lolopa died a few minutes after they brought him to safety.

Jack sat in a lean-to in front of a fire while Somatu warmed his shirt. "You did your best," O'Rourke spoke softly. "The cold killed him."

"It was a race against time, and I lost."

"You did your best, mate."

"How many more men are going to die before we get them home?"

O'Rourke said nothing and both men sat and stared stonily into the fire. Are life and death real enough for you now? Jack asked himself.

The morning broke clear and fine. It was freezing cold at that altitude. Hakea and Ange, the men constable Agoti carried into camp had died during the night.

Jack wrote an entry in his journal:

The police buried the three men on the side of the camp, and it was pathetic to see Hakea's bilum holding his belt, earrings and the little somethings that belonged only yesterday to a man full of life, stuffed into the grave. We have passed through the back door of the Purari. It is the 25th of April, Anzac Day, and I feel certain we will find our way back to the coast.

They concealed the spot with leaves. With only a handful of rice to sustain each of them, they climbed the side of a huge timbered spur and followed a gentle slope that led eastward. Through a break in the forest above the camp, the mountain presented a grand spectacle with its rocky summit and its crevices glistening ice-like in the morning sun.

They followed a new track from the south that wound downward passing through a stretch of lichen and moss forest. At about the 6,000-foot level, they came to a grass-covered spur, which overlooked a large valley. They could see a river wending its way to the southeast, draining a vast area of grassland, streams and cultivations. They could see countless spirals of smoke and knew they had found an even greater population than the Tarifuraro.

Jack glanced at O'Rourke, who was stuffing his pack with some rocks and pebbles. "What have you got?"

"Gold nuggets." O'Rourke handed Jack two large oval-shaped rocks. The carriers were also busily filling their swags.

"We'd better save room for the rice," he warned.

"What rice? We finished all but the last this morning," O'Rourke said. "There's less than a handful left for every man," as he pushed more golden pebbles into his pockets.

As the patrol came down the slopes unnoticed and approached a half-hidden dagu in the forest, they surprised a male native coming out of the dwelling. He looked frightened, but seemed to understand the greeting of "Hamena", for he did not attempt to run away. Although he tried to appear friendly, it was clear that he wanted the party to leave. Sgt. Manu signed that they wanted food. The man went back into the dagu and returned with a few handfuls of potatoes. He then gestured that they follow the track that led down the slopes to the river.

The patrol was barely out of sight when they heard the man yodel loudly. The yodeling was taken up from all the little homesteads around them, and soon scores of men began appearing. "Keep your eyes peeled, but take no notice of them," Jack instructed the constables. They marched onto the wide river flats of the valley system. "It must be what they call the 'wega'," Jack said. "It could lead to the Purari."

"It's the only way out of here," O'Rourke commented. "We'll be right if we can get past these blokes," and he indicated the increasing number of men who were beginning to surround them. The minutes grew tense as they watched the natives slowly closing in on the party. At the rear, a hundred or more truculent men were menacing Sgt. Manu and his police, but none of the policemen flinched at the sight of the drawn bows.

"You are watching, Sgt. Manu?" Jack asked.

"My eyes are there, Kiap."

"There's at least a thousand men around us," O'Rourke said, motioning to the horde lining both sides of the road.

"Have no fear," Jack replied. "As Cpl. Isi says, 'We are ten.'" They pushed on southward, and soon more people were standing by the track -- old men, women and children. "Wave your hat," Jack instructed O'Rourke, and for the next few miles they waved their hats continuously.

When they came to a park near a village they were met by a particularly evil-looking chief. A swarthy-looking character with a black wig and dried grass stuffed in his nostrils. Sgt. Manu rubbed his stomach and put a pained scowl on his face hoping that the appeal for food would end in a trade of axes for potatoes. "It no use, Kiap. They will give us nothing."

The old chieftain spoke to Jack and indicated that he wanted to see inside the medical box, his forced friendliness barely concealing his unfriendly intentions. Jack motioned with his hand

and told the man firmly to go away. Turning his back on the man, he pointed to the gardens of food and appealed to the other natives for "kai".

A young native came forward with a small bag of potatoes. The self-assured, smirking smile on the young man's face angered the policemen. He took several half-rotten potatoes out of his bilum, and placing them on the ground, demanded an axe.

"This man not come to trade, but to mock us. Ths food is for pigs," Somatu said. The man looked up at Jack insolently.

"Stand by the Kiap," Sergeant Manu barked.

All the people of this new region were watching intently as Jack took a good string of beads from his sling bag and carefully handed them to the man. He took them, but also smilingly took back half of the foul potatoes. Jack signed that the man must put back all of the potatoes, and when he did not, Jack knocked them out of his hand. The young man threw the beads in Jack's face, and turning his back, walked over to where his fellow men were sitting down. He calmly sat down with them, while at the same time making a gesture which obviously meant, "That's the way to treat these people."

"Constable Agoti, kick this man out of the park and onto the track," Jack commanded. Agoti did it well. As the policemen covered him with their rifles, he approached the native.

"Whose child are you?" he asked insolently in Motu. When the man did not answer him, Agoti pulled him up by the hair and kicked him out of the park. Cpl. Dekadua grabbed the chieftain and dragged him to the edge of the park.

"Wait until dere is a government station here," Dekadua muttered. "I will not forget your face. I have strong eyes."

The sullen expressions on the warriors' faces did not change. Then they all stood up and silently left the park. Soon the yodeling began.

"We aren't going to get anything from these people," O'Rourke replied as he calmly lit his pipe. "We have one day's emergency rations left, the biscuits. I don't want to use them until we absolutely have to."

"It's too late to go around them, Tim. If we show any sign of weakness, I have a feeling we will be attacked instantly."

"Then to hell with these bastards! I say let's fight if we're forced into it," O'Rourke advised.

"Perhaps we're about to have our problem solved for us," Jack said, and he pointed to a trio of natives crossing into the park.

Three men, carrying unstrung bows and bundles of arrows, came in and signed that they were willing to lead the patrol down the track. Sgt. Manu asked them for food, rubbing his belly and pointing to his mouth. No food here, they signed, but they would provide some further along the track.

"Nothing doing but to follow them, as long as they're headed our way," O'Rourke piped. "If we don't get food soon, the men will be too weak to walk.

Jack casually pointed to a bridge beyond two pinnacles to the east. "Maybe there's a different breed of people on the other side of the park."

"Maybe or maybe not." O'Rourke shrugged his shoulders and ordered the police to load their rifles. Sgt. Manu bunched the carriers closely together, and with the police in close-line march, started forward.

Jack knew that with empty stomachs their ragtag band of outcasts faced a long day ahead. They crossed a grass basin covered with snow-white balsam and heliotrope and followed the guides to some small limestone pinnacles. Through a gap they could see another smaller valley system, a tableland of hollows and mounds all covered with grass and cultivations. The three natives pointed to it and called the country the "wen".

A large number of men now appeared at their rear. Some of them trailed their bows behind them. When the police looked back, they would drop their weapons and stand with their arms folded across their chests. Others carried their weapons concealed in bundles of green pandanas leaves. They heard yodels in front of them that were answered by a chorus of yodelers on their flanks. "Sounds like a pack of dingos," O'Rourke said. But apart from watching the men carefully, the patrol made no sign of alarm.

Climbing to the top of the gap, where one track led up the side of the saddle, and the other down into the southeast, they encountered twenty men waiting in the path. Their friendliness was overdone, but Jack did what he could to show them he neither feared them nor desired to harm them. He knew what they were up to, and he made a slash across his throat and pointed to the rifles, indicating that his weapons were not to be despised. But their smirking, self-possessed faces showed that they were not convinced. "There are no women here, Kiap," Sgt. Manu warned.

A man wearing a crown of black cassowary feathers appeared on the saddle about twenty yards above them, riding on the shoulders of another man. He made an impatient gesture and disappeared down a sidetrack. Their guides nervously urged them to be on their way. The yodeling on the sidetracks ceased, and then the guides fled down a nearby gully.

"It is here we find it, Kiap," Sgt. Manu stated. Jack turned to Sgt. Manu whose beard was black and fuzzy, his uniform torn and dirty from months of breaking trail. His arms and legs were crisscrossed with lesions and sores, but the haggard, worn face of this grimy Papuan registered a gritty coolness.

"They won't take us cheaply, Sergeant." The patrol moved off in a close line, the carriers bunched in the middle, and O'Rourke, with five policemen, brought up the rear. Out in front, two men watched the right-hand side and two the left. They covered more than two hundred yards when they heard yodeling and war cries coming from men concealed in the Kunai grass. The ambushers had allowed Constable Nudnua, the point man, to go through the kunai, in order to surprise the main body of the party. A constable, who had been carrying his rifle with the bayonet fixed, charged into the grass where the warriors were hidden in strength. They hammered him with their stone clubs. Yet he went on bayoneting one warrior after another. His charge gave the police in front time to recover, and they opened fire.

Clusters of falling arrows splattered the ground in front of them. Then the whole line was attacked. Borege was the first man to take an arrow. Jack fired in front, and then to the rear, as men carrying short spears rushed to the line. The carriers showed their mettle, and yelled and screamed and threw their steel tomahawks at the attackers.

Constable Borege started swinging his rifle when the warriors closed in on him. He was pulled to the ground, and a man with a battle-axe was on top of him. Jack rushed to his aid, and pulling his pistol, shot the man in the head. He turned and fired at two assailants who were dragging Somatu away, wounding them both. Somatu rolled over and grabbed Borege's rifle, and fired on two men who were closing in on Jack from behind. Another group of men rushed from the front as Somatu yelled a warning.

Jack felt a blow in his solar plexus above his belt buckle as an arrow slid into his stomach, knocking the wind out of him. As he fell to his knees, a warrior jumped in front of him, fired an arrow at point-blank range into his thigh, and then pulled a war club from behind him. A muzzle blast deafened Jack as Somatu shoved his rifle into the warrior's chest and pulled the trigger. The din of battle was overwhelming. Rifle shots and the cries of wounded and dying men filled the air.

Agoti, Dekadua, and Sgt. Manu were firing rapidly at the rush of men in the front. Constable Amis charged three men who were rushing at Jack, bayoneting one man. He was hit with an arrow and clubbed to the ground. Jack staggered to his feet and emptied his pistol, killing two other men who had slipped inside their line. Arrows landed at his feet as he picked up his rifle and located O'Rourke, who was fighting a rear guard action. An arrow shaft protruded from his thigh.

"Don't let them get past you," Jack yelled to the constables in front.

All three answered, "We live. They no come."

Jack and O'Rourke reloaded just as another wave of attackers came over the crest. "Can you see the white's of their eyes?" O'Rourke yelled as he reloaded his rifle. Jack emptied his rifle point blank into three natives, knocking them down one by one. He rushed a fourth warrior who was trying to bludgeon a carrier and bashed in the man's skull with the butt of his rifle.

The struggle was over as quickly as it began. The thunder of the rifles had silenced the howling warriors. Jack pulled the arrow out of his thigh with a quick jerk. The other arrow felt like a raw nerve in a decayed tooth. He was seized by a violent and protracted fit of vomiting. When he had recovered, he moved slowly back up the track, one hand against his stomach. Dead and wounded men were scattered along the track.

"I am blind. I cannot see," Constable Emesi wailed. An arrow had pierced one eye, penetrated the bridge of his nose and exited out of the other eye. "Help me, Isi," he pleaded. "I see no more. I am no more for dis land."

Cpl. Dekadua had an arrow which had pierced one nipple and slid across his chest, piercing the other. Constable Agoti pulled the arrow through Dekadua's body, and plugged the holes with cotton wool and iodine from the medical chest. Somatu was attending to Constable Baku. An arrow had pierced his skull above his eye and fleshed out over his ear. He writhed in agony and screamed when the MO Tenoso daubed iodine on his scalp.

Blood was streaming down Sgt. Manu's cheek from a deep gash that had lacerated his scalp. "Forgive, Kiap," Sgt. Manu said as Agoti seized Jack by his arms and Sgt. Manu pulled the protruding arrow out of his stomach with a quick jerk. Jack fainted, and Agoti eased him to the ground. "It's a sharp arrow. No barb. The Kiap will live," Sgt. Manu grunted as he rubbed stinging nettles into the wounds. The nettles brought Jack to his senses, and he struggled to his feet.

Leaning against a boulder, O'Rourke watched the pair remove the arrow from Jack. Both policemen turned their attention to him. "No thank you, Constable," O'Rourke said. "I'll not be needing any treatment just now." And he slid backward against a rock.

"It is necessary, Kiap. I must remove de arrow quickly or you die a bad death." O'Rourke nodded, stuffed his pipe into his mouth and bit hard on the stem. Agoti broke the arrow in his strong hands, and Sgt. Manu removed one end as Agoti pulled on the barbed end. O'Rourke's pipe stem snapped, but he did not yell. "You be fine, Kiap, but you not move."

Sgt. Manu, Agoti and the MO Tenoso went from man to man, drawing arrows and treating the wounds. Every member of the patrol had been wounded, a few by arrows, but most were injured during the infighting. Several men had been clubbed with palm wood clubs or green stone adzes. Two of the carriers' arms hung limply at their sides. "They will not recover soon," MO Tenoso stated sadly.

Jack began to vomit heavily. The sky blackened around him. When he recovered, he leaned against a rock ledge for support. Somatu reported that the bad-talk men had carried Sevo and Eri off while they were fighting. O'Rourke squatted behind a rock on the brow of the hill. The tall Agoti lay sprawled beside him. Jack, Sgt. Manu and two constables moved behind another rock pile a few yards to their left. The rest of the patrol lay in a lone line concealed from the warriors below by clumps of Kunai grass. Atop the rocky pinnacle, Cpl. Isi and Cpl. Dekadua stood guard. Armed with Borege's rifle, Somatu crouched in a crevice to Jack's left while MO Tenoso was tending the two seriously wounded men.

"We can cover all three tracks from here, Jack," O'Rourke called. "We can hold out all day."

"Our problem now is water," Jack replied as he glanced at the sun high in the sky. "And food. We must have food soon, or we won't get out of here." A flight of arrows landed near the men, coming from their left. Agoti and Sgt. Manu fired in that direction, chasing off the skirmishers. "Why are these people attacking us? They are like bush hornets," Jack said, addressing no one in particular.

"Now, what have we here?" O'Rourke cried. A contingent of men raced down the side of a hill on their right. An odd looking hunk of meat was dangling on a long pole suspended between two of the natives' shoulders.

"It is the carrier Sevo. That is his belt, Kiap." Sgt. Manu rose up and shouted his rage. The natives stopped and slapped their bared bottoms in the age-old gesture that was their version of the *raspberry*. The enraged police jumped to their feet and began howling their own epitaphs across the vale.

"Your skin stinks."

"You steal pigs."

"You drink blood from a vagina."

The natives fired a round of arrows, but they fell far short of the patrol's position. The police, without waiting for orders, began firing randomly at the natives. Three men fell instantly and the others ran back into the cover of the tall grass.

"Cease firing," Jack shouted, and slowly the men returned to their positions.

"There's that weird devil," O'Rourke said, pointing to the black-bearded man riding on the shoulders of a strongly built native. He was gabbling excitedly and madly gesturing at the patrol.

"Sweet mother, O'Rourke, would you believe that?" Jack asked. Over the crest in front of them marched hundreds of men, big black men, faces painted with red and yellow ochre, with pom-poms of cassowary feathers on the tops of their heads. They were carrying shields, painted with a white human design, and were marching toward them. Each man carried a bone-tipped spear, shaking it in his right hand, and their black plumes swayed menacingly as they moved forward. Jack swallowed the saliva forming in his mouth.

"There must be hundreds of the bastards," O'Rourke stammered. Behind them another mob of wigged men appeared, all armed with bows, and they spread out, taking firing positions behind the shield bearers. They fired with the wind, and they even had spotters out on the flank as they lobbed clusters of arrows.

"We can't let them get close to us," Jack snarled. "Sgt. Manu, have your men lock and load." The bolts snapped home. "Cpl. Isi, are there men behind us?"

"No, Kiap."

"Somatu?" Jack asked.

"No, Kiap, there no men here."

"Constables, lower your sights to minimum range. Fire at their shields on my command. Do you understand?"

"Yes, Kiap," they answered. They watched as the black plumed warriors started up the spur of their hill. They could hear the guttural cadence as the men closed. In the vanguard a thin line of men began pounding on large garumut drums that swung between their legs as they advanced up the slope.

"Christ, I know how Custer must have felt," O'Rourke chirped, but Jack wasn't listening. The plumed warriors raised their shields. Jack could see their black painted eyes peering over the rims, then their fat lower lips, and he could hear them click their teeth aggressively. A deep throat-rattling cry "Wai--ye--ehaa," pierced the air.

"Pick your targets," Jack shouted.

"We are ten," screamed Cpl. Isi from the top of his battlement.

"Fire!" Jack commanded. A thunderous volley rang out over the valley. A row of men went down, their shields splintered and pierced with holes. "To your left ... fire!" And a second row pitched forward onto their faces. "To your right ... fire!" The blades of Kunai grass were turning red. "Pick your targets," Jack shouted again and sporadic firing ripped up and down the line. Some of the black-plumed men turn and ran down the hill. A few stood still in confusion. Another hundred or more determined men closed ranks and moved forward.

"To your right," Jack ordered, and the constables delivered round after round into the advancing warriors. The line wavered, and then broke for cover. A plumed headman, sitting astride another man shouted at the retreating warriors to no avail. He waved his spear at the bowmen and they started forward, but they would advance no further than the base of the hill, where they fell to the ground and tried to crawl forward under the cover of the Kunai grass.

Jack stood up and signaled the constables to advance down the hill. A deep, wild atavistic spirit stirred him. "Pick your targets," he shouted to the constables, knowing that the bowmen below would have to stand to fire their arrows. A few brave men got to their feet, but were cut down by the murderous fire before they could notch their arrows.

The bowmen, realizing they were about to be slaughtered, sprung to their feet and raced back down the slope their bark cloaks flowing behind them. The policemen kept up a constant fire into the retreating men's backs. Very few bowmen made it back to the top of the rise. The two-bodied man charged out onto the field, shouting angrily at the men still crouched in the grass.

"I've had enough of that fellow," Jack said.

"You take the high road and I'll take the low road," O'Rourke replied. Jack nodded, and both men calmly raised their rifles.

"One-two-three," Jack counted and their two rifles cracked as one. The two-bodied man fell forward. The warriors were silent, then began to wail, and moved off the field, leaving their dead behind.

"We are ten!" came from the top of the pinnacle. The men turned and looked up at the summit. Cpl. Isi was bent over, his skirt raised, as he *raspberried* the retreating phalanx of warriors. The kunai grass was littered with bodies.

The burial party placed their dead comrades in a deep crevice and filled it in with rocks. The three carriers, and the three constables Borege, Emisi and Enube, martyrs to the savage attack, were laid in the unmarked grave. The patrol was reduced to twenty survivors. Ten policemen, the two officers, six carriers, including Somatu, were still in fair condition. There were two badly wounded carriers, one with his arm in a sling and Constable Nudnua whose arm had been amputated by MO Tenoso was being transported in a litter.

"Head for the river," Jack ordered, fearing if they stayed on the ridge, they might not get moving again. Four policemen carried Jack on a litter on a nightmare ride through the dead and dying tribesmen abandoned on the hillside. O'Rourke limped alongside until they reached the river.

“Stop here,” Jack commanded, rising up from the litter. “I need a bath. Sergeant, have the carriers boil some water.” Somatu and two of the carriers set up the last remaining stove. Somatu gathered wood while the others hauled up canvas buckets of water from the stream.

“The Kiap is gone mad,” Somatu muttered loudly. “These bad-talk people will attack us while he washes his white hide.”

Opening his oilskin packet, Jack pulled out a bar of Life-Buoy soap. “You aren't the only one who saves things for a rainy day,” and he winked at O'Rourke.

“What else have you got hidden there?” O'Rourke asked. Jack smiled and pulled out a toothbrush and a tin of tooth powder.

“Me first.” Jack wheezed out a laugh as a look of chagrin crossed O'Rourke's face. They poured buckets of hot water over themselves and used the soap to scrub their dirty skins.

“What a sight we must make,” O'Rourke said and motioned to a number of men who were watching from the ridge beyond the streambed. Their bodies were multi-colored, red on the face and neck and forearms from exposure to the sun and the rest of their bodies, white. “Now that they have seen us naked, they know we are human beings, not gods. Even if we have two-toned hides,” O'Rourke laughed.

The two men went down to the river and slipped into the icy water. The warriors watched, fascinated as the officers swam a few yards across a deep pool, while a policeman stood guard with a loaded revolver. These mountain people had never seen a man swim before.

“Katie -- Keerist,” yelled O'Rourke, and they both withdrew from the icy water. MO Tenoso dressed their wounds with iodine and wooly cotton. Then he wrapped linen bandages around their wounds, being particularly careful as he wrapped a pressure pad around Jack's stomach.

“Does it hurt inside, Kiap?” he asked.

“Only when I walk, Tenoso.”

Somatu rummaged through the officers' packs and pulled out two neatly rolled packages of oilskins and unwrapped two crinkly shirts. "No sense saving them for a dinner party," Jack said, as the two men donned their shirts and snapped the pearly buttons shut. They stood guard while the policemen and carriers plunged into the river and scrubbed themselves clean using up the last of the soap bar.

While the men bathed, the officers kept a wary eye on a silent mob of 300 or so men who squatted on a nearby hillock and watched the bizarre scene. "We may have to fight again, Kiap," Sgt. Manu said, indicating the bunch of warriors above them. "We do not have much ammo left," he said, pointing to his nearly empty cartridge belt.

"We do not fight until we have eaten, Sergeant. Have the men break out their iron rations." A crowd of curious women joined the men on the hill as the patrol sat warming themselves in the late afternoon sun and devoured their rations. One by one the survivors went down to the river, drank water and filled their canteens.

"Sergeant, have the men put on their dress uniforms." The men pulled out small oilskin packets from their kits and prepared to don their uniforms.

Cpl. Isi pointed at the curious women on the hill. "You are without shame. Turn your heads," he yelled disgustedly in Motu.

"Be still, Isi," Sgt. Manu barked. "We have no need to be ashamed of our bodies." Each man put on his blue serge blouse and lap-lap and carefully wrapped a bright red sash around his waist.

When they were ready, Jack stood up and addressed the patrol. "Constables, you and the men of Oroko have fought bravely. I am proud of you. Each of you has fought as if you were ten," and he smiled at Cpl. Isi. "We must cross that bridge and find the Purari. It is time to go home. I will tell Judge Murray what you have done here." He turned to Sgt. Manu. "We will march away from here in close order. The men are to leave the trade goods, the stoves and buckets on the ground. We carry only the canteens, axes, guns and ammo, and our packs."

"Yes, sir, Kiap." Sgt. Manu saluted Jack and O'Rourke smartly. "You heard the Kiap," he told the men. "Fall into ranks and show these ignorant men what polismani are made of." Cpl. Isi attached the Australian Blue ensign to the top of a dry pole.

As they moved down the track, Jack watched the people on the hill rush down and ransack their cast-off belongings. He felt very weak, and his stomach wound ached as he led the men onto a flat in front of the rope bridge. A band of blue-legged warriors from the nearby hillocks raced past them and reached the bridge, crossing the track in front of them. More men carrying bows were waiting in front of the bridge.

"These are the same bastards that ambushed us up on the track. Look at their bloody blue legs," O'Rourke shrilled.

A formidable-looking man stepped forward and shouted, "Yeep," and tried to look friendly.

"Shoot him first, O'Rourke." And Jack stepped out to meet the man, his rifle at the ready.

"Yeep," shouted the man, and broke his bow across his knees. The leader turned and yelled "Yeep," and he cry was followed by a loud snapping and crackling as the warriors in front of them also broke their bows while the patrol stared in disbelief.

The warriors stepped off the track, and behind them a long row of food had been placed on the ground -- bananas, cane, spinach and yams. "Attention," said Jack. "Port arms." He heard the rifles crack in unison. "Fix bayonets." He waited until he heard the last bayonet click into place. "Ready arms." The rifles cracked again. "Quick march, on my command." Jack paused as the natives fell further back.

"Forward, to the bridge," he added and the phalanx filed through the warriors who dodged off the road. The patrol marched over a neatly piled row of food, trampling it contemptuously beneath their feet. Jack led the men single file across the bridge while O'Rourke, Sgt. Manu and Cpl. Dekadua stood rear guard. Once they were across, the patrol lined up on the opposite bank and protected the rear guard as they crossed the river.

"Cut the bridge," Jack ordered. Dekadua and Agoti fell to with axes and cut the main supports to the bridge. The whole structure toppled into the water and the patrolmen shouted triumphantly to the consternation of the abandoned warriors on the other side. An arrow whistled harmlessly across the river, but no more followed.

Late afternoon shadows crept across the hollow where Jack and O'Rourke sat on the grass by a fire. Momentarily Jack forgot the pain in his stomach. Somatu was scraping the ashes from a cooked potato for O'Rourke. Somatu handed O'Rourke two cooked and scraped potatoes, and held up a third and looked at O'Rourke.

"You eat the rest," O'Rourke said.

"Thank you Kiap," Somatu said and stuffed the half-roasted potato in his mouth.

God help them all, Jack thought. Nothing was too good for them. They had shown him just how big and how good their hearts were. They had given all their strength to protect the officers, and now it was his sacred duty to take care of every one of them.

They had made friends with an old man they had met this side of the river. He was not frightened in the least. Jack had given him an axe and told him about the fighting over on the other side of the "wen." He had placed his finger to his ear and indicated with a knowing nod that he had heard all about it. He had tugged O'Rourke's beard affectionately, and, stamping his foot on the ground, told them to camp on the spot -- that they were among friends. "I guess we made our point. We'll have no trouble tonight, Jack."

"Dammit, O'Rourke. We didn't come up here to make a point. I will always regret shooting those people."

"They ambushed us Jack. We never had a chance to work it out. If we'd followed Judge Murray's policy, we would be dead."

While the police built lean-to shelters, the old man had hurried away fast as his old legs could carry him. He returned later with a small number of friendly people who brought yams, spinach and tobacco, and laid them on the ground. None of these people carried weapons. What a difference it was. The relief of getting away from treacherous natives, and to be free from the howling and yodeling -- if only for a few hours -- was indescribable. The old man sat with them by the fire, and when he saw Jack looking at the country around them, he pointed to the southeastern walls of the basin and said, "Eloi."

Was he telling them about the Purari? Had he heard about Europeans before, and was he pointing to some place where he had seen them? According to O'Rourke's reckoning, they could not be far from the Erewa, the highest point on the Purari ever reached by white men from the Papuan coast.

The old man and his people left them to their sleep. The fires burned bright all around on the little grassy area, and carriers and police sat contentedly, eating roasted yams and parcels of broiled and slimy spinach.

"We can't cross the limestone again," Jack said. "None of us has the strength or the stamina. Besides, we can't carry enough food or water to make it through."

"Then it's down the Iehe chasm. There's nothing left but to do it," O'Rourke replied.

Jack groaned and drew his knees up to ease the pain in his stomach and thigh. "We don't know what the rapids will be like. There has to be a tremendous drop on the Purari between here and the coast."

"Better to die falling off a raft than to die of hunger and exhaustion on that blasted barrier," O'Rourke snorted. "For sure we would avoid the Kukukukus. If we run into them it'll be one face-off and ambush after another."

"Food is scarce here." Jack said. "We have no knowledge of the people or terrain in front of us. The Purari's headwaters must be somewhere beyond this damned range. It will take a mighty effort to reach it. After that we still have to make our way down to the coast."

Jack looked over the band of men. Their frames were little more than skeletons, bones protruding against the skin, and dull eyes sunken in their sockets. Death was written all over their faces, and he could picture them dragging their exhausted bodies over the limestone rocks, exerting themselves again and again, nostrils filled with mucus and no strength to clear it away. He hoped he would never have to see such tortured and pitiable human beings again. He knew they couldn't remain in this camp. They had already exhausted the spare food these generous people had given them.

"It's the chasm," he said, but O'Rourke didn't respond. He was fast asleep, his head resting on his knees. Jack pushed him gently over on his side and covered him with some pandanas leaves. Jack felt they were being watched from the forest, but he was too tired to care.

They were on the move at sunrise, descending to the floor of a large and waterless basin. There was neither creek nor stream in this region. All the rainwater ran off the slopes, where it percolated through the limestone down to some underground river.

The patrol relied on sugar cane to quench their thirst. They camped that afternoon on deserted grassland, near an old park of casuarinas trees. Contour drains, still in good condition, crisscrossed the whole of this unoccupied land, showing that it had once been under cultivation.

"Come, Kiap," Cpl. Dekadau said. "Many warriors fighting." He led Jack down the track to a saddle overlooking a narrow valley. Below them a small-scale battle was taking place. Two armies were firing volleys of arrows at each other from hillocks separated by a no-man's land, a small open basin between the two forces. As they watched groups of men detached themselves from the bowmen and armed with spears, clubs and shields, raced into the basin, howling and yodeling as they met each other head-on. They could hear the clash of shields. The patrol watched as the skirmishes waxed and waned while Cpl. Dekadua and Agoti scouted for a route that would bypass the massed warriors.

"No way around, Kiap," Cpl. Dekadua reported. "Limestone walls are everywhere."

"This is the only route to the Erewa, Jack," O'Rourke stated. "We have to take it. It can't be more than two days march from here."

"Then we are going through here. It's do or die," Jack decided. "Take the point, Sgt. Manu. Police to front, carriers behind. Cpl. Dekadua and Agoti, you bring up the rear. Detail, forward, march." The gallant but weary men marched down the track directly toward the open basin.

Crossing a small ravine, they strode down the other side in plain view of the massed men. The warriors on the left flank ceased fighting and stared at the patrol. Jack studied these big black Papuans with half-moon boar tusks though their noses. They were the fiercest looking savages he had yet seen. Numbers of them were not more than fifteen yards from the patrol, and they stood behind their grotesquely painted shields. On his right, packed closely together, were a light-skinned race of bowmen, similar to the people they had met beyond the limestone barrier. Their bows were an unusual length and arced peculiarly at the tips. Each warrior carried a large quiver of extremely long bamboo arrows with sharp tips. They could rain a cloud of death if they fired in volley, Jack thought. In front of them were several ranks of shorter men. They carried short palm wood spears and small round shields were strapped to their forearms.

Both of the war parties had grown silent and were watching them with unflinching eyes. It was a tense moment. A single wrong movement could bring death and destruction to the patrol. This basin could easily become a killing ground.

Suddenly Somatu raced to the front of the formation, blowing loudly on his harmonica. He stopped and came to full attention, and then slowly goose-stepped his way forward until he reached the edge of the war parties. He looked at both groups of warriors, and feigning fear, pulled his jacket up over his shoulders and covered his head. He gave a cry of alarm and raced back to the policemen's rank, and popping his head out of his jacket, blew his harmonica directly into a startled Sgt. Manu's face, who struck Somatu on the shoulders several times with his swagger stick.

"Stupid boy. Are you mad? Who gives you permission to leave the formation?" and he turned Somatu around and kicked him hard in the behind. Somatu promptly blew his harmonica again, raced to the rear of the formation and pulled his jacket back over his head. A ripple of laughter cascaded down the hillside. Warriors on both sides of the vale relaxed. Some put aside their weapons and squatted down on the steep incline and watched them curiously.

When Jack saw the tension easing, he held up his arm in a friendly gesture, and turned it from side to side to indicate that the patrol did not wish to be molested. He gave the command to march, and the men bunched close together and marched as fast as they could past rows of warriors who parted like the waters of the Red Sea. A few waved and jeered at the headless Somatu who, contrary to the others, was marching backwards. Some warriors adjusted their armbands and headpieces, nonchalantly acting as if nothing of significance was happening.

"Somatu is moth-crazy," Sgt. Manu muttered in Jack's ear.

"Thank you Sgt. Manu. I'll keep that in mind."

The patrol reached a stand of bamboo on the other side of the battleground. "Whew," cried Jack, wiping perspiration off his brow, as he stared at the warriors who had resumed fighting as if the patrol had never interrupted their feud. Black clouds of arrows were raining down on both sides, and a rush of spear throwers crossed the basin, driving the men with the round shields back up their hill.

"Somatu, step forward," Jack ordered.

"Yes, sir, Kiap," and he stood in front of Jack and saluted smartly.

"Somatu, if you ever pull a stunt like that again, I will have Judge Murray lock you in the stockade."

"Yes, Kiap..."

"And when you are released, I'll personally buy you a tub of soda at the Chinaman's house. Do you understand?"

"Yes, Kiap."

"Dismissed." Jack ignored the policemen's sniggers as Somatu rejoined the formation. A scowl from Sgt. Manu silenced the policemen, and Somatu did his best to look contrite.

O'Rourke turned to Jack. "The next time you're going to call a 'King's X', let me know. If I hadn't had diarrhea all morning, I would surely have messed my shorts. Why didn't you just volunteer Somatu to referee their damned scrap?"

"I didn't think of it. Next time I will," Jack laughed. "What do you say we get the hell out of here before one side or the other, or all of them, change their minds and decide to come after us?"

PART FOUR

THE PURARI TO PORT MORESBY

There was no chance for the weary men to rest as they moved on into the unknown country, wondering whether the next people they encountered would treat them kindly, or if they would face more bands of treacherous men and be forced again and again to fight. They climbed up a little grass basin, and then followed a well-worn track eastward through grassy areas strewn with rocky pinnacles that resembled pyramids in a yellow grass desert.

On the far side of this grassy basin they spotted cultivation, and then a village hidden under a grove of pandanas trees. Some women digging potatoes saw them and bolted. Sgt. Manu called and waved. But it was no use. They had been too frightened by the sudden appearance of ragged specters. The patrol followed them quietly and without haste to their village. The wide track led them to a high arch of wooden stakes. Under the archway a single man, covered with a shield and with his bow drawn watched them approach. He stood his ground until the patrol was within range of his bow, and then he lowered his weapon and fled. They marched through the arch and entered a large compound of some thirty or more dagus. A number of bowmen came out of the doorways. But when they saw that the patrol's intentions were friendly, they put down their weapons and came forward to greet them.

One man nervously caught Jack's hands, and pointing excitedly to the large river before them, said, “Erewa, Erewa.”

“It must be the Purari,” O'Rourke shouted.

“It has to be,” Jack said.

The villagers made the patrolmen sit down and passed out sugar cane. Their friendly smiles seemed to indicate that they understood what the weary travelers had endured. These new people were big, black Papuans, who wore bands of shells across their foreheads, and large headdresses of cassowary feathers. Many of them had boar tusks and cylindrically shaped pieces of quartz inserted through the nasal septum. Nearly every man carried an article of steel, mostly tomahawks. Jack asked to see a tomahawk, and one was passed over to him.

“Brodes,” said O'Rourke, hefting the axe. More of the men passed their axes forward for the Kiaps to examine, indicating they had come from the south.

Most of them were Brodes, but Jack noticed a few strong-looking axes. “Charleston Steel Works,” he said, handing one to O'Rourke. “American. But where in the hell did they come from?” Jack pointed to the Charleston axes questioningly. The natives pointed to the northeast and explained white men like themselves had given them them.

“Miners,” said O'Rourke. “Maybe the Tealey Brothers. At least they know about white men here. We're close to home.”

The villagers built fires and soon brought them yams, spinach and more sugar cane. Crowds of natives, old and young moved among the party passing out food and bamboo tubes of water. Some of the old men sat speaking with Sgt. Manu. Judging by the serious expressions on their faces, Jack knew they were asking something of him.

Later Manu reported, “They want to know why I am with you. They want to know if you are looking for the yellow sand that glitters.”

“What did you tell them?”

“I told them that the ways of the white men are strange. That their power is great. That they always asking questions and forever wanting to control things they do not understand. But they are dangerous to those who do not want to be like them. That they are like foolish children always wishing to be heard, but I have told them that you are different than most white men. That you watch and listen and learn... that the Great Mother speaks to you and that you care for her people, that you will bring them no harm.”

“Thank you Sgt. Manu. I will do my best to live up to your good words.”

Cpl. Isi sat by one of the fires surrounded by children. He kept them laughing at his antics. Cpl. Isi grinned when he saw the Kiaps watching. With eloquent gestures he pantomimed great wanderings, the dangers he had faced, and the lower Purari he was going to reach.

Cpl. Dekadua sat like a chief with his back against a clump of sugar cane and ordered special foods from the people. They fed him, too, and cut his sugar cane into small pieces to make it easier for him to chew.

As Jack listened to the scraps of talk, he thought about the dead policemen and carriers, the Orokos, the Daru men, and the Motus, left behind in their lonely graves on that cold and distant tableland. There would be no passing friends to drop little green branches of remembrance on their last sleeping places. It could have been worse. They could all have been massacred.

With luck, soon they would be back on the coast, and he would have to tell the relatives of their men's separate fates. Then Jack remembered the glorious men and women of the Talifuraro Valley. The noble Furaro, his exotic queen with the red bird of paradise feathers, and his gentle son Maibu, who guided them to the Kikuri. What a contrast of peoples we have found up here, he thought. Besoso's fratricidal mob, the noble people in the Happy Valley, the murderously aggressive people of the Wen and now these serenely gentle people here.

Are we civilized men any different? Are we not as much slaves to our environment as these people living in huts under their trees? Do we not have our ritual wars, arms races and Armageddons? Is their blood sacrifice any different than the senseless wars we've waged to determine who has the right to dispense wine and wafers, or to ordain kings? What have we to offer these people? Very little, Jack thought. In fact, these people could teach us a lot about kindness and generosity.

A cloudless sky presented an orange fireball worth watching. The tableland to the east, which had taken so many weeks to cross, now appeared like a sea of timbered valleys and pinnacles. The mountains rose high in their midst like a distant city of mosques and minarets.

"Want to do it again?" O'Rourke said softly.

"I'll settle for the Amazon next time," Jack laughed. "We've come up the Fly, crossed the Limestone Barrier and traced the river systems of the Purari. We've given it a fair go. It's time to go home and tell the government what we've found up here."

A short older native sat down in front of the patrol officers and told them, with a lot of gestures, about men down the river who stood on logs and paddled with sticks. He was telling them of the canoe people. Using twigs, he showed them a route down through the Iehi chasm. Too dangerous, he indicated with his palm flattened across his eyes. He then showed them another route which the Kiaps knew must be the Hathor gorge. Four older men joined them. They chatted incessantly, their heads bobbing all the while, giving them the news about the Hathor country. The district ahead was a poor one, they indicated. There is not much food, and there is an empty space that would take four days to cross. Bad country, they said. Few people.

"That's the way Champion came," O'Rourke said.

"Too far," Jack replied. "In our condition, with nothing to trade for food, we'll never make it. And from what I can sort out, it's mostly uninhabited country. It could take us weeks, and the wet season will be on us."

The moon rose over the tablelands to the east, and the two men sat for a while in silence, each with his thoughts. O'Rourke stubbed out his pipe. "I'm for some shut eye," he said, and crawled deep back into the shelter. Jack joined him a few minutes later, and eavesdropped on the Oroko carriers who were still eating and gossiping by their fires. Now and again, he heard an occasional laugh. The men were still in a terrible condition, but there was hope in their words.

A cold heavy rain began to fall, and the carriers moved into a hut with cold, hard floors. They were wet and filthy, Jack thought, but at least they have been well fed tonight and have shelter. He drew a layer of pandanus leaves over his body and fell asleep in the comfort of the fire, listening to the rain drum on the thatched roof.

In the morning Jack gave these kind people two tomahawks and the red sashes that belonged to the policemen. They seemed grateful to receive the scraps of cloth. After promising to return one day with gifts and trade goods, the patrol was on its way once more. Three youths escorted them across a foaming river on a suspension bridge made of Ori vine and cane. The carriers and policemen carried gifts of Kunda rope as well as small bags of sugar cane and yams. Their guides showed them the source of the Iehi creek, and indicated that if they followed its course, it would lead into Sago country.

The patrol advanced single file through a cold, damp, and dismal rainforest. They had been warned that the people ahead were not friendly, and minutes after their guides left them, the harsh yodeling they had learned to fear started up ahead.

Some odd-looking men were lurking behind the trees and oversized ferns. Most of them had braided their hair in a bizarre fashion. And worse, dead opossums and lizards dangled from their ears. Soon, scattered arrows began arching through the air. One landed at the officers' feet.

"That cuts it," Jack said, and fired his rifle at a rock near one of the offender's feet, sending a plume of white powder into the air. The lizard-man disappeared into the gloom. "Were going downstream, No more of this nonsense. I've had enough."

"So much for first contact," O'Rourke said. "However, they were the most primitive looking bastards I ever saw," he hastily added after receiving a scathing look from Jack.

The party followed the streambed. There were no tracks. From time to time they were forced to wade in cold, hip-deep water. The stream had its source on a wide platform at around 6,000 feet, and as they followed it, more and more tributaries came in from the east and west increasing its volume.

The carriers and police struggled with the litter. Nandua, the carrier who'd had his arm amputated, was a living skeleton. His eyes were yellow and sunken, and his face was ashen. Late that day Nandua called for Sgt. Manu and asked him if all the police were on guard.

"They are all on guard," replied Sergeant Manu.

"What you doing?" Nandua asked.

"Me on guard too."

"Where are de Kiaps?"

"They stop."

"All right. No matter." Nandua's eyes rolled upward and he gripped Sgt. Manu's hand. "I am leaving," he gasped and slumped back into the litter. His life had ended in this dark land so near yet so far from his home.

"When we get back to Moresby, I'm putting up a marker for him," Jack said.

"Count on me, mate. I'll go halves with you for certain. No man deserves it more," O'Rourke said. They buried the brave policeman, whose courageous defense had saved them at the ambush, under a pile of green and white limestone pebbles on a hummock overlooking the stream.

They perched underneath a rock ledge and munched their cold yams while the drizzling rain fell all around them. No one said anything. Each man sat wrapped in his particular misery, hugging himself tightly to keep warm.

Jack's stomach burned and his bowels churned miserably. His dysentery had returned, and a great weakness seemed to permeate his body, and even his mind. Malaria or Black Fever, he thought to himself. "I'm not sure I'll make it, mate," he said to O'Rourke.

"You'll make it, all right, even if I have to carry you on my back," and he coughed blackly.

They moved out into shrouds of fog-like mists. Soon the water of the Iehe disappeared, having seeped underground somewhere, and there was only the boulder and pebble-strewn course of white, water-worn limestone in front of them. They started to descend rapidly, and now they could see the entrance to the chasm. It loomed up in front of them, and they entered between its straight limestone walls.

"It looks like the gates to hell," Jack commented.

"It does seem like purgatory, that's certain," O'Rourke replied grimly. As they walked deeper into the chasm, the nearly unscaleable walls dwarfed them. Here and there small shrubs clung tenaciously to the cracks and fissures.

Worried about their slow pace, Jack said, “Cpl. Dekadua, take Agoti and scout ahead. Try to find an easier way.”

“Yes, Kiap.”

By mid-day the chasm narrowed to about twenty yards in width. They climbed, searching for hand and toe holds, over huge boulders piled on top of one another and slid down the rock faces and terraces. A cold shroud-like mist enclosed them. There were no birds or animal sounds. The eerie chasm had the silence of a tomb.

“I'll bet this place never sees the light of day,” O'Rourke commented. Jack nodded numbly, saving his breath and holding his hand against his stomach. “Do you want to rest?” asked O'Rourke.

“I'll be right once we get beyond these damned boulders.”

Late in the afternoon they came to a deep drop. Cpl. Dekadua and Agoti had gotten over the difficulty by cutting down and trimming a slender tree trunk. With the help of the carriers, they placed it upright on the ledge below. It took time, using their vine ropes and axes to cut hand holes down the trunk, so that when the last of the party was safely below, darkness was beginning to fall. Jack looked for a safe place to camp, but the only spot to camp was on a slightly elevated terrace above the streambed.

“This will have to do,” Jack said.

“Good enough,” O’Rourke agreed.

“The men have found some meat Kiap,” Sgt. Manu said. “I tell them to fix it.”

“That’s good news, Sergeant. If it’s a moraboa, just singe it a little. ”

“It’s not, Kiap. It is something that I have never seen.”

“If it walks, talks, or squawks, I’ll eat it, Sergeant.”

Dekadua and Agoti had killed a curious animal in a small cave nearby. Its body was covered with hairy fur, and but for its tail, one could have called it a black bear. Its front legs appeared to be of the same shape and length, and the imprint it left was like a baby's foot. Somatu made some soup for the officers out of its tail, and its carcass was divided evenly among the men who ate every portion except the paws, intestines and hair.

That night, sitting under the outcrop, the Oroko carriers began singing the mournful hymns from the palm-clad beaches of the gulf coast. The policemen answered with a medley of barracks tunes. Led by Cpl. Isi, they clamored: "Pack up trouble in old kit bag and smi' boys smi'."

Later the carriers moved down the chasm and climbed up into small niches carved in the limestone. The police and both officers tried to hide from the wind and rain under the large overhanging rock on the terrace, but it was useless. They were all chilled to the bone by the ceaseless wind that whipped down the chasm.

A terrific electrical storm formed overhead. Each successive clap of thunder made them think the walls of the chasm were falling. The rain fell with such a force they could barely hear each other speak. From time to time O'Rourke or Sgt. Manu would peer out into the darkness from the edge of the terrace. When lightening flashed they could see the glistening white boulders of limestone that marked the floor of the chasm.

"I don't like this," O'Rourke said, shaking off the rain as he stood under the overhang. "We're sitting ducks. A flash flood could wipe us right off this ledge. What about climbing higher?"

"Sgt. Manu, take a torch and see if you can spot a way to the top." Jack ordered.

"Yes, Kiap," and he disappeared into the rain.

"The wall is too steep. There are no toe holds that I could see," O'Rourke pointed out. "The face is too slippery. We'll lose the whole party if we try to scale it at night." Jack unconsciously held his stomach as he considered their plight.

"Cpl. Dekadua, the cave where you found the bear. How deep was it?"

"Not very deep, Kiap. De animal was resting in de mouth. It did not look like much to me."

"Let's have a look-see." Jack followed Dekadua out into the rain. "Agoti and Somatu, come with us. Bring my torch."

The four men crept slowly along the terrace and found the narrow ledge that led to the cave's entrance. Cpl. Dekadua led the way along the precipice. The Corporal and Somatu crawled inside. Agoti gave Jack a push upward, and then Somatu grabbed his arm and hauled Jack up into the cave.

The men half-stood and half crouched in the small, dim, dank-smelling interior. Jack flashed the weak torch light around the walls. The light revealed a small hollow in the rocks, room for maybe ten men to stand if they bent over, fifteen at most.

"We'd be trapped like rats in here," Jack said.

"It is better than on the ledge, Kiap," Somatu said. "We're much higher up here."

"You're right. Go back and tell Sgt. Manu to bring the constables here." Somatu left the last torch clutched in his hand. The men watched as the weak light moved across the terrace and disappeared around the bend in the rocks.

In a few minutes the torch reappeared. They could hear, but barely see, the men clambering up the rock face. One by one the constables clambered over the edge, and Agoti hauled them into the cave. Cpl. Dekadua stacked their arms and ammo on a small ledge over their heads.

O'Rourke stood by Jack in the entrance and said, "This is peachy. Cpl. Isi, take the torch and get the map cases."

"Yes, Kiap," and grunting, Isi turned and groped his way back down the slippery rock face. The men waited, hunched over, in the darkness, for Cpl. Isi and Sgt. Manu to return. There was no water yet. Perhaps Sgt. Manu has found a way to the top, Jack mused.

Above the rumbling and thunder and fall of the rain came a new sound. Faintly at first, but with each second it became louder and louder. The Sergeant's face appeared at the top of the ledge. "It comes, Kiap, the flood!" he shouted.

The avalanche of water came with a rush and a roar rising at an alarming pace onto the terrace. The strong arms of Agoti lifted Sgt. Manu up, and Cpl. Dekadua pulled him into the entrance of the small cave. Sgt. Manu was the last man over the edge.

Corporal Isi's face appeared at the entrance of the cave. Clinging to a small root in the face of the precipice, he started to pull himself upward just as a wall of water struck him. He hung there for a moment as Agoti and Jack reached for his flailing free arm. But they were too late. With a cry, the Corporal was gone, swept away in swirling mass of dark water.

Mingled with the roar of rain and the rushing waters were the shouts of the terror-stricken carriers as they tried to scale the limestone walls to safety. Jack knew instinctively the carriers were lost. The men inside the cave waited, cold and shivering for a miracle to save them from the rising waters.

“It is above my knees,” Jack heard O'Rourke's voice in the dark.

One of the policemen cried out in fear. “Save us, Kiap.”

“Be still,” said Sgt. Manu. “Maski, it does not matter.”

There was no escape unless the water stopped rising. The water reached their thighs. Then their belt buckles. And still they waited, hoping and hoping, and silently cursing every clap of thunder that seemed to increase the downpour of rain.

Quickly, too quickly, the water was level with Jack's chin. He gulped down a mouthful; it tasted like the cold salt sweat of a corpse. The mouthful struck him as the forerunner of choking suffocation. He swallowed a second mouthful and felt the outrage to his body that this gulping of death brought; a spasm shivered through him and hummed in his ears and drummed in his heart.

Jack stood on his toes. There was nothing to lean on. The ground began to sink beneath his full weight. His body danced off the floor of the cave, and his hands involuntarily grasped O’Rourke’s shoulders. Alongside him, the men were struggling for footholds and crying out for help when the water was suddenly sucked out of the cave like the flushing of a commode. Jack blocked the entrance to the cave with his body to keep the other men from being swept out.

Jack's stomach heaved under his soaked flannel jacket. Nothing remained of the floodwaters but broken brown bubbles going slowly round and round their ankles and feet in circles. The great creative force which some men call Nature, in her fathomless, inhuman compassion, had ceased her death-magic and instead had delivered salvation. For them, they had exited from her watery womb. For those outside the cave, they were swept to their watery graves.

All struggling, all beating with the arms, all kicking with their legs ceased, and the men collapsed on the floor in an incredible delicious silence. They crouched, shivering, leaning into each other for warmth, arms and legs aching with pain and weariness until the first faint light of day appeared.

The men clambered down the precipice to the terrace below. Jack waited silently until Agoti had passed the arms down to Cpl. Dekadua, who relayed them to the men. The policemen called loudly, hailing the carriers. The sound ricocheted off the canyon's walls. Sgt. Manu glanced up at Jack, and then down at his feet.

“It's no good, Kiap. They go finis.” A pang of anguish stabbed at Jack's stomach. He winced and reflexively stepped backward, jarring into O'Rourke, who stood behind him.

“Easy, Jack,” O'Rourke said, and grabbed his arms and eased him onto a rock.

Seven dead men, Jack thought. Seven more men. They weren't just carriers. They came through hundreds of miles of hostile country because they trusted me. They were Oroko men, the best of their kind. They stuck with me up on the Fly River when the Daru men deserted. They fought bravely when the shield men ambushed us and never complained when we scraped through that damn limestone barrier. They ate moraboa when the rice rations were finished. They made this whole journey possible. Then this happens. You don't take your friends out and kill them.

“We no find Cpl. Isi,” Manu said softly.

Eight men. Jack buried his head in his arms. His shoulders rocked. The policemen were visibly moved at Jack's display of grief, and they moved around the terrace self-consciously, not knowing what to say or do.

"I did not know," Somatu said, "that a Kiap could cry. I did not know they cared."

"Be still, boy," Sgt. Manu spoke. "All government men care, but this Kiap is different. He loves the people.... We are lucky to be with this man. He knows the Great Mother. She will tell him what she wants him to know."

Rousing himself, Jack stood up and glanced around the chasm. Dawn was breaking, piles of logs and debris blocked the streambed in some places, in others the streambed had been scoured clean.

"They are asking what we do, Kiap," Sgt. Manu said.

"Tell the men we go south, Sergeant. We are going home."

A grim faced Sgt. Manu walked away and ordered the men to start downstream. As they moved forward, the chasm began to widen and the walls were lowering. By mid-morning they picked up a rivulet seeping out of a streambed. It soon became a creek, then a flowing shallow river sixty yards wide forcing the men to move down the side of one bank, picking their way over the boulders.

By noon the cliff walls were wider and much lower. Agoti and Cpl. Dekadua had climbed to the top and they began shouting, "Purari! Purari! Kiap." The patrol picked up the pace.

They rounded a bend and less than a quarter of a mile ahead, a broad silver ribbon glistening in the sunlight. "Praise be. Hallelujah!" O'Rourke screamed in a rasping voice.

"When did you get religion, mate?" Jack teased as the red-bearded, barefooted tattered figure waved his battered, brimless felt hat wildly in the air.

The constables looked at the half-mad red-bearded scarecrow with alarm. O'Rourke scrambled over the rocks, and yelling "Follow me boys," led the constables on a mad charge down to the river, leaving Jack to trail painfully behind in their wake.

Jack rested on a broken log and watched the men's playful antics. The happy policemen crawled out of the stream and picked up their stacked arms. Jack led them down a narrow sandy beach where the Erewa emptied into the Purari.

"We have company," O'Rourke said as he brought his weapon to the ready. An old man with oily braided hair and a short grass sporran was sitting in front of a small fire, picking at his feet. Piles of spinach, potatoes and cane were spread in front of him. He did not look up as the wary men approached him.

Branches rustled above their heads. The constables aimed their rifles skyward. "Pack up troubles in old kit bag and smi' boys smi'." The leaves parted. "Don't shoot. It's me, Isi." With that, Isi jumped from a low branch, landing in a heap on the soft sand. The police howled and piled on top of Isi, rolling over and over in a mass of arms and legs.

Corporal Isi broke out of the pile and, trailed by the grinning constables, who pounded his back and pulled him forward by his arms, approached the officers. "Good dai, Kiap," he said, saluting, with a lopsided grin on his face.

"Where have you been, Isi?" Jack shouted.

"I fall in de river, Kiap. Dat water was strong. I catch a log and end up here. Den I find dis man and tell him to bring food for the men. He knows about polismani."

"Polismani?" queried the old man, nervously.

Raising the old man to his feet, Jack handed him his steel tomahawk and his last swatch of red cloth, and put his worn out bush hat on the man's head. He gave the man all he had to give. The old man nodded his thanks for the poor presents.

The men fell to and demolished the meal. The old man watched the ravenous men, and then went back into the forest, promising to bring more food when he returned. It was a relief to be in the quiet forest again, out of the treacherous gorge and to hear the birds they knew so well.

Jack sent Dekadua and Agoti to scout downriver. The constables reported back late in the afternoon.

"Dere is no road." Agoti reported. "It is rock and rock and trees and trees. De track is badaga. No more."

“We have to raft,” Jack said to O'Rourke. “We could spend weeks cutting a trail down the Purari. The men are too weak.” They spent the rest of the afternoon searching for rafting material. The constables found a few suitable trees and a copse of bamboo a few hundred yards inland from the river.

They spent the next two days constructing rafts, and during the night they slept under ledges of rock or in rough shelters. For food they ate the stringy potatoes, wood mushrooms and cabbages of the guru palm that Cpl. Isi and the old man gathered.

“Dere is no more cabbages or spinach. Dere is not much food here,” Cpl. Isi reported.

By the end of the third day, three large rafts had been completed. The next morning, as they prepared to move off, the old man came up and hugged Cpl. Isi affectionately. He spoke in soft melodious tones while tears coursed down his brown cheeks. He turned to Jack, and by signs he explained that if the men remained in his country, he would take care of them and not let them starve.

Jack signed that they had to go on. The rafts would take them. The old man grabbed Isi's arms more firmly. He must come back with him. The river was no good. He looked at Jack again, his eyes pleading. Jack shook his head and pointed down the river. The old man nodded his head slowly in understanding. He threw a stick into the river, and he pointed to it as it floated away with the current. Then he pointed to the rafts and looked to see if the Kiap understood. Jack nodded.

He then took up two small pieces of wood, and he made a wavy motion with his hand, let it drop to the ground and, touching a limestone rock at his feet, snapped the pieces in half.

“He's telling us there's a big drop somewhere below,” O'Rourke said.

“I know,” Jack replied. He touched the old man on top of the head and said, “Thank you, friend.”

They boarded the rafts with their rifles and what little gear that was left. The last they saw of the old man, he was still standing alone on the bank, holding the box of matches, the empty canvas bag, the axe and the few poor presents in his arms.

"This is it -- the Homestretch," O'Rourke said to Jack as he looked happily around him while endeavoring to make a leaf tobacco cigarette. They shared a raft with Cpl. Isi and MO Tenoso. Their rifles, ammo and net bags were tied to a pole in the center of the raft.

They had been on the river a short time, and were passing through a stretch of calm water. "The rafts seem to be holding up," O'Rourke said.

"I don't want to dampen your enthusiasm," Jack replied, "but we must be at about 4500 feet in elevation. The Purari as we know it must be about 2200 feet lower. There has to be a drop somewhere."

"At this rate, we will be at the mouth of the river in a week." O'Rourke hummed, ignoring Jack's remark, overjoyed as he watched the great walls of honeycombed rocks slip by them.

"Keep your eyes open," Jack shouted ahead to the raft manned by Dekadua and Agoti. Sgt. Manu and the rest of the constables were behind them on the largest raft. They entered narrow stretches of slow-moving water with unscaleable limestone walls rising high above them. At times they rushed past narrow razorback limestone islands rising from the center of the river.

Every bend was a nightmare to Jack. He expected to see a tremendous drop from which they could not escape. They entered another narrow and rapidly moving stretch of water between high walls of rock when they heard rifle shots. Jack could hear a thunderous sound that was growing louder as the rafts began to move faster in the water. "A waterfall! Make for the bank!" Jack shouted.

The men began to paddle harder with their rough blades, making for the shallow water. The raft's response was maddeningly slow, but they brought it safely to a shelf on the bank, just above a point where the two constables were waiting. Sgt. Manu's raft was unmanageable. The men abandoned it and swam for the bank.

Somatu struggled toward a rock. He clung for a moment, and then fell back into the stream. He reached back for the safety of the rock, but his fingers slipped off the edge. Somatu can't swim, Jack remembered. He raced down the bank and dove into the water, stroking wildly. He reached for Somatu's hair and grasped it firmly in one hand, turned and tried to swim backward, his free arm flailing weakly behind him.

The treacherous water gained momentum. Someone shouted and extended a paddle toward them, but it was too late. A giant hand seemed to reach up and pull the two struggling men forcibly over the lip of a waterfall. Water cascaded over Jack's face and body. He closed his mouth and eyes. The sound was deafening.

Down, down they slid for what seemed an eternity, and then they crashed into a pool of water. The air was smashed out of Jack's lungs. They spun around and were pushed forward through the foam and swept outward and downward through another cascade of water and rocks. They landed in a deep cauldron of frothing, swirling water and were sucked down and pounded under another set of falls.

The men were dragged down, down, deeper and deeper into the darkness. Jack felt like he was being pulled apart by two opposing forces. As his consciousness was fading, a watery figure came toward him.

"You must not drink."

"Save us," he gasped as a searing pain cramped his lungs. "I don't want to die," he prayed and began flailing with his free arm. His fingers tightened on Somatu's mop of hair. A thin, long, rippling surge of energy poured through his flesh and shivered into his arms and legs. His feet touched bottom as his head struck a rock, sending a shock wave into his brain.

A red wave of rage drove him upward, tearing, dividing, and rending the water overhead. "I won't be conquered by you," he screamed inwardly. He broke through the surface of the water with a gasp. Grasping Somatu's hair more firmly, he redoubled his strokes. Twenty yards. Thirty yards. “I can't go on,” he thought, and he almost let loose of Somatu to save himself.

Slowly Jack worked his way into a brown flood of calm water, still deep enough to drown him. His legs sank slowly beneath as they were swept downstream. Then he felt his feet dragging on the riverbed. Slowly he dug in and found he could stand up. As the water tugged at his weakened body, he crawled through some watery reeds, dragging Somatu behind. A startled heron rose with a scream and flapped out of the rushes.

Grasping hidden roots and the stalks of last year's reeds, Jack glanced down at Somatu's corpse-like face. Some power deep inside was making Somatu's lips move, but no sound came out. Jack collapsed face down on the riverbank. The pungent smell of muck filled his nostrils. The river sobbed as it licked the edges of his boots. The waterfall sounded faint in his ears.

He grabbed the green shoots of a coconut palm in his hand. He turned his head and it seemed as if the earth had fallen asleep. The black void lifted and he heard a voice deep in the caverns of his mind: “You offered your life to save one of my own even as you strove to become one with the force. I give you the light of full consciousness. You will always know that living is merely to be always on the edge of death's darkness. You will be awake, aware of pain, of the life force. You will not always believe so but you are blessed, not cursed. The cosmic mystery is beyond meaning, but the truth is that we are both one with the transcendent.”

Jack felt as if the primal force of all life had touched him. An unknown ecstasy flooded into the arteries of his soul. The Great Mother spoke again, “You are reborn. The water has cleansed you. You are free to make of your life what you will.”

Some time later Jack was vaguely aware that strong hands and arms were lifting him. He remembered tasting sweet coconut milk, drinking from a coconut shell until he could drink no more. He felt strong hands place him in the bottom of a canoe, and he dreamed of paddles swishing through the water, of voices calling in Motu, and then in English. Then he dreamed of food.

Chocolate cakes and meat pies. Were there really such things? Then he dreamed of plunging downward through water, gasping for air.

He awoke with a scream. A black, bushy-bearded man was bending over him, a small torch in his hand. "Mr. Reed, I presume." Jack's eyes took in the white walls, the sunlight streaming through a window. Tall white cabinets full of jars fringed the room. White mosquito netting surrounded the cot where he lay.

"Where am I?" Jack asked.

"You are safe, Mr. Reed. You are here at the Purari Mission." Jack's head fell onto his pillow.

"Somatu?" He started to rise.

"He is fine. He is resting in the next room."

A kind-looking woman opened the net, propped Jack up with a pillow and began spooning warm broth into his mouth. Jack swallowed some and then collapsed back onto the pillow. It was dark when he awakened. The friendly woman fed him again. He sucked the juice from a strip of pineapple and swallowed gratefully. "How long have I been here?" he asked her.

"Nearly two days. The Motus brought you here."

"My men. They are still up there." Jack started to raise up.

"Mr. Jefferson sent a party of carriers upriver right after you arrived. Your man told him where to find the patrol. They should return soon."

The rain was drumming down on the corrugated steel roof. Jack pulled the warm blankets over his shoulders and slept soundly for the first time in months. He awoke to nearby cries of alarm. A bell was sounding somewhere nearby.

"The polisemani is coming," he heard a child yell. Jack sat up and momentarily lost his bearings. He pulled on a pair of cloth slippers he found beside his bed and, pushing through a set of curtains, he stepped out onto a wide veranda that surrounded the infirmary.

Somatu was there before him, and he put his arms around Jack and led him slowly down the narrow path and out onto the wharf. The natives gave way when they saw Somatu and the Kiap coming. The women and children watched as the white pajamaed figure, supported by Somatu, waved to the ragged dirty officer with the red, bushy beard and to the equally dirty policemen with black bushy beards, sitting in the midst of twenty paddlers who had brought them down the river.

A terrible tension broke in Jack, and he leaned with relief onto the shoulders of Somatu. O'Rourke staggered up the bank and embraced the two men. They were too excited to speak and Mister Jefferson led them back to the residence, where the kind lady laid out a breakfast of bacon and eggs, food they had been craving for months. They sat in comfortable chairs while the missionaries told them the news and gossip from Moresby. What a relief it was to be free from want and treachery, to taste good food again and to rest under a strong roof.

They described their journey to the couple, from Daru, to the barrier, through the highlands, to the Iehe chasm. They told them about the people they met, the hardships, the tragic loss of lives, the desertion of the carriers, the landslide, of the savagery and kindness of the tribes.

"A terrible saga of hardship and suffering," the kind lady sighed.

"A piece of cake," O'Rourke smiled, and scraped some crumbs of chocolate off his plate. Jack laughed easily for the first time in months.

"I've sent word by radio that Reed and O'Rourke have come down the Purari. Moresby will send up a plane in the morning."

The Sea Cloud landed on the Purari shortly before noon the next day. As the party boarded the plane, Jack shouted farewell to the missionaries standing together on the wharf. The seaplane turned around on the broad flat Purari, and with a roar it skipped down the river and was airborne. O'Rourke was up front in the cockpit talking excitedly with the pilots. Jack was in the cargo bay strapped to a stretcher.

The policemen were seated on canvas seats suspended along the hull. Over the roar and rumblings of the engines, Jack listened to the start of an argument as to the number of "months at fifteen shillings," and realized that the topic of most absorbing interest to the policemen at that moment was the computation of pay they would receive when they reached Port Moresby. Some said "six moons" had gone by since they left the coast. Others argued that there had only been five. Yet the most remarkable thing was that these unschooled natives had, without any calendars and without the actual money in their hands, arrived at the correct amount of money due to them.

"When we find Port Moresby, I will buy white man's tobacco and six tins of meat," he heard one of them say. Another said he would buy a tilley lamp and kerosene, and some white man's biscuits.

Cpl. Isi announced that he was going to buy a pair of trousers and a black singlet. No, he would not buy a shirt; he liked the black singlets. He was going to "get a paper from the judge" so he could wear his purchases in public without going to Gaol. "And when I get to Moresby I will buy a motor car," he boasted.

I'm glad these men survived, Jack thought, but what will I tell the Oroko widows and orphans? He could hear only too keenly in his mind, the wailing of the women; he could hear the old men making speeches, and see the fathers plucking their beards in grief. A blow to the "funny bone" would numb the hand and then the smash of an adze would take off a finger below the joint from a young wife or from a sister to honor the departed husband or brother. The Government will give the widows a fiver, a sack of rice, and a tin of tea. Something for the chief and sticks of tobacco for the fathers and our obligation will be satisfied, until the next time. God, what are we doing here? What right have we to take these men from their homes and families to help us search for ways to exploit them and their land? We don't belong here.

Tugging on Jack's sleeve, Somatu brought Jack back to the present by saying, "With this much kona, will I be allowed to attend school, Kiap? I wish to learn how to read the tracks white men make on paper."

Jack touched Somatu's shoulder wishing he could slap his back. "There will be enough kona for you to go to school. I will speak to Judge Murray."

Somatu jumped to his feet, his eyes flashed and he grinned as he proudly told the constables, "I am going to school and someday I will be a government man." He went forward to the cockpit to share his good news with Kiap O'Rourke.

The Sea Cloud turned into the wind and landed in a deep lagoon inside the harbor. The pilot slowed the engines and taxied the sea plane toward the Burns' Philips wharf where Jack could see officials and business men in white duck suits standing like isolated islands in a crowd of natives dressed in lap-laps.

The Sea Cloud wigwagged its way to the wharf. The co-pilot weaved his way through the tangled bodies, and opening the side hatch, stepped out, hawser in hand, onto the dock. He was back in a moment.

"All ashore that's going ashore, gentlemen. Welcome to Port Moresby." He grinned and extended a hand to Jack as he stepped onto the gangplank. A blazing sun, the stifling humidity, the blaring band, all fused and Jack felt his eyes blurring. A sudden surge of darkness filled his brain and he felt himself collapsing.

"Give a hand," he heard the co-pilot say, and he felt himself being picked up and heaved onto someone's shoulders like a sack of potatoes and his mind went blank.

Strong arms laid Jack gently on a table. He opened his eyes. When they focused he could see a mirrored operating lamp over his head. A freckle-faced red-bearded giant was peering closely at him. "O'Rourke!" he exclaimed.

"You'll be right," O'Rourke reassured him. "You're in the hospital. Brought you in on my back. Just like I promised Murray I would," and he laughed nervously.

"Stand back, man," a voice barked, and a sallow, gaunt-looking, black-mustachioed man with an optic mirror bent over him, flicked on a small torch and began to peer into his eyes.

"What on earth have you done to your hair, man?" Doctor Pitt asked after he quit squinting into Jack's eyes.

"Parted it with an arrow," Jack responded as the MO carefully examined his scalp.

"Good God, man. That's a nasty wound in your belly. Did you fall on your bayonet? Nothing for it but surgery... Sister. Prepare him for the operating room." He was out the door to check on the other men.

A beam of sunlight cascaded through the soft gauze netting that surrounded Jack's hospital bed. Outside the open window, a slight breeze pestered the green banana leaves. He could hear the soft melodic voices of the grounds keepers chatting as they policed up the compound. "God how peaceful it is here," he thought. No scout reports from Cpl. Dekadua. No Sgt. Manu requesting march orders. No concerns over rations. No log bridges to cross. No yodeling to startle the soul. He felt his body. He was covered with bandages.

Jack moved his leg; it was stiff. He pressed and probed his stomach. It was tender, but the gnawing pain was gone. He felt an urge to go back to sleep.

"Well, how's my sleeping beauty?" Pitt's abrasive nasal voice intoned jarring Jack out of his reverie.

"I'm alright, I think."

"Well, let's just see," and Pitt began examining Jack's wounds. He checked his scalp. Then his legs, his thigh wound and then examined his abdomen carefully. "Aside from an arrow in your gut, one in your thigh, and that abrasion on your scalp, not to mention a few pock marks where the maggots festered in your leech bites, and a touch of malaria, a heavy dose of dysentery, and a bit of scrub typhus, you'll be right."

"Where's O'Rourke?" Jack demanded. "Oh, he's been in town celebrating I think for the past few days while you slept. In fact, we had to track him down and medicate him twice.'

"I've been here three days?"

"Four to be exact, sleeping your arse off for most of the time, that is when you weren't delirious and raving about crocodiles and sorcerers."

"Sgt. Manu and the men?"

"Discharged. All of them and spending their pay in Hanuaba Town." Jack sank back into his pillow. A long sigh of relief escaped his lips.

"Well nurse, I think our man is fit enough to meet the ladies auxiliary and the gentlemen from the press."

"What press?" Jack blurted.

"Why the Moresby people and the Sydney bunch. Everyone wants to meet the man who discovered the Garden of Eden. Your story is out to the world. O'Rourke's had his share of the glory. Now it's your turn." He opened the door and called gaily to the people waiting outside. "Ladies and gentlemen, Mr. Jack Reed, our honored guest awaits you, he said, and with a peevish flourish, directed them into the room.

Several ladies and journalists surrounded Jack's bed. "Poor man," tutted the women, as Lady Stoddard plumped his pillow.

"I never thanked you for helping me that evening at the hotel," she clucked, reminding him of Assistant Administrative Officer Townsend.

"What was it like up there? Did you run into any headhunters? Did you find any gold?" The reporters bombarded Jack. After ten minutes of incessant questioning, Jack gave the Sister a beseeching look. Ignoring their cries of protest, she came to the rescue and shooed the lot of them out of the room.

He overheard one of the dowagers cooing in the corridor. "He is so young; he's just a boy. Imagine having to suffer so much to bring his men home." The fuss astonished Jack. The Sister returned and handed Jack a copy of the *Moresby Courier*.

“Shangri-La Discovered” a headline blazoned across the front page. There was a longer article in the *Pacific Island Monthly*: “Patrol officers Reed and O'Rourke discover a vast fertile territory, densely inhabited by skilled agriculturalists of a peculiar social type ....”

For the next hour, Jack read a fascinating and highly imaginative account of the patrol's adventures in the Highland that recounted a saga of hardship and adventure that as far as Jack could tell had occurred only in the mind of the journalist, who at one point depicted Jack firing pistols with both hands into an oncoming band of berserk skirmishers. The article captured nothing of the hardship and dangers they had faced together; the terror, the terrible waste of life; the hunger, their grief for lost comrades. Instead the reporter had painted an exaggerated vision of Shangri-la, soon to be made accessible to tourists via the airplane. There was little mention of the brave porters and constabulary without whose courage, loyalty, and extreme efforts they would have all perished in the high country.

Jack gathered his pillow into a tight clump and sat propped up in bed, staring out the window where a vague diffusion of sunlight danced and floated on the fronds of a banana tree. A sweet and sticky smell of mud came up the river and mixed with the sweet ether-smelling corridor outside his room. He could hear the orderlies shuffling by, but no one disturbed him.

The beaded curtains at his doorway parted, and a rakish-looking native attired in a grass skirt, a large circular pig's tusk adorning his chest, and with a bushy mop of hair enlivened by flowers, stepped into the room. “Good morning, Kiap. Are you right?”

“Sergeant?” Jack examined the gaunt near-naked figure in front of him. “I hardly recognized you.”

“That is good to hear, Kiap, for I do not wish to be recognized,” and he moved close to Jack's bed.

“Why not?” Jack asked. “Has something happened? Tell me.”

Sgt. Manu paused and then began to speak slowly. "There is much wrong, Kiap. Some big things and many small things. For some days I have been thinking. I have decided I no longer wish to be a policeman. I no longer wish to stay in Moresby. I want to return to my people."

"But why, Sergeant? You are an honored policeman. You are the best of the constabulary men. What has happened?" and Jack swung his legs over the bed.

"Please, do not stand, Kiap. I will tell you. You are a good man. You are not like other white men. When we were trapped in the cave, you drank from the Great Mother's cup and in the waterfall she cleansed you. Her wisdom has seeped into you like water into limestone. She has set you free. You are one of her warriors. That you will care for her people I know. You are our friend. But I have been thinking long on this thing. The white man is destroying my people. We no longer have a voice. The white man does not listen to us. He only listens to his own voice." Manu paused and thought for a moment, and then began again.

"I was born free. When Judge Murray first came to our village he brought us medicines, and then schools, and took young men like me into the constabulary. I thought the white man's magic was good. My people wanted the tinned milk and the tea and the trade goods too much. But now I know these things are chains. We are no longer free. The mountain people are wise to reject the white man's steel. In my village now, we must obey the white man's law and believe in his god. I no longer want to be a polisemani. I betray my people when I go get troublemakers, men who only wish to follow the old ways. Our spirits get trapped in our bodies. We can speak of them, but the white man will not listen. We are only half-men who are scorned for our beliefs. My people no longer know who they are. Our god is everywhere! He is in the birds, the trees, the wind. He is not in a book or a building. I go back to the hills and cleanse myself. I help my people find their spirit. If you are with white men, you cannot find your spirit. To stay here is to die from the worms inside. I will burn my house and take my family up into the hills, far from the white man's words. The white man is too clever. Someday we will find out which people is the stronger, or maybe the Great Mother will make us one. But the time is not now." Manu grasped Jack's hand. "I am gone. You will see me no more unless you come alone to the hills. May the Great Mother forever dance across your path."

Before Jack could react, Manu stepped over the windowsill and disappeared into the lime-green illumination caused by the bananas leaves as they whirled in the sunlight. Jack glanced down and saw the brown leather swagger stick lying at the foot of his bed.

"Sgt. Manu," he called but there was no answer, just faint footsteps in the hall. Jack began to cry softly. Then giant sobs made his shoulders heave. The best man I ever knew, and I never even thanked him. Manu is right. What might we learn from these people if we weren't always trying to show them our ways?

Later in the afternoon, the nurse led Jack around the little park outside the hospital. Aside from a slight tender spot in his gut, he felt fit. When they returned from their jaunt, Jack found Ah Chin, the Chinese merchant, trader, and tailor, waiting for him in his room. The obsequious little man fawned over Jack, and smiling unctuously began to take his measurements.

"Not to worry. No charge," he assured Jack with a knowing wink. "No cost to you," he cackled gleefully as he and his assistant bowed out of the room. "Tomorrow we bring back," and he was gone.

MO Pitt stepped in for a moment. "I've advised the AO that you're fit to report for duty, but I've recommended a convalescent leave. You are scheduled to meet with him tomorrow after big tea."

A resplendent scarecrow dressed in a white linen tropical suit, fitted cream-colored silk shirt, and silk tie stared back at Jack from the wardroom mirror. The bowing Ah Chin and his assistant had brought the suit along with a considerable wardrobe. "Not to worry," was all Ah Chin would say when Jack had inquired about the payment.

Jack walked outside to the hospital porch and was about to start down the path to the Administrative Headquarters when O'Rourke drove through the compound gates in a late-model Buick and slithered to a stop in the sand. "Where did you find this?"

"No time to palaver. Let's just say I inherited it." The two men walked side by side to the AO's office. "Let's get this over with," and O'Rourke buried his cigarette in the dirt with his heel.

The two men stood erect, but not at attention, in front of Acting AO Townsend's desk. He turned and fixed them with his best officious stare and tossed his notepad on the desk. "I'll be brief gentlemen, and to the point. I've read Patrol Officer O'Rourke's preliminary report of the expedition. I will expect a complete report from the both of you by the week's end, but from what I've read so far," and he pointed to O'Rourke's notes.

"I can only say that I'm shocked. The patrol officer in charge and his second in command in my opinion were totally incompetent and are guilty of extreme malfeasance. There is the matter of the desertions, the loss of valuable equipment and trade goods. Your men didn't even bring in their handcuffs! There are absolutely no maps or diaries indicating any reasonably reliable information about terrain, population, or resources. Your expedition should have been dubbed the 'Lost Patrol' and it will certainly be your last if I have anything to say."

"You abandoned men and are responsible for their deaths. The fact that you, by this report, against all orders provoked and fired wantonly on unarmed native populations time and again is lamentable. For this and a variety of reasons, I've ordered a Board of Inquiry to determine your fitness for future service. Until then, your pay and service records will be sealed and held in this office. You may draw health and comfort funds from the commissary and you may bunk if you wish at Constabulary Headquarters. I am admonishing you to keep this matter strictly to yourselves until the proceedings. You are not to discuss this with the press or any private individuals. Dismissed."

"You sawed-off pint of piss," O'Rourke lunged across the desk, but Jack pulled him back.

"I'll handle this, O'Rourke. Don't be foolish. He'd love to stick an assault and battery charge to his tic sheet on us. Wouldn't you, Townsend?"

Townsend's look of alarm lessened and he shrugged his shoulders. "Only doing my duty, gentlemen. Constable, please escort these men to the exchequer."

The two white-faced, grim-lipped men stalked out the door and down the street to the Buick. "Pile in, mate," O'Rourke said and Jack opened the door and settled into the seat. O'Rourke drove silently past the saluting guards at the compound gates and broke out in a mirthful smile.

"What's so funny?" Jack snapped and O'Rourke pulled a crumpled radiogram out of his pocket and handed it to Jack.

Jack spread it open and read: "Thank you for your radio advisement. Am fully aware of your predicament. I will personally conduct any inquiries if I feel it is warranted. Please keep me advised of P.O. Reed's condition. Congratulations. Am looking forward to hearing the details. Sec. Gen. Murray."

"He's been appointed Secretary-General?"

"Yes, but Townsend doesn't know it yet!" O'Rourke laughed. "Murray flew in on the Sea Cloud yesterday evening. He kept me up all night, but I couldn't fill him in completely. It was his idea that we front Townsend and he has scheduled you for a visit when we are finished here. Townsend isn't to know a thing. There will be a formal announcement of the changing of the guard this evening. Townsend isn't the only one in the Moresby crowd that is due for a few surprises," he chuckled. "When you're finished with Murray, I'll be with the mates at the hotel."

They sat on the veranda of the Moresby Hotel, a dozen empty beer glasses in front of them and watched a mob of frantic miners, ships boys, and transients trying to cram into Ah Chin's Mercantile Store. Furtive men with packs of supplies, trade good, and shovels in hand piled excitedly out the rear.

"Gold fever. There's nothing like it," Jamison commented. "They've gone nuggety all right. The fur will fly when those boys hit the Upper Purari," McCarthy predicted.

"What started it?" Jack asked.

"Some bloke cashed in some gold nuggets with Ah Chin. All he told him was that he found them somewhere up the river," O'Rourke said slyly.

"How did you know to order shovels from Brisbane?" Jack asked Woodsen.

"Oh. Maybe a white cockatoo told me," and he grinned.

"A white cockatoo with a red beard I'll bet," and Jack stared hard at O'Rourke.

"All's well that ends well, I always say," O'Rourke coughed and swallowed the last of his beer. A model T Ford pickup truck sped past the hotel. Standing in the back, holding onto a rack on the roof, a mound of hair blowing in the wind, wearing an open black shirt and black shorts, grinning madly, was Cpl. Isi. Three Hanabua women were seated in the bed, hanging to the side of the truck, obviously enjoying themselves.

"Good dai, Kiap," he shouted and waved to the men on the veranda.

"It looks like Isi struck it rich too," Jack said wryly and waved back. "Maybe they found something in their ruck sacks," and Jack suddenly recalled the men and O'Rourke filling their empty sacks with yellow nuggets up on the plateau.

"I heard that Constable Agoti and Corporal Dekadua bought a small copra plantation." O'Rourke said.

"Now how did they manage that?" Jack mused aloud.

"It also seems that Somatu has been selected to stand for an advanced school in Brisbane. Wants to be an exchequer or Prime Minister someday or something like that."

"Did Murray put it to you?" McCarthy asked.

"Hmm...." Jack sighed and raised his hands in the air.

"Go on."

"I made my speech and handed him my resignation. But he put it in his pocket."

"Good on 'em," McCarthy said.

Jack leaned back in his chair and studied the porch railings. The other men grew quiet. His thoughts drifted back to his meeting with Murray. As usual, Murray had the final say. "There will be no official inquiry, Jack. I've seen to that. I'm convinced that the patrol was carried out with the skill and forbearance that is characteristic of this type of endeavor. You and your men acquitted yourselves with honor throughout the patrol. You could not prevent the attacks on your party and you are not accountable where natural events are concerned. What has to happen, will always happen. How you react to disaster is what counts... and in my opinion, you persevered and brought your men out, as I knew you would. At this point in time, I cannot accept your resignation out-of-hand. I hope I've made it clear, Jack that there is no need for your resignation from the Service, either from my viewpoint or from Canberra for that matter."

"Judge, I've been doing some thinking. I'm not sure I belong here anymore. In fact, the farther I am from civilization, the better I feel. I'll always be an outsider. There are wonderful people up there in the Highlands. They are untouched by us and have no need of us or anything we in our wisdom think they need. We are not their benefactors. I've discovered somehow what civilization is by seeing what it isn't. The people I met are neither noble nor ignoble. They aren't perfect. They are making their own mistakes. Often warlike, they are nonetheless deeply human. We cannot dismiss them lightly. They offer us a great gift... a different view of the world than ours and I won't let it be destroyed by our view of things. I don't want them subjected to our form of violence and genocide. They live the way we used to before we called ourselves civilized. Their myths are just as true for them as our myths are for us. Like them, we are lost Adams without regenerative grace. We will bring them first native-development and follow that with Euro-development. Why is the white man's way always the right way? My view of the world is changing. As far as I am concerned, it's everyone's world, not just the white man's. As I see it in our society everyone and everything has its price and living a good life has no value. The more we sell ourselves and sell others, the more robot-like we become. We so-called "civilized men" are in danger of losing our souls. And I for one am not going to help turn their culture into a pale reflection of our own, not me. I want no part of it and in my opinion if they understood what will happen to them, they wouldn't want any part of it either!"

"You both underestimate and over-estimate them Jack. They live according to your own account in a brutal world of payback, an eye-for-an-eye and a tooth-for-a-tooth existence. Every murder and killing is avenged by ever more killing and raiding. It is our duty to bring an end to it... You value curiosity and so do they. It is not the nature of man to want to be sealed off from knowledge that widens his horizons, however upsetting that knowledge may be to his pre-conceived ideas. True, he may fret and fume at the new ideas, but in the end, he accepts them and is glad to have them. There is no question that in the beginning they should fear us with our superior weapons and inventions. They have to feel inferior and for certain they have to fear that we might enslave them. The impact our civilization will make on them is a disturbing, frightening impact on people so like ourselves that differences don't matter. Don't overlook the fact that your Shangri-La is not peopled by men who want lives of bliss and contentment. In truth, they want to pursue lives of self-expression.

"Otherwise, they wouldn't have constructed bridges, refined weapons, and concocted the high art and music forms you discovered. The few who showed no interest in your steel axes simply didn't grasp yet the differences between the two technologies. Those men who fired on you, thought you were unarmed; now they understand the difference. The damage has been done. They know about us now, and in most cases will welcome us back, even if somewhat reluctantly. Like all men everywhere, they have a thirst for knowledge. Nature abhors a vacuum, Jack, and man, the status quo. If it were otherwise, men all over this planet would still be painting their bodies blue and counting on their toes.

Murray continued, "Contemplative inertia is not the answer, Jack. You're too young to be a hermit. When you are young, it's all ego, vanity and idealism. Then some damned unforeseeable event, person, abomination comes along and shoots the lights out of your dreams, your hopes, your vision. Mother nature, social injustice, it doesn't matter, its all mystery.

"The fact is, Jack, that we live in the age of the alibi. Action ... altruistic action ... love, if you will, is the only answer. Fruitful activity is the only way through the maze. Freedom lies somewhere on the other side. We haven't evolved enough to be compassionate with ourselves. We keep mutilating each other's hopes and dreams. We haven't learned to love each other or die well. So live as fully as you can, while you can. Don't dwell on the morbid possibilities past or future. Become your own experiment in living, not someone else's, or society's, for that matter. If you want to be alone, then go back to the high country and confront your isolation and loneliness. That's the road for you. It's the road to connectedness. Up there you can become a teacher, a creator, or a prophet if you want, not a destroyer. Better still, become an Outside Man. Become a bridge between our two peoples. Civilization is still on the road from intolerance to tolerance. One day civilization will come to mean the kinship of all men. We'll be right when we start calling these people men and not bois. Try and break, if you can, the circle of misery, fear, anger and violence. That way, at least you can catch a breath of freedom and do some good for the Papuans. Buy them some time until we can work it all out.

"Don't decide now, Jack. Take your leave and come back and give me your answer. The trick is, Jack, to know when you've found what you're looking for... and I think you have. The bigger trick is to know what to do about it. You're the best of the lot, Jack. I'm counting on you, and so is Sgt. Manu wherever he is, and all the rest of your men. By the way, I'm secunding Townsend to the sanitation and cemeteries section. Garbage to garbage, I say," and he laughed and waved Jack out of his office.

“Well, what was it like up there, boys,” queried Bill, the barman, as he brought them a fresh round of beers.

“A piece of cake,” O'Rourke said nonchalantly. The men all looked away as Jack's eyes welled up with tears.

“To the Outside Men,” Jack said and they all stood and raised their glasses.

EPILOGUE

The constabulary band stood at Parade Rest beside the reviewing stand watching the "Grand Parade". Tens of hundreds of men in full ceremonial finery, with high plumes and ritual wigs, great trident spears and shields, war bows and arrows, axes and bone daggers, faces painted, shells shining in the fierce sunlight passed in review.

They were like some wild army, waving banners over their tossing plumes. Moving and halting to the surging rhythm of their chant, and crashing their hands on the drumheads of their black kundu drums... their face paint was brilliant, startling in some of its design of red against yellow, green, black, and blue. Headmen's noses were pierced not only with thin crescents of pearl-shell but with the sweeping curves of enameled bird of paradise plumes. When the drumming and the roar of the sing-sing paused, a jingling, as from a thousand hard-toned bells arose. This came from pieces of tambunam, the iridescent seashells each man wore tied to his waist.

Leaning his chin on a walking stick, Jack stared across the crowded arena, looking beyond the big shelters that housed the exhibits. The golden gong swung on a blue velvet ribbon beneath his chin. "The sunset has fallen on the old days, Jack," the Prime Minister pronounced. "In the old days, they would have killed a thousand pigs or more," and he pointed to a band of men who before the show had ended had ran wild all over the grounds, chasing a pig, which they caught and killed with shouts and laugher.

Jack didn't reply. He was studying an elderly but somehow familiar-looking Papuan who was moving purposely toward them. The thin aged man's waist was sheathed in a peculiar grass skirt. He wore a worn European style suit coat. A mop of gray hair was covered with a 1930s N.C.O. constabulary cap. The lithe apparition paused in front of Jack. He drew himself to attention and saluted smartly.

"Good afternoon, Sirs," a familiar voice that crackled with age rang out, and a grin spread across the man's wrinkled features.

Jack returned the salute automatically. His voice broke..."Sgt. Manu, is it you?"

"Yes, Kiap, it is truly me."

The two men embraced. Jack shivered in the older man's still-strong arms while onlookers stared curiously at the oddly disparate pair of men. "Where have you been? I have looked for you many times."

"In the mountains, among my people as I promised. I came here today to see you get your gong, Kiap. And you, Somatu, you have come far. I remember when you were a cook-boi who dreamed of reading the tracks white men make in books. You are now a big-man in our people's eyes; you are the Prime Minister. I am proud of you both. I tell my grand-children many stories about you." Sgt. Manu eyed the two men carefully. "The Aussies go finis here. Today the big-men all have much kona, but they will be bigger when they give it all away. We once belonged to the sky and mud. Now we belong to the generation of the setting sun. After the sun sets, darkness comes," Manu warned. "We must become lamps in the night. Our stories have told us a time would come when we must share our wisdom and way of living to save the earth. That time is now. All the people must speak and all men must listen because dark times are coming."

Prime Minister Somatu drew himself up with dignity; towering over both men, he removed his top hat, his "official hat". "Sgt. Manu, I am not a Government man. Nor am I a coconut man, brown on the outside and white on the inside. When I let go of my resentment of what the white man did to me and to our people, all things began to come to me. I do not know everything, but I will not see this land tamed, its resources used up with no regard for the future. This earth belongs to everyone, not just us and not just the white man."

"I know this to be true, Somatu. You are a true son of Iunagazia. I know you will protect all the peoples." The three men stared into each other's eyes. Each man instinctively knew that the bond forged so long ago would stand in good stead now. "What of Kiap O'Rourke?" Manu asked. "I have heard that the Japanese took him prisoner and cut off his head at Rabaul."

A sharp pain surged through Jack's chest and arced its way down his arm. He waited for the pain to subside before he replied, "Yes, Manu. It is true. The Kiap was captured and beheaded. He was serving as a coast watcher. Since he had no uniform, the Japanese Commandant claimed he was a spy."

"And Isi?"

"Yes, Isi, too. They were together."

"They were truly brave men... It is a pity. It is said that Isi gave the Japanese a raspberry -- and O'Rourke did so as well."

"I have heard that," Jack said. "They were truly brave men."

When Manu spoke again his eyes misted, "Once we were all Judge Murray's men and although we have walked different paths, we all were born here and now we are free! We are truly what Murray called us, Sons of the Tropics, are we not? We are no longer sons beeches sitting around campfires eating moraboas." The men laughed at Sgt. Manu's joke.

Pulling his baton from under his arm, "I have something that belongs to you I think," Jack said and he handed Sgt. Manu the old leather swagger stick he had carried since the day Manu disappeared into the bush.

"Thank you Kiap. I will keep it with me always. One day I will be buried with it in my hands. If you or Somatu ever act like stupid children, I will use it to remind you of who you are," as he touched them lightly on the shoulders. "I must leave now. My people are waiting," and he pointed to an entourage of grass-skirted, heavily plumed band of men and women on the far side of the Parade Ground. "Good dai."

"Wait," Jack said. "We must talk some more."

"I am living with the Chimbu people near Goroka. You must come to our village. You will be welcome. We will chew the fat. Good-bye Kiap. Good bye Somatu," and he saluted the men and turned and walked back to his people.

"Whew, I thought he died 30 years ago. He must be at least 80 years old or more," Somatu said.

"He will never die, Somatu. Remember he always told us that death is only an illusion. Living life well was the only reality for Sgt. Manu."

"I think we think too much, Jack. For me, it is life that is often the illusion."

Late in the afternoon Jack stood alone on the old jetty, camera in hand waiting for the sunset. The new yacht club was all that remained of the old hotel that he and his mates had frequented. The old deserted village of Hanuabua Town silhouetted to the south, added to the feelings of loneliness. Ah Chin's trading emporium was gone finis. So were the white merchants in their straw hats, sitting on the verandas with their fly whisks and glasses of gin. There were no more ladies with umbrellas leading a parade of haus-bois down the boulevards. Gone finis were all the administrators and civil servants who had accepted the Golden Handshake and returned to Australia. Gone were those who had said they loved this place, who were going to die and be buried here. When they realized they were no longer Mastas, but aliens without power or authority, they sang their Old Lang Synes and left.

When Jack looked back at the civilized town of Port Moresby, he felt a heavy sadness. In my lifetime these Papuans have traveled from the Stone Age to independence. Soon all this will be no more than a dream, another vision in the gallery of memories. Our ambitions have been realized and our labors done, he thought. We made mistakes, but all in all, it was a fair go Australia.

The sun was passing down over the horizon, far off the shore an ineffable calm like a soothing sleep fell over the world. The birds were coming home and the lotus flowers exhaled their evening fragrance. From the distant breakwater a solitary figure paddled out in a canoe, faintly calling across the waters, "Sambio! Sambio!"... "Peace! Peace!"

THE END

POST SCRIPT

The exploration and gradual development of the Central Highlands continued until the invasion of New Guinea by the Japanese in the early years of WWII. Many patrol officers volunteered as coast watchers, taking part in the world's most hazardous spy operation. Their knowledge of local terrain and populations, bush craft and leadership skills enabled them to render an invaluable contribution to the Allied cause. The coast watchers saved Guadalcanal and Guadalcanal saved the Pacific. At the base of the Coast Watchers Memorial Light, a plague lists the names of the fallen men. The inscription reads: *They watched and warned and died that we might live.*

In 1975 under heavy pressure from third world countries led by the Indonesians, the United Nations forced the Australians to precipitously leave Papua New Guinea. They left behind what has been called "briefcase independence" and walked out of the haus. Inside the briefcase was a copy of the Australian Constitution. Overnight the most able of the Papuans in the civil service were tossed into key government positions. Local leaders who won national positions in the elections, soon discovered it was easier to lead a village than to lead a nation. Somehow the "new breed" has managed to carry on.

Most of the Australian expatriates, in spite of their proclamations that they loved Papua and wished to be buried there, accepted the Golden Handshake and crossed back over the Torres Strait. They had passed in one generation from being Mastas to being foreigners in their beloved Papua New Guinea.

Today the Japanese, who lost the war, are busy converting one-fifth of the world's forest into toilet paper and wood products. Their fleets of fishing trawlers sweep the seas and reefs off New Guinea unchallenged, leaving a marine desert in their wake. The only resistances to their incursions come from a few independent leaders and a handful of followers. The neo-colonists from Indonesia have swallowed the former Dutch colony in New Guinea. Their militiamen impose "Indonesian civilization" from heavily armed helicopter gun ships. In most instances, conquest would be a better word for civilization.

Without substantial aid and an improved transportation system, the newly independent Papua New Guinea cannot flourish in the modern world. Tribalism is returning, dividing the districts, and cargo cults flourish. In Moresby, sorcerers appear out of the jungle and direct traffic; tourists buy art and souvenirs; and brawls frequently break out in the movie theatre. "Big Men," native plantation owners in full regalia, ride around in the back of Mazda trucks. Weeds grow across the Australian-American cemetery.

AUTHOR'S NOTE

My primary purpose in writing *Sons of the Tropics* was to draw attention to the island, the peoples, and the rainforests of Papua New Guinea, largely forgotten following World War II. Today Papua is an emerging democratic third-world nation struggling to develop economic, social, and political security for its people.

American, Australian, European, and Asian corporations are engaged in exploring, developing, and exploiting the mineral, fishing, and forest resources of Papua. The result is a rapid destruction on an unheard of scale of the New Guinea rainforest, one-fifth of the world's lungs. Ultimately, threatening the stability, if not the total collapse, of all life forms on our planet.

To create an awareness of the impending danger that the destruction of this environment presents is a stupendous challenge. Our global political leaders need to catch the vision wave to enable them to make the hard decisions required to preserve all our futures.

One has to wonder what would happen if some of us, if more of us, or even if all of us communicated the vision wave of a better ecological future to our leaders. As Judge Murray would say, "There's nothing to do, but to do it!"

To that end, the profit from this novel will be donated to environmental organizations that support this and similar causes.

ABOUT THE AUTHOR

Drs. Wayne and Berta Parrish have lived and worked in Mexico, in the Caribbean, in the South Pacific, and in Europe, studying indigenous cultures, focusing particularly on myths, legends, and artifacts. Often serving as consultants, they helped create cultural centers for the tribal peoples of New Guinea, the South Pacific, and the American Southwest. Their publications include articles, texts, and novels on aviation, ecology, education, mysteries, and legends.

Currently living on the central Californian coast, Wayne is writing a sequel to *The Blue Owl, The Golden Eagle*, a novel blending an ancient Native American myth with a contemporary mystery. Berta is teaching, conducting workshops, and writing *The Elder's Way* – an archetypal approach for creating purpose and passion in elderhood for the Baby Boomer generation.

If you enjoyed *Sons of the Tropics,*
then sample the following excerpt from
Legend of the Blue Owl

LEGEND OF THE BLUE OWL

By Wayne Parrish

PROLOGUE

Night came and with it a cold wind. I'itoi sat in the entrance of the cave and warmed his gnarled hands over a small bed of glowing mesquite coals. Earlier he had smoked the strong tobacco that made him listless. He watched the bright warriors and the winter moon move across the sky. All the signs and omens told him that the bad times had come again.

I'itoi held up a fiery ember and stared owlishly at the figures the cave guardians had drawn over the millennia on the smoke-blackened walls. A horny toad, beads of water pecked on its back, marked the departure of the Old People. They left after the Great River had run too low to feed their canals and the lakes had turned into salt marshes.

Pale half-men, half-animals, carrying sticks that belched fire and thunder had appeared in the south searching for yellow stones and slaves. These fearsome monster-men had put their marks over those of the Wanderers and the Old People who were there before them on the sacred boulder that stood beside the marshy lake. A spotted lizard symbolized the plague that had struck down the Wanderers. Their young had died clutching their groins, fire arrows protruded from their bellies. The carved faces expressed shock and horror.

The rock drawings told I'itoi many things: of a man struck by lightning; of a child killed by a rattlesnake; of eclipses, floods, droughts, earthquakes, and meteor showers. In the moon following the meteor shower, the Yumans had attacked and stolen the harvest. In the spring, the floods came and destroyed the fields.

Much later, the brown-robes had ventured as far north as the earth dwelling of the powerful shaman-chieftain, Morning Blue, which sat some distance from the wide bend of the river. They begged for food and the people had given them baskets of corn, pumpkins, mesquite beans and the agave fruit. The brown-robes had gone away, but they left behind a coughing sickness that killed young and old alike. Even Curing Woman's skills could not prevent the deaths.

Morning Blue blamed the disaster on HA-AK, the evil giant girl-child of his unmarried daughter, Woman-Who-Makes-Sleeping-Mats. Morning Blue told I'itoi to inscribe these tragic events so that the rocks would speak of them forever.

I'itoi prepared for the arduous work by fasting and smoking strong tobacco. He had let his heart tell his hands what to do. First he selected large rocks in the right shapes from the holy mountain on the east end of the vast valley and had them carried to his cave on the lone butte that overlooked the marshy lake.

Using a hammer and an awl made from the sacred stone that fell from the sky, he inscribed a different figure on each rock. He scraped the soft metal from the yellow cross and the other foreign objects that the brown-robes had left in the pit they had dug near I'itoi's home in the earth. He hammered the filings into the eye sockets of the blue owl that he had inscribed so carefully.

After finishing this task, I'itoi had prayed to the Earth Mother and the Sky Father for a vision, and the Earth Mother had blessed him. Once again, he would be a savior to his people. According to his vision, the people must break up into clans and scatter in the directions of the four winds. He told the people they must collect their shields, leave their houses, and each clan should separate. One to the east; another to the west; the third to the north; and I'itoi's clan to the south.

The Earth Mother told I'itoi that the clans should not return to this place, the center of everything sacred, until she sent them a sign. They must leave behind the objects that once belonged to the Old People. All the rag-dolls and kick-balls must be placed in the cave along with the glass beads and bells the brown-robes had given them.

All this I'itoi devotedly inscribed on the chosen rocks and boulders inside the cave. Only in this way will the clans be forgiven for burning HA-AK. The Earth Mother had told I'itoi that he must remain there forever and guard the rocks that speak.

The sun came up sluggishly. The first rays cast a reddish glow on the lone butte, dispersing a false gray dawn, changing into paler hues of bluish-gray. A velvety shadow at the cave entrance contrasted with the brilliant incandescent light as the sun climbed higher.

Overhead an eagle soared across the cobalt sky, creating a dark shadow that sliced across the yellow ochre earth below. A green-gold eyed lizard slithered inside, and after a brief halt, sped swiftly past I'itoi into the darkened interior and perched beside a small pool of water that had seeped down from a crevice above its head.

Outside the cave a drum began to beat. A singer's song lifted in the air:

> *"Hear I'itoi our prayer, purify the land, water, and air.*
> *Protect us on our journeys to the four directions.*
> *Spare us from enemies, sickness, and witches."*

At the beat of the drum, the men smartly raised their shields and pounded the ground. The dancers had wood coverings on their heads, woven bands on their arms, and rabbit fur bodices and kit-foxtails on their rumps. The deer bones on their ankles jangled as they imitated the movements of the deer and other creatures. Their bare arms and breasts were painted with red ochre from the canyon walls, with black mud from shale, with white made from pale clay, with brown from the sandstone, and with yellow and violet made from cactus flowers.

I'itoi tasted the sacred pollen made from the blue corn flowers and blew a handful into the air. He tossed his prayer bundle made from owl feathers onto the fire. The blue smoke drifted upward through the spirit chimney as he began his song:

"Tcutcunoni ko'kovoli sis'vunuka-a
Apu tuvavki wunanita.
Apu tuvavki wunanita.
The Blue Owl is bright
And happy when we leave her home alone.
And happy when we leave her home alone."

The first baskets full of stones that would forever separate I'itoi from his world tumbled down and blocked the cave entrance. Morning Blue's voice rang out and echoed in the chamber: "Farewell I'itoi. You are no more, but you will be remembered… forever.

CHAPTER 1

A cloud of caliche dust floated behind the 1936 Ford pick-up, obscuring the overpass where Ocotillo Road crossed over Interstate 10. Jack Reed centered the truck on the washboard road and tried to avoid the deeper ruts. He dodged a pothole and the back axle shuddered as the rear wheels scrambled for a grip on the shale surface.

A cattle pen, with a stack of dog-eared straw bales, cow piles and human detritus bordered the left side of the track. On the right, a ragged curtain fluttered out of a paneless window of a demolished Airstream trailer. Rusted bedsprings and a rotted mattress rested under a palo verde tree. Dashing out from under a tractor tire, half buried in the sandy wash, a roadrunner outpaced the truck and veered into the brush.

The road dropped down into a gully, crossed a cow-guard and climbed straight up the face of a second ridge. A twelve-foot wide, brightly painted white gate blocked the road. The truck skidded to a halt in front of a large sign that was riddled with bullet holes:

Ocotillo Ranch
No Trespassing
No Hunting
No Shooters
No Motorcycles
No Off-Road Vehicles

"Someone doesn't believe in signs," Jack said. He reached out the window, pulled a bar and swung the gate open. He drove through the wide gap and stopped the truck. The door creaked when he pushed it open with his shoulder. As Jack stepped out, a puff of powdery silt covered his boots. He put a foot on the bottom rail and rode the gate while it swung backwards and slammed into the support post.

"Damn," Jack said, rubbing his shinbone and focusing his eyes on the crude drawings etched on a huge half-domed boulder that sat at the base of the ridge. A pair of incised eyes stared owlishly back at him. An arrow pointed to a double spiral higher up the face of the rock. A stick-figure man, drawn by some ancient hand, had been blasted by shotgun pellets. Bullet scars also marred the other figures on the rock. "Jerks, mindless macho jerks. Hurray for the NRA!" Jack shouted. He reached into the truck, grabbed a bottle of spring water, and swallowed deeply, clearing the dust from his throat.

Jack crossed a narrow gully and climbed to the top of the ridge. The desert flattened to the south, forming a basin that lowered gradually to the well house and beyond to Mollie Gentry's dairy farm where a laborer was tossing bales of hay off the top of a massive haystack to the cattle milling below.

Beyond the dairy, white-topped cotton fields stretched for another five miles before the land turned brown and barren, marking the beginning of the Indian Reservation. The San Tans stretched in a long line eastward towards the Superstitions; all but the tips were lost in a cloud of dust and brown haze. On the other side of the freeway, an endless sea of pink tiled roofs marched westward. "The Californians are coming," Jack said. The South Mountain range ran from east to west for twenty miles, cutting off any view of Phoenix.

A dust devil swirled across the alkali sand in the lakebed where the ancient HoHoKam canals ended their journey. To the west, broken glass glazed purple by the searing desert sun glittered in the graveled shards. Two gigantic eucalyptus trees towered over the adobe ranch house, stable, tool shed, ramada, and orchard. Terraced cactus gardens surrounded the buildings, the verdant blue-green contrasting vividly with the whitewashed adobe walls and rock buildings. A bent figure of a man was raking the gravel yard.

"Old Ruiz!" Jack almost shouted. The roadrunner approached the top of the ridge, eyed Jack warily with one eye, and turned the other towards a blue-green lizard with golden eyes. "What will I tell the old man?" Jack asked the roadrunner. "This place is mine now, Ruiz. The entire 160 acres. Mine to live in, mine to sell, and mine to pay the taxes. Why did they build here? They might as well have built a ramada on the rim of Popocatepetl."

The roadrunner rushed the lizard and dashed off into the brush holding a quivering blue-green tail proudly in its mouth. The tailless lizard scrambled under a rock. "Everybody's a winner," Jack said. "God, how I hate this place!"

Paco, Ruiz's dog, part-Aussie and part-coyote, raced out of the yard barking furiously. Jack parked the truck under a rustic ramada. Aged ironwood posts supported a roof of ocotillo branches, covered with long palm fronds that offered some protection from the blistering summer sun. Sunbeams filtered through and danced across a perfectly stacked cord of wood. Jack stepped out of the truck and dropped one knee to the ground, "Come here, boy." Paco hesitated for a moment and then rushed forward, nearly bowling him over. Jack wrapped his arms around the dog and hugged him as Paco affectionately licked his face.

Ruiz was waiting for him, his straw cowboy hat crossed over his chest. "Buenos dias, Jefe," he said solemnly, his eyes twinkling.

"Buenos dias, Ruiz," Jack replied and the two men hugged each other.

"It has been too long, Jack."

"Nearly three years this time."

"You have filled out even more," Ruiz said stepping back and sizing him up. "You are a jefe now, but there is still a little jefito in you. Only a jefito would swing on a gate. I used to tell you that often when you were a boy, but you were so like your grandfather, El Jefe. He was stubborn. He was muy hombre. Your grandmother was even more stubborn. We called you Jefito – Little Boss."

Jack laughed. "How do you know I swung on the front gate?"

"Some things never change, Jefe, but I heard the gate slam shut. Then I heard the truck. I knew you would be coming soon."

"I saw the sign at the gate when I drove in. Looks like we've had visitors."

"That is not all, Jefe. Last week someone shot some milk cows the Gentrys were drying out in the pen by the big haystack. They set fire to it and tore down a mile of fence."

"Who would do that?"

Ruiz hesitated, "Someone who wants to make life hard for you and Mollie. Making it easier for you to sell your land. Are you going to sell the ranch, Jefe?" Ruiz asked softly.

The question floated in the air. "I may have to, Ruiz. My mother left a warehouse full of antiques to my stepsister. She gave me the ranch but no cash, so I'm up to my ears in taxes and debts. I may have to sell, unless I find water, a lot of water, Ruiz. Even then I need financing to develop the ranch. You see, I've left the university, and I don't know what an oceanologist can do in the middle of the desert."

"When the time comes, you will know what to do. It is good that you are here. Someone wrecked the pump house, Jefe, and they shot up the water tank."

"The water tank? When?"

"Sunday, Jefe. Maria and I went to mass in Guadalupe. I was not here. I could not fix it. Too much damage," he said shaking his head sadly. "But I cleared out the old tank and started the pump in the orchard. There is enough water for the trees and the house if you are careful."

"Let's take a look," Jack followed Ruiz down an irrigation ditch on the backside of the citrus grove.

"Careful, Jefe, that old grandfather rattler still lives under the tool shed. Someday I'll catch him."

"You've been saying that for ten years," Jack said as he made a wide circle around the shed. "I saw him once, Ruiz. He was sunning himself on that flat rock. I went after a shotgun, but when I came back he was gone. He must have been five feet long."

"Maybe seven feet now, Jefe. I caught him one day. I grabbed him by the tail and pulled him out from under the shed. The devil turned on me and chased me all the way to the stables. Your grandfather thought that was very funny. Every year he would ask me 'Have you caught any snakes by the tail lately?' and he would laugh. It wasn't funny. I can tell you that much."

The two men entered the clearing where a large steel water tank lay on its side. The supports had been chopped through with an ax, and several large holes perforated the sides.

"Someone used a howitzer on that tank. From the size of the holes maybe a .458 Winchester or a 45-70," Jack said. Ruiz nodded.

"They smashed the batteries and poured acid on the generator. It will cost a lot to fix."

"We won't fix it, at least not soon. We'll use the back up. I can carry in bottled drinking water. I'll survive." Jack listened to the pump on the back up tank; it ran smoothly. "You've done a good job, Ruiz."

Ruiz smiled. “Gracias, Jefe.”

“If we drill for water, I think we should try somewhere else.”

“Where will you look, Jefe?”

“I think there might be an aquifer under the old lakebed. There should be a lot of water trapped there.”

“I think you’re right, Jefe. I dug the first well here behind the stable. We found water at twenty-five feet and this well was only eighty feet down. When it dried up, your mother brought in a rig. They had to go to 600 feet. I told them not to drill there, but no one listened. That is the way to go,” Ruiz finished and pointed at the dry lake. “No need to pump uphill from there either.”

“I’ll get some hydrographic maps; maybe they can tell us where to look.”

“A willow wand is better,” Ruiz said, but Jack didn’t reply. “I really hate to see you sell this place, Jefe. Your mother wanted you to have it someday. So did your grandmother.” Ruiz made the sign of the cross. “They were good women. Sometimes a little loco.” Ruiz grinned at Jack. “Your grandmother made me plant the orchard and the bushes and those eucalyptus trees. Then your mother brought this cactus. It comes from all over the world, from Africa and Baja, California, even some from Asia. ‘Ruiz,’ she would say, ‘I’m going to have the best damn cactus garden in the world.’”

“It must have been a lot of work.”

“A lot of work, Jefe. It’s been the work of my whole life. But it is done, and it is the best damn cactus garden in Arizona, if not the world,” he said proudly. “It will be here when both of us are gone.”

“You’re right, Ruiz. If I do sell the ranch, we’ll save this piece. Make it into a public park. Whoever buys the ranch won’t miss a few acres. Tell you what, we’ll call it the Vargas Cactus Gardens or Ruiz’s Arboretum.”

"Thank you, Jefe," Ruiz said quietly and put on his hat. Jack could see the old man was moved by his spur-of-the-moment gesture. "I will tell Maria. She will be happy to know this thing. Adios."

"Adios, Ruiz." Jack carried the groceries into the house through the back door and waited while his eyes adjusted to the darkened interior. After popping open a can of beer and swallowing deeply, he turned on the oven and opened the door. The oven coughed, and he opened a side oven door, hoping to find a plate or a pan to heat a burrito. He bent over and looked inside.

"Keerist," he yelled and jumped backwards, his can of beer sailed upward dousing the ceiling. A spotted skunk was staring directly at him and sitting in the middle of a round copper bowl surrounded by her litter of black-and-white kits. Jack kicked the door shut, but it was too late!

Jack retreated into the dining room and put the burrito on the table. He raced back into the kitchen and opened the dutch door and windows. The skunk odor quickly permeated the entire house, forcing him outside.

The evening star followed a blazing sunset as the sky turned pink, purple, blue, and then black. Jack lay in a hammock swung between the two heavy posts at the end of the front porch, taking advantage of a slight westerly breeze. It was a warm July night, too hot to sleep outside, but inside, the cool adobe still reeked of skunk. He watched Altair, followed by Vega, and then the Pleiades, as they marched across the sky.

REVIEWS for *Legend of the Blue Owl*

"Readers will find no dull moments in *Blue Owl*. Parrish's entry into the fiction field is filled with action and credible characters. More importantly, it's based on original plot ideas"

--- *Tony Hillerman*

"From the prologue where the vision of the shaman I'itoi leads him to voluntarily sealed in a cave as the perpetual guardian of its secrets, *Blue Owl* draws the reader inexorably into the story, all the while teaching those same secrets to a society as far removed from I'itoi's as the stars…Parrish's plot, based on a Native American legend, is stretched across its framework as tightly as the skin of a tribal drum. *Blue Owl* could establish Parrish as a legend himself."

--- *New Times*

"Anyone with the remotest passion for the Southwest will enjoy the *Blue Owl*. In his novel, Parrish has masterfully composed a story that blends authentic desert history with engaging fiction. *Blue Owl* weaves a tale of suspense and intrigue involving ancient storytelling combined with archeological and scientific knowledge. Parrish's new book is crammed full of fascinating gems of information involving the present Southwest and also of a time gone by."

---- *The Arizona News*

"Parrish has a passion in his works that flows through as if the man is on a mission to convince the world that his corner of the world is the most beautiful place to be. And with each locale, it is. He gets across his point about environmentalism without beating the reader over the head. He doesn't preach, instead he gives you something to think about. The author's love of his subjects shows through in the words. The book is lyrically written, almost musically. You will love the personable characters, get a feel for their lives and they will have a lasting affect on yours. A very good read."

--- *San Diego/La Jolla Light*

"Storytellers are the voice of the past, present, and future. Visionaries walk a long, difficult and often lonely road, but their road is the high ground. Parrish is a natural storyteller."

--- *The Columbus Dispatch*

“ What we are doing to the forests of the world is but a mirror reflection of what we are doing to ourselves and to one another.”

Mahatma Gandhi

www.ingramcontent.com/pod-product-compliance
Lightning Source LLC
LaVergne TN
LVHW050532100826
845148LV00002B/525

* 9 7 8 0 9 7 2 5 0 0 0 3 6 *